Jenny Lloyd is the author of the acclaimed novel Leap the Wild Water. She was born in Powys, Wales.

BY THE SAME AUTHOR

Leap the Wild Water

The Calling of the Raven

JENNY LLOYD

Published by Jenny Lloyd

ISBN: 978-1-291-87988-9

Copyright 2014 Jenny Lloyd

Jenny Lloyd asserts the moral right to be identified as the author of this work.

Thanks to all those who had enough confidence in me to buy Leap the Wild Water, on a wing and a prayer, not knowing if it would be any good or not.

Special thanks to those who have let me know how their hearts and minds were touched by Leap the Wild Water. Your praise was my encouragement to go on writing and publish this sequel.

Author's Foreword.

Though The Calling of the Raven is set in a time when women were mere chattels of men and had no rights of their own, domestic abuse still goes on today, in all parts of the world. Those who perpetrate domestic abuse are as guilty of denying women their basic rights as those who denied women any rights in the past. Every man, woman and child should be afforded the right to live without fear.

The Calling of the Raven is dedicated to every woman, past, present, and future who has been constrained and subjugated by fear due to the perpetration of physical, mental or emotional violence.

Prologue

Oh, dear, what can the matter be?

There's not much I don't know about people and their ways. I've seen plenty, I have, enough to know when things are not right with a person. I could tell, the moment I saw her, you see, could tell that something was wrong. Six years or more it must have been, since the last time I laid eyes on her. Oh, it was a shock, I can tell you, to see her turn up at my door! Good friends we became, back then, and I missed and worried about her sorely when she stopped coming to market. One week, she was there as usual, and then we saw her no more.

So there she is, standing in my doorway with a dog standing beside her. There's something about the glassiness of her eyes that makes me think perhaps she has a fever. I usher her inside my little hovel. Embarrassed, I am, for her to see the lowly place where I do dwell. For she is dressed all fine, not like in the old days, and I think to myself; she married well then, that's good.

"I've come bearing gifts," she says, with a smile that doesn't sit right on her face, as though she struggles to keep it there.

She comes inside, the dog at her heels, and I tell her, sit down, and give me your cloak, for it is far too hot to be wearing such a thing.

"It's to keep me warm at night," she says, that smile still struggling to stay put.

I lift the cloak from her shoulders, and she sits down on the chair by the smouldering fire. The dress she wears is even finer than her cloak. Yet, now she is right beside me, I see that her hair is not brushed and her face is in need of a wash, and all. There is a scratch along her cheek. It is beaded with dried droplets of dark red blood. I don't know quite what to make of it all. Her hands are full. She has a basket full of something or other, and carries a bundle wrapped in a shawl. The dog has lain down on the floor beside her chair, its head resting on its paws. She places her burdens beside her, on the mud floor of my little room, and reaches into the basket.

"I brought you tea! And I bought these candles at the chandlers round the corner. They're good ones that burn clean and won't sting your eyes or stink up the room!"

"Girl, bach, there was no need to bring anything but your self. But, oh, I am glad to see you!"

It is as if she hasn't heard me.

"And look, there is a whole ham in here, and a cheese, too, I bought them in the market place! The preacher in our chapel says that money is the source of all evil! But I must confess, I find the spending of it the greatest pleasure there is!"

Her voice is too high, her speech so fast it leaves her breathless. Though it is gloomy here in my little room, I can see the beads of sweat glistening on her brow.

"I'll brew some of that tea. Proper stuff is it? There's a treat! The only tea I get to drink is the dregs leftover from the gypsy's teacup. Do you remember her? No, perhaps she came after you left. The things she can read from the bottom of a cup, you wouldn't believe!"

Megan's smile wavers and gives up the fight. She gazes into the paltry flames of my fireplace. "I dread to think what she would read in mine," she says, so quietly I have to strain my lugs to catch it. I brew the tea. I have nothing so fancy as teacups, so I pour it into a couple of bowls. She takes hers and places it on the floor beside her, and then she pulls a small flask from her skirt pocket, and pours a little of the pungent smelling, brown liquid into her tea.

"Here, have some of this. An old friend of mine, Dafydd, taught me to drink tea this way. It much improves it! I bought this from the inn."

"Is that brandy? Go on then, good girl!" I say, taking the flask from her and pouring a good measure into my own.

"I bought it to warm myself, for I am chilled to my bones," she says.

I take a good look at her. She doesn't look well at all.

"I fear you have a fever, Meg, for it is a warm day."

"I feel, every minute of every hour, that someone is crawling over my grave," she says, gazing into the fire again. Her words make me shiver too, and I rub the gooseflesh that has risen on my arms. Then she looks up and she looks so close to tears, I can stay silent no longer.

"Are you going to tell me, then, what you came here to confide?"

"I hardly know where to begin," says she.

By the time she has told me all that has happened since I last saw her, the daylight is failing and I am lighting one of the candles she brought. I've tutted with outrage, and wept tears to hear all that has happened to my friend. She tells me how her young man, the farm manager, upped and left her carrying his child. She tells me how her mother and brother stole the baby from her and boarded it with a whore, and how she almost went mad with the grief and the rage. Six years passed, of which she can remember little, and then her Mam died and her childhood sweetheart returned, begging her to marry him.

"I did try to tell him but I did not try very hard. I let him marry me without telling him about the baby," she says.

The omission weighed hard on her conscience, she said. And her brother started threatening to bring the child home, from the moment she told him she was going to marry. She thought he was just trying to keep her from marrying.

"We'd only been married a couple of months when Morgan brought little Fortune home. I was so a-feared, Myfanwy, of Eli finding out she was mine," she pauses, "I was going to throw myself in the river. I wanted to die rather than see Eli reject me when he found out."

"Oh, cariad!" is all I can think to say, but I am shocked to the core to hear her speak of such. There's plenty round here have ended up in the river on being abandoned in the family way. It breaks my heart to think my dear friend nearly went the same way.

"Then Morgan, somehow, I don't know how, but he sensed what I was going to do and he came looking for me and shouted my name and … and so I did not do it."

She looks away and reaches down to stroke the dog's head, hiding her face from me so that I do not see the pitiful anguish there laid bare.

"Thank God you did not do it, Meg!"

She does not agree with me but carries on as if she hasn't heard.

"And right then, it came to me, what I must do. I had wanted to die rather than tell Eli the truth. So I thought the only answer was to tell him all."

"Oh, dear," I say, wondering how he will have taken it and thinking he would not have taken it well at all.

Then she tells me the rest and what she has now done, and a cold chill runs down my spine. Her eyes are like those of a wild animal, cornered and waiting its fate. I look at her again, taking in her unkempt hair, the dirt and blood on her face, the glassiness in her eyes, and I see her in a new light. It is no fever of the body she is suffering. I have had but a few hours with my old friend, after all these years, and now she will have to go. This time, there will not be any coming back.

"You must give yourself up, Meg. There will be people looking for you."

"Haven't you listened to what I've said? They will lock me up and throw away the key!"

"Oh, love! You shouldn't have done what you did!"

"Will you not help me, then? Can I not stay here with you?"

Her eyes beseech me. She sounds like a lost child, I think. And lost she is, for certain.

Chapter One

The truth is not always ours to tell

The longest walk of my life is the short journey I make back to Wildwater and the telling of the truth. The house-martins swoop in and out of the eaves. The rustling leaves of the sycamore behind the great barn glisten in the sunlight. The sounds of Gwen clattering about with pans drift down from the kitchen. Eli's trap stands outside the barn, still harnessed to the restless pony that claws at the cobblestones and tosses his long white mane.

Down in the meadow, the dairy-maid sits on a stool beside the cow. Her bonneted head rests on the cow's flank as she brings the frothing white liquid gushing into the pail. Across the river, a sheepdog barks and the shepherd whistles a merry tune.

All is as it should be, and as it has always been. Here I stand on the cobblestones with the hot summer sun beating down on my head, yet I shiver, as though a trampling foot has trodden upon my grave. I take a deep breath. How to tell the husband who worships the ground beneath your feet, that you are not the pious women he believes you to be? How to explain the burden of guilt, of allowing him to marry me without his knowing what I did?

It is with gnawing dread I approach the front door of the house which has become my home. Like a hen scratching for worms, I scrabble about in my mind for the right words to tell such a wrong. I attempt to imagine his reaction but cannot imagine his face, only feel the pain I will cause him. There is no easy way to say a thing which will break another's heart; no easy way to tell the thing that will smite the love light from his eyes.

When this truth is told, I fear he will loathe me, but I am resolved. From the moment Morgan brought me back from the brink of that crashing, dark death in the Wildwater, I decided if I was to live at all, then I must do so honestly.

Oh! How my heart does hammer inside my chest when I enter into the dark, windowless hallway. The parlour door is ajar. Eli stands with his back to me. He is stooped, his head bowed, his arms stretched out and gripping the mantle-piece over the fire, as though the mantle is a wagon of hay he is pushing. I walk into the room, my skirts rustling against the door. I force myself to speak.

"Eli. I have something I must tell you."

Now the first words are spoken, I feel quite dizzy in my head. How terrible that the telling of truth should strike such fear in a person's heart. I think he has not heard me for he does not move or answer. Out in the hallway, the clock ticks away the lengthening seconds.

"Eli?"

He turns now and when I see his face I think something terrible has happened, and wonder how I can tell him now when he clearly has enough to trouble him. Relief floods through me at the thought of a possible and legitimate reason for delay, while at the same time I am thinking, no, I must not delay any longer.

"What is wrong?" I ask.

He stands with his hands folded behind his back, and I cannot put a name to the look on his face for it is not one I have seen before.

"I've been to the hiring fair, today, to hire a new dairy-maid," he says.

I nod for him to go on. His eyes dart towards me and as quickly look away. I wonder what it is that I have done, for it seems that I am the source of his agitation. He stares at the floor between us, tight-lipped, a tic pulsing away at his temple.

"I bumped into an old friend of yours," he says.

He goes over to where the portrait of his parents hangs upon the wall. Looking up at them, he clasps his hands again behind his back, clenching and stretching his fingers.

I think he must have met Myfanwy but cannot think what she may have said or done to so upset him.

Myfanwy knew nothing about what happened after I stopped going to the market.

"Oh, did you meet Myfanwy? How is she? It is so long since I last saw her."

Eli swings round, his long frock-coat swishing like a devil's tail. "Your friend's name was Iago and he had a great deal to tell me about you," he says.

I feel the ground shifting beneath my feet, and fear I will fall.

"You should sit down, my dear, you look rather faint."

He does not speak with his usual tender concern. He speaks with more than a hint of sarcasm in his voice. I swallow hard and my mouth is suddenly so dry I cannot speak. This very morn, before I went in search of a place to end my life, Eli would have rushed to me with tender concern at the sight of my nearly fainting. Now he stands firm, fingers tucked into his coat pockets, his eyes black with anger. I grope behind me for a chair and sit down before my legs do fail me.

"Remember him?" Eli goes on. "The rogue that stole from me, when I employed him to manage this place for me?!"

Eli's voice quavers with each rising note and I cast a wary glance at him. My heart swells with pity, for his eyes shine with unshed tears.

"It would seem my profits were not the all of what he stole from me."

"What did he tell you?" I ask, my voice barely more than a whisper.

He clears his throat and swallows hard.

"More than I wished to hear."

He sits down heavily on a small chair beneath his parents' portrait. He tells me of his trip to Dinasffraint, for the hiring fair where folks come from far and wide to look for work. Eli had gone to find a replacement carter, his old one having taken ill with little hope of recovery; and to hire a new dairy-maid, for the old one was leaving to marry.

"Who should be standing there but that rogue himself, as bold as the brasses on my horse's harness?"

From the moment Eli set eyes on Iago, Eli went about the market place, putting out the word that Iago was not to be trusted or hired. He and a few others were all for running Iago out of town, he said. When Iago realised what was going on, he retaliated.

"I hear you married Megan Jones. Partial to another man's cast-offs, are you?" he'd said, grinning.

Eli had taken Iago by his shirt collar and threatened to run him through for insulting me.

"Rough with her, and all, are you? I seem to remember she liked a bit of that!"

"You're a liar!" Eli shouted at him.

Eli knocked him to the ground which only served to loosen Iago's tongue further. He cited knowledge of a birth-mark, high up on my inner thigh, to prove he was

17

not lying. Eli threatened to kill him, his hands around Iago's throat, just to silence him.

"Ask her who the father of her bastard is, if you don't believe me!" Iago tells him, struggling for breath.

Eli loosened his grip, stunned by Iago's words. Iago scrambled away across the cobblestones, like a frightened dog. Child or no child, it was Iago's knowledge of that birth-mark which wormed its way into Eli's mind and proved my guilt.

"I was going to tell you. I was coming now, to tell you!" I say, lamely.

He moves so fast and the slap is so hard, it knocks me from my chair and I crash upon the floor. He stands over me, panting. Then his eyes fill with tears and he turns away.

"You should have told me before we married. You should have told me then."

I begin to say that I had tried but stop when I see his look of contempt. I get up from the floor, right the chair, and sit down. My cheek is hot and stinging, more from shame than the slap he'd given me, I think.

Let that be a lesson to you, I hear Mam say, as if she is stood right here beside me.

"Is there anything else you have not told me? Though I can't think there could be anything worse."

I stare at my distorted reflection in the polished surface of the table. I tell him Iago spoke the truth about there being a child, steeling myself should he strike me again. I watch his face contort with disbelief and puzzlement, and he asks, but where?

"They stole her away from me, Morgan and Mam, rather than have me bring shame on them."

"Ha! Can you blame them?"

"Please do not say that. It nearly killed me."

"That's what comes from being loose with your favours!"

I am silent for a time, tracing the outlines of my reflection with my finger.

"Morgan took her to a woman who takes in such children for money."

"Best place for her!"

"All these years, six years, he and Mam knew this woman was neglecting and ill using my little daughter, yet still did not bring her back to me."

Eli shrugs as if it is of little consequence.

"Until Morgan discovered that woman was laying with men for money. Only then did he decide to bring my daughter home."

I pause and look up at him, to see if he understands the full import of what I am telling him.

"He brought her home three days ago, Eli."

His face sags with surprise, then he looks at me with narrow-eyed suspicion.

"So that is why you were going to tell me so late in the day; before I saw the evidence with my own eyes!"

"No, that wasn't my reason…"

"By God, you'd never have told me, would you?"

"Morgan has offered to claim her as is his own…"

"Has he indeed!"

"…but I refused because I was tired of the lying, couldn't bear deceiving you anymore. I decided it was time to tell you the truth."

"No, Megan. The only right time to tell me about your whoring was when I asked you to marry me. You kept quiet about it for the sole purpose of getting that ring on your finger," he jerks his head towards my hand, "and for that I will never forgive you."

My mind is thrown into a whorl as I try to find words to convince him my intentions were not bad.

"I believed we could turn back time and begin again. I see now that I was wrong. But it did not seem fair that I should go on being punished for the rest of my days, for something that would never have happened if we had only been allowed to marry long afore."

"Didn't seem fair that you should pay for your sins? Who in hell are you to decide whether you should be punished or not? It is for God to decide, Megan. GOD SHALL DECIDE!"

I am reminded of Mam's words. God shall decide if she lives or dies, she said to Morgan outside my chamber when I was giving birth to Fortune and screaming for help. God shall decide what you will or will not have, she said, when she stole from me every penny I had earned. All the while she was preaching, it was her own plotting and scheming that decided my fate for me. To the self-righteous, God is always on their side.

I think all this but say nothing for I know that in Eli's eyes, in anyone's eyes but my own, there is no excusing what I have done. Eli begins shouting again, and I wonder if Gwen is listening on the other side of the door.

"You went chasing after some ne'er-do-well, lay with him like a common whore, decide I need not know a thing like that, lest I should change my mind about marrying you; and you think it not fair that you should be punished for your sins?"

As he screams this last at me, he is red in the face, spittle flying like wind-blown raindrops from his mouth. The sinews in his neck are swollen like the ropes that tie up the wool packs. It is an ugly and terrifying sight.

It is all lost, his love for me, smashed like my bonnet on the Wildwater torrent, broken by the unrelenting surge of my own sorry fate, hurtling me forward, always towards disaster. I hear myself speak the same feeble words I once said to Morgan after he found I was with child.

"He told me we would be married. He told me that he loved me."

Like my brother before him, he snorts his contempt and replies;

"And that makes it all right in your eyes, does it, Megan?"

How can I say that, for me, it did? If I told him the truth it would only incite more condemnation and anger; that I'd been swept along on a torrent of lust, love, and promises of forever; a torrent as forceful as the Wildwater itself.

"I believed you had abandoned me with no explanation or excuse. I had no reason to think you would come back to me. My heart was broken!"

"Well, you've had your revenge now, Megan, for you in turn have broken mine."

He turns and walks towards the door but not before I have seen all the pain I have caused, laid bare upon his face.

"I never meant any harm, ever, least of all to you. I love you, Eli, you must know that."

He pauses with his hand on the door knob. He looks in the direction of my feet, unable to look at me directly.

"If it wasn't for revenge, Megan, then why did you lay with him here, in my own house, and on my own land?"

Was there any detail Iago had not told him? Did that rogue have no mercy? How I loathe Iago in this moment, when I see what his words have done to my beloved Eli. Words I could not deny, for I know if I open my pitiful mouth in defence, my stammering denial would only serve to give me away. Instead, I say I understand if he cannot forgive me, and tell him I will go and pack my things.

"You're not going anywhere, except to tell that brother of yours that I accept his offer to claim your bastard for his own. You have privately made a fool of me, Megan. I'll be damned before I will let you make it a public exhibition."

"You want me to continue as your wife?" I say, hope rising in my throat.

"Oh, aye, Megan, but for appearance's sake, only."

Chapter Two

A life is carved up according to the wishes of others.

When the front door slams, Eli's parents tremble within their frame and the parlour doors shake upon their hinges. I hug myself against a chill that comes from deep within me. No thoughts scramble for attention. My mind is empty. I feel I should be weeping for all I have lost but I am numb. It is the shock, I think, and raise my fingers to my cheek. It is blazing hot to the touch.

How long have I sat here staring at the walls? I must stir myself and go and tell Morgan that Eli has accepted his offer. In my mind I know this must be done but my body is unwilling to do my bidding. How will we go on, I wonder, after this? My humiliation and shame are such that I do not think I can face Eli when he returns, let alone share this home with him for the rest of my days.

Time may heal, I tell myself, and this thought provides some comfort. Eli is a good man. Perhaps he will find it in his heart to forgive me, in time.

I hear movements in the kitchen beyond the parlour door. At last, I stir myself and go out there to tell Gwen I am going up to Carregwyn. She is stood at the fire, her back to me, stirring a pot of broth hanging there. She does not turn when I speak but nods her head sharply.

"Aye, alright," is all she says.

My innards lurch with fear that she has heard it all.

"I'll just wrap a little bread and cheese…" I say.

"Help yourself," comes her curt reply.

Until now she has fussed over me, urging parcels of food on me, admonishing me for climbing that hill in all weathers. She continues to stir the pot. Her back turned toward me is as stiff as a besom handle. Will she tell? Surely she will not tell, out of loyalty to Eli. God help me, it is as if my life is repeating itself, over and over. Before, it was Mam and Morgan who could not bear to lay eyes on me. Now, it is my own husband and his housekeeper.

I feel sick to my bones and do not bother to get bread nor cheese for my journey. I walk past Gwen and out the back door. How am I to live in this house?

When I reach the edge of the Wildwater the full awfulness of my predicament does come bearing down upon me like the torrent crashing over the boulders below. The water bubbles and foams like a boiling pot of stew. I wish now that I had thrown myself in. If only Eli had not met Iago at the fair; if Eli had heard the truth from me first, and only from me, perhaps it would not have hurt him so much. My poor Eli. How will he forget

I laid with Iago in his very house, on his own land, much less forgive it?

I turn from the river and begin the climb up to Carregwyn. I have not seen Beulah since Morgan told her of Fortune's identity. I don't know how I shall face her. I don't know how she will receive me, now. I am no longer the Megan she thought I was. She has seen me in a different light. It is a strange feeling indeed, to present oneself anew, like a stranger. The truth of it is, I feel shame and expect to see it reflected in her eyes.

Only when I reach the heath do bitter tears of grief and remorse begin to flow. The joyous warblings of the sky-larks, and the warm breeze kissing my skin, only serve to bring home to me all that I have lost. I knew real happiness once, I think, then quickly correct myself, for I was never happy in that home where Mam tormented and scolded me from morn 'til night. But here, up here on this hill, where I could walk free and unfettered by my duties; here, with the wind in my hair and the world at my feet, I snatched moments of pure joy.

I reach the outcrop of rocks overhung by the hawthorn tree, where I looked down and saw Fortune for the first time since she was stolen from me. How am I to go on, now I am not allowed to acknowledge her as my own? How will I bear to have her know me only as Aunt Megan, when all I long to do is gather her up and hold her close and never let her go?

I fear I shall go mad for I have an urge to tear the hair from my head, fingers clawed and screaming. It is all so wrong and will never be put right, for she shall never again be mine.

The fields below are full of Morgan's sheep, panting in the late afternoon heat. I wonder why they are not up on the heath, then remember with a jolt; the shearings are about to begin, when the neighbours will encounter Fortune for the first time. This thought hurries me onward, down the hill, for Morgan must be told before his shearing begins.

As I come near, I see Morgan is sat in the shade behind the barn, sharpening the blades of his shears. He is leaning forward, elbows on his knees, swiping the blades across the sharpening stone with long, slow sweeps. His thick curls tumble over his forehead, and his brow is furrowed in concentration. Watching him, I feel my old rage dissipate and sisterly affection takes its place. He has tried so hard to make amends, has even saved my life, though it was not worth the saving.

The house door is closed, and I am both relieved and disappointed all at once. I long to see Fortune up close, yet at the same time I dread that I will, for I do not think myself strong enough not to crumple like a withered leaf falling to the ground. How will I look into her sweet face and be able to compose myself and behave as an aunt would do? This question rises like a scream within me.

I wipe the tears from my face but there is a weight on my chest that makes me feel I shall never breathe freely again. Morgan hears my footfall on the cobbles and glances up, his face registering surprise to see me.

"Megan!" he says, and gets to his feet, looking awkward, his eyes searching mine for the answer to the question he has yet to ask.

"He didn't take it well then?" he says, seeing the answer written in my face.

I flop down on the bench and tell him of all that has transpired in these past few hours, and that Eli accepts his offer of claiming Fortune as his own.

"Aye, alright, you know I will do that. Dear God, Meg, of all the things to happen; for Eli to find out the way he has, I'm not surprised he's taken it hard."

"He hates me. I wish..."

I was going to say I wished he had left me to the Wildwater, for I don't know how to go on, but I do not want to seem ungrateful so keep my thoughts to myself.

"Come on over to the house. Beulah has been longing to see you. And you have to meet Fortune! Oh, Meg, she's the spit of you!"

"No!" I say, suddenly panicking. "Not today. I can't, I am not able..."

And then she appears. She comes running around the corner of the barn, abruptly stopping when she sees me. I am frozen to a stillness in which my heart barely beats and I am holding an eternal breath. I look into her eyes and am thrown headlong, back to the day when I found her gone, and the shock of it knocks the breath from me and I gasp. In those seconds that we stare at each other, in my mind I am gathering her into my arms, burying my face in her hair, breathing in her scent; but only in my mind, for that is as close as I shall get to being her mother from this day.

"This is my sister Megan, say hello," Morgan tells her, and the spell is broken.

She is shy of me and looks at me with the wariness of a stranger that rents my heart in two. I get to my feet, making my excuses for having to hurry away. I can hear the break of my heart in the cracking of my voice.

"You has to see Beulah first! She been telling me all about you. She been missing you something terrible," Fortune says, grabbing my hand and pulling at me with all her might.

Her hand in mine! It is the sweetest, silkiest thing, like the new leaves in springtime. It is the first time I have touched her in over six years.

"Is that so? Beulah has missed me? Well, I have missed her too!" I say, trying to control the tremble in my voice, trying to sound normal, trying to sound as though my heart is not bursting.

She talks nineteen to the dozen as she pulls me along. "Our shearing is starting soon, and Beulah says she will be up to her eyes in it then and I has to be good and help and not hinder her and I'm a big girl now and I can do all sorts of things."

"Can you indeed?"

I lift my face to the sky and blink back the tears I do not want her to see.

"I's going to tell her you's here!" Fortune says with a gleeful grin, freeing my hand and running ahead with a skip.

I flick away the tears and take a gulp of air. I do not know Morgan is behind me until I feel his hand upon my shoulder.

"Be brave," he says, and I answer with a sharp nod of my head before carrying on towards the house.

Beulah comes rushing to meet me, quickly drying her hands on her pinafore before wrapping her big arms around me in a hug. A sob escapes from my throat and she hugs me tighter. Then she stands back, her hands gripping my shoulders.

"Oh, Megan bach, you have no idea how I've missed you! Come on! Come in!"

She ushers me in through the door, telling Morgan that Tom has been up to say they'll all be up for his shearing, two days hence. Fortune is tugging at my skirts.

"Come and sit down, Megan!"

She rushes to pull out a chair from the table. I sit down in a daze, and hear Morgan ask Fortune if she'd like a ride in the cart with him, to go and fetch a barrel of cider for the shearing. She squeals and shouts yes, jumping up and down on the spot, clapping her hands together. Then her face falls and she looks at me.

"But I wants to talk to Megan."

I feel an overwhelming rush of love for her. I am on the verge of spreading my arms out to scoop her up when Morgan speaks.

"There'll be many more chances to speak to Megan, won't there Meg?"

"Yes. Yes, of course," I say, though I don't believe I will be able to bear it.

Beulah and I are left to ourselves, and in answer to Beulah's questions, I find myself retelling the sorry events of this day, all over again. With the repetition, my awful predicament becomes all the more real to me.

"Eli will forgive it, Meg. That man worships the ground you walk on."

"I do not believe he will. The Megan he worshipped was the good and pious woman he left behind, not me, flawed and tainted sinner that I am."

"The way that I see it is this; I am a widow and if I were to marry again, my future husband would not torment himself or seek to punish me for the fact he was not my first love. I don't see why your not having been married to Iago should make such difference. Eli's a reasonable man, Megan. I'm sure he'll see you have done him no great wrong. I believe he loves you enough for that."

"You are such a good friend, Beulah. There is no other in this parish who would not shun and condemn me if they knew what I had done."

"Aye, well, they will never know now, will they?"

Her words do not reassure me for I have not told her all of it; that I laid with Iago in Eli's own house and on his own land. I do not tell her for I know how it will seem, and I dare not risk losing her sympathy and friendship. It is this which Eli will not forgive because of the conclusions he has drawn from it. And why would he not? I cannot explain or excuse it to myself. Nothing that I say or do can prove I did not do that with any intention of harm.

"We shall have to tell Fortune before the shearing, that Morgan is her Da," Beulah says, breaking into my thoughts.

I stare down at my hands folded in my lap, the hands that have longed to hold my baby daughter again. I know I should thank them for doing this for me, but it is not what I would wish for myself. It is to be done for Eli's sake, for everyone's sake but mine. It means I will have to pretend for the rest of my days, to my own daughter and everyone else, that I am not who I really am. I cannot say thank you for that.

I leave with a promise to return and help Beulah with the preparations for the shearing. It will be the start of my new life as Fortune's aunt. Like a carcass, I am carved up and shared out, and these pieces of me are called by names that others wish me to be. The who that I am is to be that which is most convenient to others.

Chapter Three

Dead woman walking.

Eli has spoken to me but once this evening and only to tell me that Gwen has handed in her notice. We are sat at opposite ends of the polished table. He has not looked at me since my return from Carregwyn. As he eats, his gaze moves from the table to the window, but his eyes remain averted from mine.

"All my life she has been our housekeeper, even coming along with me to my Uncle's farm," now he looks at me, and it is a glare of such ferocity that I do feel myself shrink. "What have you done to upset her?" he accuses.

"I fear she overheard our quarrel," I say with my gaze downcast.

I look up to see the shock in his face, his forkful of food suspended in the air. He places the fork back on his plate with a clatter and pushes the half-eaten plate of food away from him. Then he gets up from his seat without another word, and goes out into the kitchen, closing the door behind him.

I sit still as a mouse that has caught the scent of a cat, hardly breathing, straining to hear the conversation out in the kitchen. I can hear Eli asking Gwen if she will change her mind.

"I'm not getting any younger, Eli," she says," it's time I hung up my apron springs."

"Is it something I or Megan has said, perhaps, that has made you think of leaving?"

I hold my breath in the long pause before she answers. I get up from my chair and go nearer the door, the better to hear. I strain to hear it, for her voice drops to a loud whisper.

"There's things I can't help but overhear, that I'd rather not have known."

There is another short pause then Eli says, "I see."

I press my ear against the oak of the door. It is as shiny as glass from the years of polishing that Gwen has given it.

"You deserve better than that, Eli," she goes on, "far better. I'll never think the same of that one again, I can tell you that."

Her voice quavers and I hear her blow her nose.

"I'd throw her out on her ear, if I were you..." she says, her voice louder now and full of moral indignation.

Eli butts in. "And have the whole parish laughing behind my back at how she fooled me? I think not, Gwen."

"She does not deserve to be your wife."

She is crying now and I strain to hear Eli's reply, praying he will disagree.

"No, I know. But what can I do? I've married her for better or worse, 'til death shall part us."

Gwen makes a noise of disgust, from deep within her throat, as though she is about to spit.

"It's a sorry state of affairs is all I can say. In all my years as housekeeper here, I never imagined I'd see such a day as this!"

Again, she blows her nose.

"I'm sorry, Gwen, sorry you should have to know it. But you'll not tell a soul, will you?"

"She would be shamed in front of the whole parish, if I had my way! But no, of course, I'll not breathe a word behind your back, you know that. You've been as a son to me. When I think how that...that...trollop in there has tricked you...it fair breaks my heart!"

She is sobbing heartily now.

"I wish you would stay, Gwen. It will be harder for me without you."

I press my ear tight against the door, waiting to hear her answer. I don't think I could bear it if she stays now, having to face her cold condemnation, day after day.

I feel my body sag with relief when she speaks.

"No, indeed, I cannot bear to lay eyes on her another day. I don't know how you shall, either."

"I have to bear it, Gwen, for appearances sake," he answers.

I do not wish to hear any more. I sneak out of the parlour and go up the stairs, avoiding the creaking step near the top. I go into my bedchamber and close the door behind me with a soft click. I undress and go to the window. Gwen has not been up to shut it as she usually would. I'll have it all to do now, the running of this house, heaven help me.

I lean out of the open window. A warm breeze blowing up from the valley snatches at my hair. I can just barely hear the Wildwater. From here it sounds like wind blowing through leafy tree tops.

There will be no more time for long walks along the side of that raging torrent. No time to pick flowers or watch the sun making rainbows up by the Giant's Leap. My life is to be a continuation of the drudgery before I came here. I should have done it, when I had a mind to, should have thrown myself in that water. I can do it still if I can no longer bear this life I am now condemned to live. It brings me some comfort to know I still have one choice; one escape from this vale of tears. It is a sin to take one's own life but what is one more sin to add to the rest I have committed? God will surely not forgive what mere mortals cannot.

Lamplight from the kitchen is spread out over the cobbles below, like milk spilled over a table. Muffled conversation drifts up to my perch, and I wonder if they are talking still about the sorry state I have brought Eli to.

Beulah is wrong. Eli does not love me enough. He has never loved me, the Megan who strayed and was betrayed. He never loved that Megan because he never even knew her until this day. He only ever loved the Megan who is long gone and never will be again. That Megan is lost forever, destroyed by a lying, cheating ne'er-do-well.

It is grown dark outside, save the light from a crescent moon that has risen. It is suspended in the dark sky above the sycamore tree behind the barn. I have not lit a candle; I stand with my back to the darkness of my room. The lamplight from the kitchen dims then goes out and I am plunged into a deeper darkness still. I fumble, feeling my way towards our bed, as I hear Eli's footfall on the bottom stair. I long to try to comfort him, here in the darkness of our feather bed; to stroke his hair and tell him I love him, have always loved him, and always will. Here in the darkness, perhaps we can find light.

The light of his candle flickers beneath our bedchamber door and I hold my breath. The light moves away and I hear the door to the adjoining bedchamber open. When I hear that door click shut, I am filled with fear and foreboding for it means he has utterly rejected and forsaken me.

I cannot face Gwen before she leaves; do not want to see the thin line of her lips clamped shut with condemnation; nor see in those grey eyes, that looked on me fondly just a day ago, the icy glare of hostility she feels toward me.

I get up and dress and sit by the window, and watch as Eli brings the pony and trap up to the front door. He disappears from view as he enters the house, then emerges again with two, large, leather bags containing the grand sum of Gwen's belongings. One at a time, he lifts them onto the rack at the back of the trap, and straps them down.

Gwen emerges onto the damp cobblestones which are wet from the overnight dew. It is early still, at that time when the sunlight is soft and casts a haze upon the misty air. Gwen dabs at her eyes, and then blows her nose. I am struck by how different she looks without her apron, for I have never seen her without it. She wears a grey dress, the colour of her eyes, and her white hair is drawn back in a neat bun at the nape of her neck.

She seems smaller than I last saw her. I think of all the kindness she has shown me since I came here. It is me that should be leaving, not her. It is not right that she should leave on account of me. As this realisation dawns on me, I get up and run down the stairs, and dash out of the front door.

"I'll go. Gwen must stay!" I say to Eli.

He is sat up on the trap beside Gwen. Her whole countenance bristles at the sight of me. Her slumped shoulders rise up and her back stiffens. She turns her face from me.

"Gwen should not leave on my account."

"No, she should not, but you are going nowhere. I'll not be made a fool of."

He flicks the reins and the trap moves forward and I have to jump out of its path or be run over. I gasp with shock at this blatant display of his disregard for my wellbeing.

"Run me down then! I wish you would!" I shout after them.

I go back inside the house and out to the kitchen. Gwen has left a stack of unwashed pots and dishes at the sink, out of spite, I suspect. There is no water in the pails, the floor is not swept, and no food prepared for the day.

The old bitch, I think, when I go to the larder and find the cold ham that hung there yesterday is gone, so I do not even have that to fall back on. There are no vegetables dug up from the garden, either, and only stale bread to eat. The new dairy-maid who is due to arrive today will not receive a good first impression.

Gwen has done it on purpose, left everything undone, so as to make things harder on me. I am promised to go up to Carregwyn to help Beulah. I'll wager Eli told Gwen to leave things as they are. Her

41

pride in her work would not have allowed her to do it, otherwise.

Well, let him punish me if that is what it takes to make him feel better. I lift the pails and stomp outside to the well. The day is warm so early, it will be hot as the fires of hell by the time my chores are done and I have to climb the hill.

To my dismay, when I re-enter the house to fill the kettle, I find they have left the fire to go out and all. I don't even know where Gwen kept the kindling. She would never let me lift a finger to help when she was in charge of things. It is too mean, I mutter to myself, as I go in search of kindling. I find some in an outhouse and get the fire going again. While I wait for the kettle to boil, I go out to the garden to dig up vegetables for the day. The soil is crumbly and dry from the spell of hot weather. As I plunge the fork into the potato patch, sweat trickles down from my brow, stinging my eyes. I pause to wipe it away with the back of my hand. My back aches, already. I am grown soft, unused to work, since I left Carregwyn.

I do not reach Carregwyn 'til mid-afternoon. I find Beulah out in the cool of the dairy, churning butter. Coming into the dairy from the heat outside is like taking a dip in the river. But Beulah is red in the face and I can see right away she is not best pleased by my tardiness. I see Beulah is alone, and my heart sinks. I wonder how I will ever quell this longing to be near to Fortune. In answer, Beulah tells me Fortune will soon be back, she has sent her to look for cleavers to strain the milk.

When I tell Beulah that I am late because Gwen has upped and left, she lets go of the churn handle, and her arms fall limply to her sides.

"I give up now, I do. That is the last straw, that is. Here am I, up to my eyes in it, and I know what's coming, I do. You're going to tell me you won't have time to help me, now."

I tell her that Eli will have to find a replacement for Gwen, for Wildwater is twice the size of Carregwyn and I shall never manage it alone.

"Well, I hope that he does, for if he does not I shall be for packing my bags, I will. If I'd known the work with this place, I don't think I'd ever have agreed to come."

"You don't mean that."

"Indeed I do! You kept that from me and all, didn't you? The carrying of the water up from that gorge in all weathers, and all the dairy work, and all!"

"I know it's a lot of work, but…"

"And now, that brother of yours tells me I'm to go to market to sell cheese and butter, else we shall never make ends meet. Where am I to find the time to do that? I asked him."

"Oh! You'll love the market…"

She has her hands on her hips, now.

"And on top of it all, I'm to cater for those snooty-nosed neighbour's wives who look down their noses at me, as if I were something the barn-cat spewed up at their feet!"

"I'm sure they don't…"

"To have to serve up food for that Mary, the Mill, is enough to make me puke. Did I tell you? What she did when she was here last, rooting for gossip like an old sow after acorns?"

"Yes, I think you may…"

"She ran her finger along the dresser, and held it up to her nose, inspecting it for dust, the old bitch. I said to Morgan, I said I'd rather pull out all my own teeth than make food for that old sow to gobble. And do you know what he did?"

"No, I…"

"He laughed! Laughed hard enough to crack a rib. Tears streaming down his face there were. Well, I'll give him tears. He'll have something to really cry about when I walk back down that road."

"He's in love with you," I say, never knowing those words were going to come from my mouth before they were spoken. Surprise and consternation wash over her, and tears spring to her eyes. She is now lost for words.

"Huh!" is all she can manage to say before sitting down hard on the milking stool by the door, looking utterly glum and sorry for herself.

"It's the truth," I say, swallowing hard on the swelling in my throat. I go over to her and rest my hand on her shoulder.

"I know it is hard toil here, but where is it anything else? I'll come and help as often as I can, I promise.

"I don't think he's in love with me, as you say. He hides it well is all I can say, if he does."

She sits with her arms outstretched, her hands splayed on her knees. Her hands are red raw from the work. The hem of her skirts, where they trail the dairy floor, is ragged and threadbare. She is not half the woman she was when she came here. Hard toil has chiselled her features into a fine-boned beauty.

"If he doesn't show it, it's because he is afraid," I tell her.

"Afraid of what?"

"Afraid you will abandon him; pack your bag and leave, as you say. Afraid you are going to break his heart asunder."

Beulah gazes at the ground at her feet and lets out a heavy sigh.

"Sod it! I've got to finish churning this butter," she says, using the hands on her knees to push herself up.

Beulah goes back to churning the butter. I see her then, my Fortune, skipping up towards the yard gate, her arms full of cleavers.

I recall one of Mam's favourite sayings and it strikes fear in my heart. 'The sins of the fathers shall be visited upon the children unto the fourth generation'. I want to gather Fortune up in my arms and carry her away, far away to another world where no one can ever punish her for that which is not her fault.

Tears well up and I shrink back against the dairy wall as Fortune comes through the yard gate. The whitewashed wall is as cold and damp as a grave against my back. Beulah glances over at me and I feign a fly has entered my eye.

Fortune does not see me standing with my back against the wall. She places the armful of cleavers on the milking stool, and runs to Beulah, flinging her arms around Beulah's waist, and burying her face in Beulah's apron.

"What's that for?" Beulah asks, laughing, stroking my little girl's hair.

"Cos I does love you!" Fortune says, pulling her head back and beaming up at Beulah.

It is like a blow to my stomach, knocking the wind out of me. It should have been for me; that embrace, that declaration of love. Robbed is what I feel; robbed of my daughter's love, and I have to look away.

"Get away with you!" Beulah is saying, giving Fortune a gentle shove away.

"We've got a visitor look! Megan's here."

46

Fortune turns with surprise and smiles with delight to see me, making my heart swell fit to bursting.

"I's going to make a nest from the cleavers, for Beulah to strain the milk through!"

"That's clever of you!" I say, my voice breaking. I make a big show of coughing, so that she will not know I am on the verge of weeping.

Beulah instructs her to sit quietly on the milking stool and get on with the job. I make my excuses to go to the house and begin preparing the feast for the shearers.

By the time they have joined me back at the house, I have composed myself, distracted by the work to be done. Beulah kneads the bread dough, while I stand over the kitchen table, stirring cake mix in a large bowl. Fortune is sat at the end of the table, waiting until the mix is in the oven when she will be given the wooden spoon to scrape out the leavings from the bowl.

She is playing with a ball which Morgan has fashioned from woven straw. She tosses it up in the air and catches it.

"Morgan is my Da! That means you is my aunty!" She says out of the blue. So he has told her then, I think.

"Yes, I suppose so."

"Morgan says," she tuts and shakes her head, correcting herself before going on, "*Da* says that my Mam died and that is why she did never come and fetch me from that nasty, fat pig, Nesta. Otherwise, she would have come and got me, she would. But dead people can't do nothing, because they is buried under the ground."

She tosses the ball up in the air again, but misses to catch it and it lands on the floor. Beulah and I exchange glances. So, I am dead and buried in the ground. Fortune gets down from the chair, picks up the ball, and scrambles back into her seat. She tosses and catches the ball again.

"I was sad and did cry a lot when he did tell me that, but Da says Beulah is as good as any Mam, so I mustn't take on."

It is Beulah's turn to look surprised and somewhat apologetic towards me. In a loud voice, Beulah tells Fortune to come quickly and help her gather vegetables from the garden. Fortune places the ball on the table, and follows Beulah out through the scullery.

I let the mixing spoon drop into the bowl, and lean with my hands flat on the table, letting it take the weight of me, as I try to quell the rising tide of grief that threatens to engulf me.

Oh, aye! Her Mam is dead, alright! Her Mam died the day they stole her away from me. Her Mam will be forever more a ghost, now, shadowing me, haunting me for the rest of my miserable days. The deed is done, my fate is sealed, and I must accept it. But it is a strange thing, indeed, to be dead and yet feel such agony.

Chapter Four

Morgan has an announcement.

With Morgan's shearing comes the dread of what he is to say. I'll get it over with, he'd said, while they are all gathered in one place other than the chapel. They'll have heard already from Mary, the Mill; that Morgan has a little girl staying with him. I can well imagine Mary going to each of them to break the news. There's something odd going on up there, if you ask me, she will say, raising her eyebrows, drawing in her chin to meet her wobbling neck.

How she will relish the scandal of Morgan having an illegitimate child, but how much more she would have enjoyed it, if she knew that Fortune was mine. I shall never forget the look of rapture on her face when Sian was shamed in front of us all in the chapel. Poor Sian, who threw herself in the Wildwater rather than live the blighted life of a spoiled woman.

There are yet worse fates, I think to myself, remembering the words my husband spoke on my return last night. On telling him we would need to leave early for Morgan's shearing, he said he would never go again to that place where my bastard resides, for Morgan and I to rub his nose in the evidence of my philandering.

I do not tell Beulah this on my arrival alone, when she asks where Eli is, though she guesses at the reason well enough, I think. While we stand together, cutting portions of bread and cake, I tell her of the new dairy-maid, who was there when I got home.

"A big lump of a thing with a pasty, round face. She has the look of a lump of bread dough," I say, remembering how she had fluttered her eyelids at Eli, every time he spoke with her.

"She flounces about the place, wiggling her backside as though she has an itch on her back she cannot reach to scratch. Like this!"

I demonstrate by walking across the kitchen with my bosom thrust forward, my back arched backwards, while wiggling my hips from side to side.

Fortune laughs with glee at this, "Like one of the ducks by the pond!"

She laughs with her head thrown back and mouth wide open, and I glow inside to think I have made her laugh. But Beulah laughs half-heartedly, not really paying attention, for she is preoccupied and nervous about the impending rush of neighbours. She lays her hands on each piece of bread, counting each one in turn. She is a bag of restless nervousness, rightly believing the neighbour's wives will be looking for reasons to find fault with her.

"We're going to be short!" She says with exasperation.

"We are not. I've been doing this since I were ten year old, Beulah. Please have some faith in me."

If I speak with impatience, it is only that her nervousness is increasing my own growing agitation about Morgan's impending speech. Fortune goes off in search of him, leaving Beulah and I alone.

"As I was saying, about the new dairy-maid..."

"You want to watch that one! I've met her sort before!" Beulah interrupts.

I fall silent, remembering how Eli spoke with her at our table, as if I was not there, and the hot surge of anger I felt at the time is reignited by the memory.

"She has barely said two words to me. I said to her, this morning before I left, to be sure she closes the dairy door when she is finished in there, lest the flies will get into the milk," I tell Beulah, "there are so many flies this year."

"Aye, that's right enough. A plague they are."

"I take me orders from Mister Jenkins, she said, and turned on her heel and flounced out!"

"The brazen madam! You want to put your foot down with that one, Megan, nip it in the bud. Tell Eli how she spoke to you. One word from him will set her straight."

Fortune comes back to tell us, with great excitement, that she has seen some men coming round the bend in the track. Beulah and I each take a stack of plates and carry them down to the table set out in the orchard. It is an old barn door set up on some makeshift trestles which Morgan has fashioned from interlocking branches of a tree. Fortune trots along behind us, carrying a clean linen sheet to throw over the table.

In Fortune's presence, I cannot tell Beulah that Eli does not speak to me, can hardly bear to be in the same room as me, and sleeps in another room. It is not for the ears of my little girl to hear.

Beulah spits on the corner of her apron, then uses it to rub a mark from one of the plates.

"This can be Mary's plate," she says with a wink, making me laugh and dispelling the grief I feel whenever I think of Eli.

Beulah sighs as we walk back up to the house. I notice she has not had time to weed the vegetable patch and know it will raise a few critical eyebrows among the womenfolk.

"God help us, the womenfolk will be arriving soon wanting to know more than is their business to know," Beulah says, casting a knowing glance from me to Fortune.

I feel a fierce, protective urge surge through me as I imagine how they will look on Fortune, as if she is not the innocent in all this. *Tainted by sin from conception*, I can hear Mam say, and that is what they will all think. There is not much the little one misses, more the pity for her, for I'm certain she won't fail to notice how she will be stared at by the neighbours this day.

We have only to wait. I sit in the chair by the window, watching the men arrive in dribs and drabs, being greeted loudly with hearty slaps on the back from Morgan which makes me suspect he has been drinking the cider already. Some have brought young lads with them, whose job it will be to help catch the sheep for the shearers. Fortune is sorely disappointed when told she cannot do this job as well.

The men are soon assembled on the benches around the shady side of the barn, and the madness and mayhem begins; with the sheep kicking up a fuss and noise enough to wake the dead, and the dust from their hundreds of hooves rising in the air. When I hear Morgan set them all off singing hymns while they work, I am surer than ever that he has been drinking to steady his nerves.

Ceridwen, from a farm down the valley, is the first of the women through the door.

"So this is Morgan's little visitor!" she says, looking from Fortune to me, eyes wide with curiosity. I feel certain she is noting the likeness between us.

When Mary, the Mill, arrives, it is with a haughty flourish, chin thrust up, striding into the house without knocking, and I see Beulah's hackles rise.

"I've brought cake," she says, laying her basket on the table, "I didn't want the menfolk disappointed."

"They shall have cake coming out of their ears, then," I say.

She turns with surprise, not having seen me sitting in the chair by the window.

"Megan! What a surprise!" she says with a tight smile, "I didn't expect to see you here. I'd have thought you had more than enough to do down at Wildwater, now your housekeeper has packed her bags and gone."

I wonder who it is that told her. Was it Eli? And if it was, what reason did he give for Gwen's departure?

Mary turns to Fortune. "Fetch me a cup of water, girl, for I am parched from the climb up that hill."

How dare she speak to Fortune so, I think, and rise to my feet.

"I'll get it!" Beulah says with a warning look at me.

"And how is our little orphan girl, today?" Mary asks Fortune.

Fortune opens her mouth to answer, and I fear she is going to tell Mary what Morgan has told her. Bessy walks in at that moment, and the moment thankfully passes.

Bessy pats my cheek. "I've brought a jug of our best elderflower cordial. See?"

She sets the jug down on the table and I thank God for the Bessys of this world, with their unwavering kindness and generosity. The little room is soon filling up with new arrivals and I suggest they all make their way to the barn. Their sidelong glances at Fortune, and sharper looks in my direction, are not lost on me, and I cannot bear to be cooped up in the kitchen with them a moment longer.

I usher them all out to the barn and our share of the work begins. Fortune runs back and forth, her arms full with the fleeces of wool that she picks up from the ground at the men's feet. In silence, we wrap and roll the fleeces at a steady pace until the wool packs are full to bursting. When we are done, we wash the dust and grease from our skins before heading down to the garden to eat.

Beulah and I carry the baskets of food down to the orchard, and it is clear that Fortune is the topic of conversation, for they fall silent on our approach, and resume their subdued chatter when we walk back to the house. I long for the day to be over. It is with growing dismay that I see Morgan has got himself drunk with the cider. I watch as he stumbles into the orchard, ahead of the shearers.

"Tuck in, neighbours!" Morgan says, sitting down on the bench with a thud, when they are all assembled at the makeshift table.

For all Morgan's attempts at cheer, it is not like the merry gatherings of old. There is a quiet tension in the air, like before a thunderstorm, a tension that makes the hairs stand away from the skin of my arms. Furtive glances are cast in Fortune's direction. I feel each of them is waiting, waiting for someone else to ask what they all want to know. Who is this Fortune, where is she come from, and why is she here? The air bristles with unasked questions.

Then Morgan rises, swaying on his feet. He rubs at the stubble of his chin; as he is want to do when anxious. He clears his throat. I exchange a look with Beulah. She understands my meaning straight away and urges Fortune to go with her, back to the house.

"I have..." he says, swaying backwards and throwing out his open hands in a theatrical gesture, "...an..." here he pauses to belch, and the ladies present do tut and share glances of disgust, "...ANNOUNCEMENT!"

His voice rises with each syllable of the word and his emotion. I have begun to tremble. No slight tremor in the hands is this, but a terrible quaking that begins in my knees and runs up through my core, as if all the pent up emotion of the past days is about to erupt from me.

It is like the tremor of the earth, I think, which happened when we were children; a tremor that began with the rattling of the plates on the dresser until they began to fly from the shelves and smash upon the floor, their sharp shards flying in every direction. One shard caught Morgan and caused blood to spout from the corner of his eye. If you look close, you will see a small scar there still. We fled from the house to run for Mam who was working out in the fields. We thought the house was about to fall in on our heads, like in a fairy-tale. And so we fled, without a thought for our Da, lying on the bed upstairs and sleeping off the drink of the night before. Only when we were a safe distance from the house did we stop and look back, astonished to find it still standing, apparently unscathed. I felt a pang of guilt, afterwards, at not having thought to save our Da. The whole bed shook, he told us later, as he explained to us what an earthquake was.

An earthquake it was, rumbling through me now. I clasp my arms tight with my hands and clench my jaw, lest my teeth begin to chatter from the trembling. Morgan clears his throat again.

"I know…" his chin drops onto his chest for a moment as if it is too great an effort to hold his head up "…you are all wondering…" another belch which he attempts to stifle with his fist, "…who the little one is!"

He takes them all in with a wide, benevolent smile which is not returned. There is a long pause in which it appears he has lost his train of thought, and I believe I will surely faint if he does not get this over with soon.

"Aye. So. I shall tell ye. I have a confession to make, you see. And I hope you can find it in your hearts to forgive me!"

I take a furtive glance at his enraptured audience. Morgan looks at them all with a sheepish grin, as though he is really guilty of the sin he is about to confess. They, in turn, look back at him with grim curiosity.

"Fortune is my own daughter! There, I've said it! I am not the pious man you believed me to be."

Morgan sits down so heavily he almost upturns the bench and everyone sat upon it. The quaking inside me ebbs away. The thing is done. The small gathering is shocked into silence. I glance around at their faces. They are embarrassed; do not know where to look, as if Morgan has loudly broken wind in their presence. The women begin gathering their belongings together, picking up their baskets and their knitting, self-consciously busying themselves with these activities, so they do not have to look at Morgan or myself.

"I must be getting along, I've a mountain of chores waiting at home," Blod says this to Gwyneth who is sat beside her, and they all follow Blod's cue and get up, one by one, to leave, making their excuses for leaving to each other but not to us. They keep their gazes averted from Morgan and me.

Twm is the first of the men to rise to his feet. As he passes behind Morgan, he does no more than glance at him when he speaks.

"I'm ashamed to know you," he says, and walks up the path, knocking the dust from his cap against his leg.

"I, too," says Elgan as he gets up from the bench. He pulls his cap onto his head, looks over at me with hostility in his narrowed eyes, and then follows Twm.

"I'm sorry, Meg, but we've a lot to do," Bessy says, hurrying past me, her face mottled and red, and her sister bustles after her.

One by one, they all leave, stiff-lipped and straight-backed, their bodies speaking of righteous indignation. I notice Dafydd has not got to his feet yet, is still sat on a low branch of the apple tree. He turns his cap round and round in his hands and gazes at the ground. Then he looks over, straight into my eyes, and there is such knowing sadness and pity in his; I know that he knows the truth.

Mary speaks his name and tells him to get moving. "I do not want to spend another moment in this…this den of iniquity," she says to him, and he slowly gets to his feet. Morgan is holding his head in his hands and does not see the way Mary looks at me, and I think she knows the truth too, and is not finished with me yet.

Dafydd pauses behind Morgan, and rests his hand on Morgan's shoulder.

"That was not an easy thing to do, but I see why you had to do it," he says to Morgan, all the while looking at me.

Dafydd slings his jacket over his shoulder, and follows after Mary with that long, slow stride of his.

Dafydd will not tell a soul of what he knows, I am certain of that, but Mary is a different thing altogether. I am quite certain she suspects Morgan did not tell the truth this day, but will she have the gall to voice her suspicions without sure foundation?

Morgan believed he would solve a problem, once and for all, this day, but things have not turned out as expected. He expected the womenfolk to condemn him for a time, only to excuse him later, on the grounds that he must have been seduced by an evil temptress. But the reaction he's received from the men of the parish, he didn't expect that. He had flinched when Twm said what he did.

Morgan is sat there still with his head in his hands, staring at the table as if he can see his sorry future mapped out there.

"They will come round," I say, with a certainty I do not feel. "It is always the fault of some wanton women with them, at the end of the day."

He lifts his head and glares at me before issuing forth his tirade.

"Well, they'd be bloody right there, and all. Don't look like that. It is your fault, all of it. They all think ill of me now and I haven't done a damned thing! And where was your precious Eli, eh? I've done him and you a great favour this day, and he didn't have the good grace to turn up."

He is shouting, and from the corner of my eye I see Beulah and Fortune emerge from the house. On hearing the unfolding argument, Beulah hurries Fortune back inside.

"It was your notion, not mine, to claim her as your own. Have you forgotten that? It is not fair to lay blame at my door for something I did not ask for myself."

"You damned well had her in the first place! Out of wedlock! How is that not your fault?"

"Why are you and Megan shouting?"

The sound of Fortune's voice pulls us up short. She has sneaked back out here, unnoticed by Beulah. Her little face is pinched with worry. I open my arms to her, telling her not to worry, it was just a silly argument. But she does not come to me; she takes a wide berth, sidling around me, then runs and flings her arms around Morgan's neck.

"Dada!" she says, hugging him tight.

My empty arms fall to my sides. She is lost to me, lost as surely as if she had died. My brother robbed me of her once, and now he has done it again. He looks over at me and must see it all, written on my stricken face, for I see it register in his. He lets go of Fortune and says, "Aw, Megan!" but I have picked up my basket and fled.

Chapter Five

The reaper's blade cares not what falls beneath
its brutal blow. Weed or little flower, the reaper
he doth mow.

They sit side by side, my husband and his new dairy maid. He is complimenting her on the butter she has made and so lavishly spread atop her oatcake. She blushes and simpers, wriggles and giggles, and I feel a strong impulse to slap the smile from her face. Instead, I get up and go to the sink, and begin to vigorously scrub the pots that were all left undone while I was at Morgan's shearing.

I shall never go there again, never. Beulah will have to manage without my help, and I must learn to endure without her friendship. It is better that I not see Fortune again, than to witness the love, that should have been mine, be showered upon others. What mine eyes do not see, my heart will endure.

I have lost my daughter. I have lost my husband's affection. I have lost everything worth having; accepting that this is so makes it curiously easier to endure. It is like the acceptance that a person is dead, knowing we cannot bring them back. Or it is, perhaps like moving home. I have shut and bolted the door on that other life that might have been, and moved into this other empty life. It is a cold, unwelcoming, and barren place but it is the only place open to me now.

"You have a good and healthy appetite. I like that in a woman," Eli is saying to the dairy-maid. He is doing this to hurt me, this I know. He wants me to feel the pain of betrayal that he is suffering. It is his way of punishing me. Knowing that, does not make the medicine any easier to swallow.

The dairy-maid giggles and pops another piece of oatcake into her voluminous mouth.

"I'd better get back to the dairy," she says.

"Take your time, Branwen," says he.

Such a pretty name it is, for such a lump of a girl. Methinks her parents must have been blind, for her name means 'beautiful raven' though there is nothing beautiful about her. Like herself, the name is a contradiction in terms, for it seems strange to me that a raven should be described as beautiful; scavengers and harbingers of doom that they are.

I watch her glance at Eli from beneath her lashes as she hoists up her stays, pushing up her breasts. I fear they are about to spill out of the top of her blouse. Eli has his eye on them, as if he thinks the same.

I will not let him see my jealousy and anger. I think he will sooner give up this game if he is not rewarded with the desired effect. I rinse the scrubbed pots in the water bucket and stand them on the side to dry. I will not rise to his bait. I shall pretend I have not seen.

Eli gets up and leaves for his precious fields. He used to return a half dozen times every day, just to see me, for he knew I became lonely. Now he takes his bread and cheese with him so he does not have to return, even for his mid-day meal. I dry my hands and follow after him, calling his name. He does not pause until he reaches the gate.

"I wondered when Gwen's replacement might arrive," I tell him.

"Replacement?" he says, his eyes dancing as if I have said something to amuse him.

"Yes, replacement. There is too much for one woman to do..." my voice trails away when I see the look of scorn on his face.

"You complained often enough when Gwen was here, that you had not enough to occupy your time. Now you have plenty to occupy you, I do not think you have reason for yet more complaint."

"But I cannot possibly manage such a place on my own, Eli."

"I daresay you imagined you would live a life of idle luxury once you had my ring on your finger."

"No! I did not imagine that, but you said yourself, make the most of things, for there would be plenty to do once the ..."

I do not finish saying 'once the children come along' for there will not be any children between us now.

He tells me I will have to manage, as there will not be another hiring fair this year.

"But surely, there must be someone local."

"And have the whole parish know about the sham of our marriage? I think not, Megan."

"A maid, then, from the village, just for a few hours a day! She would not have to live in."

"I have said all I shall say on this matter. Gwen managed perfectly well without a maid and so shall you."

"But Gwen had not a moment's respite!"

"As I said, Megan, if you hoped for an easy life when you tricked me into marriage, you can think again."

He is too cruel, I think, as I watch him stride away down the lane. I turn back to the house and the mountain of chores that await me. The house seems so tall and foreboding, suddenly, looming up there on the rise of the hill. It is as well I have already decided I shall not go to Carregwyn again for I will not have the time to help Beulah as she would like.

I go in search of kindling for the bread oven. I climb, pulling the small gambo, to a place on the hill where the ground is littered with dead branches of gorse. They are like bleached, white bones strewn upon the turf.

I gather them up in armfuls until the gambo is filled to the brim. When the last armful of sticks is thrown in, I stand and stretch my aching back. My gaze wanders over Eli's meadows below and comes to rest upon the dairy maid, milking the cow in the bottom meadow. She sits on the stool, amid the glowing buttercups, her head resting on its flank, the bucket beneath its udder.

Perhaps I should try to make a friend of her. It would make the living with her easier. I have resolved to do this when I see Eli approach her across the meadow. They are far away but I can tell from his gait that he is sneaking up on her. He sneaks up behind and I imagine he must say 'boo', for she leaps up from her stool in fright. She doubles over, no doubt laughing. Neither seem to care about the wasted bucket of milk the cow kicked over when she, too, was startled.

I stand and watch them idly talking as if they are the best of friends. He has his hands clasped behind his back, one foot resting on the milking stool. She leans against the cow, with one arm thrown over its flank and one hand on her hip. A knot of fear worms itself inside me. If he seeks her out when I am not there, then his flirtations are not only for the purpose of irking me. It is something more, something more intolerable, something which thwarts any hopes I have that, deep down, he may still love me.

It is by the light of the lamp that I take the last loaves of bread from the oven. Eli and his dairy-maid (it irks me too much to call her by name) have gone their separate ways at long last; he up the creaking front stairs, she up the back stairs to her sleeping quarters above this kitchen.

They have chattered and laughed away the evening, sat here at the kitchen table, while I attended to the baking. They talked until the window panes turned the colour of ink. They have much to talk about; for she is no stranger to him, it transpires. She was the dairy-maid on his uncle's farm when he was there. They have much remembering to do in their conversations about places and people they knew there. I am excluded, for they are people and places of which I know nothing.

They have six years' worth of shared memories. With her, he speaks fondly of things he has never shared with me. When he returned here from his uncle's farm, wishing to marry me, all he would say of his time away was that it was dull because I was not there.

Yet, it seems, his days were far from dull. She speaks of times when he and the rest of the maids and farm hands went trundling off to merry market days and fairs in Cardigan, stumbling their way home in the early hours. She laughs with her mouth so wide I can see down her throat to her drawers, I think, glancing over at her as Eli recalls a farm hand falling into a ditch on one of their forays home, no one having missed him until the next day.

"And there he was, still snoring off a belly full of mead when we found him!"

She laughs that laugh again. Her voice is so loud and her laugh is a cackle which all but pierces my eardrums so that I want to cover my ears with my hands.

"Oh, we had some good times, you and I," she says, and there is something in her tone of voice that makes me look over at her, and I see her wink at him and nudge him with her elbow.

He casts a quick look in my direction, as if worried that I have seen. It is the deep red that flushes his cheekbones that tells me it was something more than friendship between them, back on this uncle's farm. I feel a dark, dark rage swell up inside me, to think of how he is punishing me for something he saw no harm in doing himself; and with that common lump of dough sat at my table.

When she rises in the morning, her eyes encrusted with sleep and yawning widely, I think how much of her time she spends with her mouth wide open and feel a strong desire to clamp it shut. She has yet to greet me with a 'good morning'. Instead, she casts a sweeping and sly glance at me which travels from my feet to my nose, but she never looks me directly in the eye.

Seeing that look, I do realise with astonishment that she thinks herself better than me! Because HE has shown her that he thinks more of her than me. Thus, the stupid girl thinks me beneath her in the pecking order of this house. I don't know yet just how I shall do it, but I determine that she be made aware of the error in her thinking.

When I at last entered my bed chamber last night, leaving the loaves lined up on the table to cool, I was overcome with exhaustion but sleep eluded me still. The harder I tried to sleep, knowing the pile of laundry that awaited me this morn, the more elusive did sleep become.

I turn this way and that, thinking of my husband lying there in the chamber next to mine, and recalling what passed between them. The more I thought on it, the more consumed by self-pity I became. I could not reconcile the injustice that he should punish me for one mistake while admiring this trollop who thinks nothing of having been loose with her favours.

She sits there now, cramming the freshly made bread into her mouth. She slurps a great gulp from the jug of buttermilk. She is a common, ill-mannered thing, I think, as I watch her chewing with her mouth open; a common thing who does not have an ounce of table-manners.

It is hypocrisy that he should think sauce is good for the gander but not the goose. I resolve to tell him such, when or if we have a moment alone, out of shot of the maid's prying ears. Not today, for he has left for his fields already, before the two of us had risen from our beds.

She has eaten half a loaf of bread, and a large quantity of cheese. I am busying myself at the sink, but have her there in the corner of my eye. She yawns again and stretches like a contented cat, as well she may, with all that cream out there in the dairy. I watch as she gets up, scraping her chair along the flagstones. She waddles off to the dairy, scratching her rump as she goes.

With my hand, I sweep up the breadcrumbs she has left all over the table, and throw them out onto the cobbles for the birds. The sun is not up from behind the hill yet, but it is warming up already. There is not a cloud in the brilliant, blue sky. It will be hot again, and I with a great heap of laundry to do.

There is a great, cast-iron pot, built into the outside of the scullery wall, for heating water for the washing. I carry pails of water from the well to fill it. I light a bundle of straw beneath and lay kindling on top to get a good fire going. I go to fetch the baskets of dirty washing, and at the sight of what I find in there, my rage boils hotter than the water in the pot outside.

Branwen has dropped her filthy monthly rags in there. I am incensed with rage and disgust at her, that she should imagine I would wash her personal things for her.

Between finger and thumb I remove them from the basket. Then I storm up to the dairy.

She is stood skimming the cream from the milk. I throw the rags down at her feet.

"If you think I am doing your filthy washing for you, you can think again."

I am spitting with rage as I speak, but she merely narrows her eyes at me, her face full of spite.

"We'll see what Eli says about that!" she says, placing her hands on her hips.

"Oh, aye, alright. Let's go fetch him right now, and hand him those!"

I point to her bloodied rags and she blushes to the roots of her hair.

"You'd do well to remember who is mistress here," I say, turning on my heel and flouncing out of the door.

Hot tears flow as I scrub at Eli's shirt collars and work breeches. It is his fault that madam has ideas above her station, leading her to think she could treat me as though our stations were reversed. It is all his doing and he will have to put it right.

When the washing is all done, and my knuckles are scraped raw, I spread the clean clothes out on the bushes to dry. Then I go in search of Eli in the far flung fields. I sight him down in the hay meadow where a group of men are cutting the hay.

I keep back, out of sight of the men, for I know that it takes only a small distraction to break a man's concentration and cause a fatal accident. They work the field in an orderly row. Eli is up ahead, keeping the men working in an orderly rhythm. There is a loud swish as they swing their scythes in unison, and a row of hay is felled with one swoop. They stand a safe distance apart from each other, for fear of lopping another man off at the ankles. The rhythm of their sweeping scythes lulls me into a daze as I watch grasses, clovers, vetches and buttercups all fall at the reapers' feet.

I am reminded of a verse spoken in the chapel when a child dies. It says the reaper's blade cares not what falls unto its blow; weed or little flower, the reaper he doth mow.

In the heat, the men work with their sleeves of their smocks rolled up and their buttons undone. Already, the air is filled with the sweet scent of hay as the cut grasses and flowers begin to dry in the sun. I sit down to wait, on the step of the style, and look down the valley towards the Wildwater valley in the distance. Such a beautiful valley it is, with its meadows rolling down to the river's edge; small coppices of hazel, hawthorn and sisal oak; the hills rising sharply above and beyond; and there at its heart, the relentless, tumbling wild water.

All my life is there spread out before me, I think, all that turmoil being played out amidst such beauty. Why can life never be as we'd wish it?

"What are you doing here?" Eli's voice breaks into my thoughts, his tone accusing.

But days ago he would have smiled with delight to find me come to meet him. How long have I sat there dreaming I do not know but the field is all cut, and the workmen packing up their things. I get to my feet, brushing the creases from my skirts. Eli picks up his jerkin from its hanging place on the branch of a tree. He slings it over his shoulder and begins to walk on without me. Up the little narrow path that cuts across the field behind the house he strides, with me running along behind.

"Please wait! I need to speak with you," I shout after him.

He turns and looks at me with barely concealed impatience.

"What is it now?"

"You must speak with that maid of yours; let her know who is mistress of this house. She is uppity, and will not take orders from me!"

His expression is one of disinterest and boredom which reignites my anger.

"She left her filthy rags for ME to wash, as if it is I and not she that is the maid! I had to remind her, in no uncertain terms, of her place."

His look of disinterest turns to one of irritation.

"I hope you have not been upsetting her, Megan."

"Upset her? She has upset me!"

"I will not have you upsetting her. She is an old and dear friend."

His words work like a spark to a tinder-box.

"Oh, aye! I saw that for myself alright. Tell me, Eli, whilst we are on the subject. Do you not think it hypocrisy that you think no ill of her, though it is plain that she is more than loose with her favours, while condemning me for ONE mistake?! How is that you condemn me without doing the same to her?"

I am panting as though I have run up the hill but he is as calm as you like when he speaks back.

"Because there is a world of difference, Megan, between you and she," he says, leaning in closer to me, "*she* never pretended to be anything but what she is."

Chapter Six

The ill wind doth blow and the cock he doth
crow.
(Beulah does a-calling go and learns a thing or
three.)

Since Morgan told Fortune he is her Da, she has not let
him out of her sight. Whether he is off up the mountain
or to the wheelwright with the cart, up she jumps and
goes skipping after him like a faithful puppy, and never
mind me , left all alone here with the chores to do by
myself.

I have such a bad feeling about it all. No good
ever came from lies, my Aunt Suzannah used to say.
And no good will come from his spoiling her, indulging
her every whim. I know too well what it's all about. He's
still trying to assuage his conscience for having taken
Fortune away from her mother when just a babe, and
leaving her with that harlot for nigh on six years.

"No amount of spoiling will give her back what
she has lost," I said to him.

He went off to his bed in a sulk. It is only the
truth that hurts us, and which he may try to run from but

cannot escape in the end, I think to myself, listening to him shifting about in the creaking bed above.

I do not intend to be harsh, but some things are better aired in the light of day than left to moulder in the darkness of silence. From the day he and his Mam changed the course of Megan's life, things have but gone from bad to worse. 'Tis as changing the course of a mountain spring by interference. The spring may change its underground course but only to emerge somewhere else where you least expect it and don't want it. Such things should be left alone to follow their rightful course of events, for better or worse. What will be, will be, for all the wishing it will not.

Though it seemed the only thing to be done was for Morgan to claim Fortune as his, now I fear I have made matters worse for it was my own idea. I should have known better than to imagine yet more lies would provide a solution. I put down my knitting and get up to bank up the fire for the night. I am all of a muddle for this must surely be the most muddle-headed family I ever knew in my life.

My thoughts turn to Megan down there at Wildwater. I don't know if Eli is the forgiving kind, but I hope for her sake that he is. She has not been near since the day of the shearing, and left then without a bye or leave. Morgan thinks she was upset to see Fortune calling him Da. I've never been blessed with a child of my own, but imagine that if it were me it would be a torment to be near my own child and not be able to love and care for it myself.

I take up the candle to light me to bed and resolve to rise with the dawn, get my chores done early, and go down and visit. I'll wager Megan will be pleased to see a friendly face and I have a favour to ask of her.

It's the first and last time I do this, I think, on the long walk down to Wildwater. I have wandered from the true path it seems, for I have ventured into some tall bracken and have to wade my way through. Parting it with my hands, and with my skirts getting caught and snarled, I feel as though I am being pulled backwards with every step. Cobwebs brush across my face and I bat at the flies that buzz about my head, threatening to kill every last one of them if they do not let me be. It is with relief that I emerge again onto the open heath and I am thankful for the dappled shade when I enter Eli's wood. I follow the path that edges the mountain stream.

I preferred village life; that is certain. I am not cut out for the hard toil of farm life. I would never have taken the post if I'd known how hard it was going to be. But then, I remind myself, I don't know what else I would have done; widowed and about to be turned out of my cottage as I was.

Be thankful for what you have, Beulah, I tell myself, lest you find yourself in a worse situation.

Though, I don't believe I shall feel thankful when I have to climb back up this hill, later in the day.

I avoid looking into that terrible, tumbling river when I have to walk alongside it for a short time. I wonder if the ghosts of my own great-aunt Mary, and that poor young Sian Williams, are roaming its banks, never able to rest their weary heads. It might have taken Megan too, according to Morgan's account of that day, so recently, when he arrived in the nick of time.

I am greatly relieved when the path meanders away from the river's edge and the big old house comes into view. Other than Megan's wedding night, I have not been here since the days when I was a child, when I used to roam from door to door, selling great-aunt Suzannah's stockings, when she grew too old and stooped to do it herself.

Eli's parents were still alive then, but I rarely saw them for I had to go around the back entrance to sell my wares. Gwen was a youngish woman still, and she'd always give me some morsel to eat along with payment, to see me on my way.

Gwen never married or had children of her own; devoted her whole life to the running of Wildwater house. That's a housekeeper's lot in life, I remind myself. I'll grow old and grey, looking after Morgan and Fortune, and then be put out to graze like his pony, when I am all worn out with the work.

The front door is open wide and I peer inside, calling Megan's name. I see the flagstones have been scrubbed and are still wet further inside the hallway where the sunshine has not yet dried them. When there is no answer to my calls, I go round to the back door that leads into the kitchen. This too is open and the flagstones here are scrubbed and drying in the breeze. They must have got themselves a replacement housekeeper, I think, seeing the kitchen so neat and clean. It will make life easier on Megan, and make it easier for me to ask the favour I want of her.

There is no sign of Megan, so I walk up to the dairy. The door here too is open, and no one inside. I see there are flies swimming about in a large bowl of cream. Megan will be furious when she sees that. I walk out and go round the corner at the back of the dairy, thinking Megan might be down in the garden, and almost trip over the legs of the dairy maid.

She is sat with her back to the white-washed wall, legs splayed out amid the dandelions, her head lolling onto her milky bosom and snoring loudly. I give her feet a hard rap with my boot which startles her awake.

"What do you think you are doing sleeping when you should be at your work?" I say to her.

"What business is it of yours?" she asks, scrambling to her feet and picking up her bonnet from the ground.

"I'm a friend of your mistress. That makes it my business, I think you will find."

It is at such times I am grateful for my unfeminine height as I tower over her with my hands on my hips.

"I was only having a rest while I waited for the cream to rise," she says, bustling past me and heading back into the dairy.

"The cream's risen, alright, and thanks to your leaving the door open, the flies are having a nice swim in it, and all."

She shrugs, "I'll take 'em off with the skimmer."

Her devil-may-care shrug makes me want to cuff her about the ears.

"You want to watch yourself, young woman, or you'll be down that road without a reference to keep you company."

"Eli would never sack me! He says I'm the best dairy-maid he's ever had." She pulls herself up all straight and proud when she says this.

"Then Mr Jenkins can't have been looking further than the end of his nose! I shall have to help him see what he has hitherto not been able to see for himself."

She clamps her mouth tight shut and a blush rises to the roots of her hair. She does not know who I am or whether I have any influence with Eli.

"Where is your mistress?"

She shrugs again, her face sullen. "How am I supposed to know?"

"You'd do well to be more mindful of where she is, for she and I will have our eyes on you from now on."

Of all the insolent strumpets, I think, going out again in search of Megan. Well, that put her in her place. If Eli has any sense, he'll show that one the road. At last, I spot Megan down in the garden, bending over the vegetable patch, her hands sifting through the soil and lifting potatoes. She is mightily surprised but does not seem too pleased to see me.

"Oh! Beulah!" she says, straightening up and rubbing her back with one hand. She swipes the back of her other hand across the sweat on her brow and leaves a smear of mud there. Tendrils of hair fall down over her face and she swipes those away too, oblivious to the dirt on her hands. She scoops up the potatoes she's placed on the ground, and places them in the swoop of her apron.

"I'm sorry, Beulah," she says, walking back down the path towards the house, "I know I said I'd come and help but there is so much to do here..."

Her voice trails off and I think, so, that is why she is not pleased to see me. She is afraid I have come to plead for help.

"I can see that!" I say, laughing. "Oh, Megan, you do look a fright! You have mud all over your face."

"Oh, have I?" she says, emptying her apronful of potatoes out onto the scrubbed table. She goes over to a small looking-glass that hangs by the door. "Oh, yes. I'd better wash my face."

But she does not go to the sink. She goes to the table and looks perplexed.

"Now what was it I wanted these potatoes for? I've quite forgotten!"

She has trodden dirt from the garden, all over her lovely clean floor.

"What do you say I make us some tea? I'll wager that Eli has plenty of tea in the house – not like Morgan, who says we can't afford such a luxury. I'm fit to drop, I am, from that walk down the hill."

"What? Oh, oh yes, of course. I put the kettle over the fire before I went out. The tea is in the caddy up there on the dresser shelf."

The kettle is not over the fire, it stands empty on the board beside the sink. Without a word, I lift the water pail and pour enough water into the kettle for our tea and hang it over the fire. Then I gulp down a cup of water to quench my raging thirst while we wait.

"I ran into your dairy maid when I was looking for you," I say, stretching up to reach down the tea caddy from the top shelf; Megan being small, she must have to stand on a chair to reach it.

"Oh, yes? I'm sorry, Beulah, I meant to fetch carrots and swedes, too. I'll have to go and get them."

I follow her back down the garden and talk while she fills up her apron.

"She's a little madam, I must say. I gave her a piece of her mind, though."

Megan looks stricken. "You didn't upset her, did you? I hope you did not, for Eli will not like it one bit."

"Don't talk daft, Megan, if he had seen her sleeping while the flies were swimming in the cream, he would have fired her on the spot. I shall tell him when I see him."

Megan hurries ahead of me, back to the house, all of a fluster.

"Please do not, Beulah. It will only cause trouble if you do. They are old friends, it seems, from when he lived on his Uncle's farm. He won't hear a word against her."

She tips the vegetables out of her apron onto the table and does not seem to notice that some miss the table altogether and go bouncing across the floor. I stoop down to pick them up, wondering how much I dare say. I'm seeing the way the land lies around here these days, and I don't like what I see one bit.

I place the stray vegetables on the table, and push the whole lot to the middle to make room for our tea. Without another word, I set about making the tea. Spooning tea into the pot, I think that I knew what I would do, if my husband was being over-friendly with the maid. I would not wait for his permission to throw her and her bags out of the door. And I'd tell him I'd be packing my own and all if he didn't like it.

I glance over at Megan. She is standing with her back to me, at the sink, gazing out of the window that overlooks the garden, lost in thought. I set the teapot on the table and fetch two dainty cups and saucers from the dresser.

"Well! This is a rare treat," I say, taking a small jug and going out to the pantry for some milk. "Are you going to join me then?"

I tap her on the shoulder as I go past. She turns her head.

"Oh, thank you, Beulah. If I'd known you were making tea, I would have given you a hand."

Lord God, I think, things need a good shaking out around here, and the sooner the better. I reach for her cup and take a good look at her; sat there with her faraway look, curling a lock of hair around her finger. I pour her tea and push it across the table to her. She gazes at it and says;

"I do not really like tea. We never had it at home. Could never afford it. It makes me think of dying."

"Why, in heaven's name?"

"Funerals. It was the only time we drank it, at other people's funerals."

All the more for me then, I think, taking a good gulp from my cup.

"I'll ask around the village. There'll surely be a young girl or two falling over each other for the dairy-maid's post."

Megan pushes the cup of tea away from her and I think I'll be damned if I let that go to waste.

"If you're not going to drink that...?"

I pour it back into the pot and pour myself another cup.

"Eli won't allow it," she says, "I suggested a girl from the village to help me in the house."

"That would be grand! You'd have more time to visit us," I say with a grin but she does not seem as enamoured with this idea as I. She shrugs her shoulders and tells me Eli will not hear of it, anyway. He will not employ a local girl, says he doesn't want his business the subject of local gossip. Megan will have to wait until the next hiring fair before they get another housekeeper.

It is the way of this world that a wife must acquiesce to her husband; that a husband must rule the roost like a cock amongst the hens, so that he might strut about the place, preening himself, and let the world see what a fine-feathered man he is.

Now, it's a good thing to keep a rooster among the hens, for he will keep the hens peaceably together and stop them wandering too far from home. And, of course, without him there would be no little chicks. But every now and then, you will find yourself with a rooster who is a bad 'un. All that preening and strutting goes to his head, and he will start throwing his weight around. I've known such a rooster attack his hens, viciously pecking at them and drawing blood. I've known such a rooster to kill a little hen. There's only one course for such a rooster and that is the chopper and the cooking pot.

I see which way the wind is blowing and I don't much like what I smell on it. If Eli Jenkins thinks he can bully this little hen, he can think again. Our little Meg deserves better, far better, than that.

"Oh Lord! I must peel these vegetables else we won't eat tonight." Megan says, leaning back in her chair and retrieving a knife from the table drawer in front of her.

"Give me a knife, we'll do it together," I say, holding out my hand.

I see very well how things are. A man holds all the power in a marriage, and in a world where only last week, at market, a man sold his wife to another he owed money to, so Morgan informed me on his return. Morgan thought I would be as amused as he until he saw I was not laughing.

There is too little love in this world where too many scrape and struggle to put food into their bellies. It is a heartless bugger that would sell his wife, I said to Morgan. Sometimes, he is blind to the suffering beneath the spectacle. Too many marry out of need because there's no alternative. Women marry men because it is that or end up an old maid in someone else's house until they die, as I shall, no doubt. Men marry so they do not

88

have the expense of employing a maid and so that their other needs are met.

How it pains me to see Megan go from skivvying for her mother to doing the same at her husband's behest; and he one of the wealthiest farmers in the parish, able to employ as much help as is needed. Not like Morgan, piss poor and barely able to make ends meet. If ever a couple married out of love, I thought it was these two. But then, Eli did not know of Megan's past, and that has changed the balance of things.

Slicing the feathery green leaves from the top of a carrot, I tell Megan I will have words with Eli.

"You can't go on like this, it will make you ill," I tell her.

"No, Beulah! Please don't say a word. It will only make things worse."

"How could things get any worse?" I ask with exasperation.

She looks away from me and fixes her gaze upon the table between us.

"He is angry with me as it is. He will hate me all the more if he thinks I've been carrying tales behind his back."

"What are you speaking of?! That man worships the ground you walk on. He likely has no idea how much work there is with a house like this and..."

"Shouldn't you be getting back? I can manage this perfectly well on my own!" she says, glancing up at the clock hanging on the wall behind me. I'll wager Eli is due to return soon.

"I'll walk with you now, as far as the Wildwater," she says, getting up from her chair and standing there, anxiously waiting for me to rise.

"I'll just finish this tea, first, to see me on my way," I say, pouring myself a cup. I have yet to request the favour I came here to ask her. Morgan will not be pleased if I return without having asked.

Megan stands fidgeting with her apron, looking from the clock to the door. It's clear she wants me gone. Anxious or not, I'm in no hurry to climb back up that hill.

"I've barely had time to sit down and you're bustling me to be on my way. If it's because I said I'll talk to Eli, I promise I won't say a word if you don't want me to."

This appears to reassure and she sits back down while I ask if I can make a little more tea before I go.

"Now, I have a favour to ask of you," I say, pouring myself a nice, fresh cup. Oh, I could live in a house like this, I think, leaning back in my chair and taking a sip. I'd drink tea all day, until it was spouting from my ears.

"I'm sorry, Beulah, but you can see I haven't time to come up and help you," she snaps at me.

I tell her that is not what I'd come to ask. Though, if I have my way, she'll have plenty of time to come up to Carregwyn. Though I have said I will not say anything to Eli, I will be having words with him. Things will be easier for Megan after. I tell her how Morgan needs me to start selling our cheese and butter at market, like she used to do, to make ends meet.

"But I haven't driven a pony cart in my life and have no intention of starting. I'd likely die of the fright. So we were hoping you would do it."

"Best days I ever had were those Fridays at market," she gazes out of the door with a wistful look on her face, "I should have been grateful for what I had."

"You'll come then! Morgan will be over the moon when I tell him. And as for Fortune, well, she can hardly wait!"

She gets up from her chair and begins throwing the vegetables into a pot. I don't know what I've said now to upset her but it is clear from her face that I have.

"I can't do it. I'm sorry but I really won't have the time..."

"Won't have the time for what?"

Megan visibly jumps and almost drops the pot of vegetables at the sound of Eli's voice. He is stood in the open doorway. "Hello, Beulah! This is a nice surprise," he says, walking in and gracing me with a smile.

"I was just asking Megan if she will drive me to market once a week, "I tell him, "but she says she has no time."

"Nonsense! Of course, she has the time. It will be good for her to get out of the house."

"That's settled then, Meg," I say, with a sigh of relief.

I imagined she would be pleased but I can see by her face she is anything but.

"You would like that wouldn't you?" I ask her.

"She'd love to!" Eli says, without waiting for Megan to answer. He offers to drive me home in his pony and trap and I almost fall over myself with relief, for I'd been dreading that climb back up the hill since the moment I'd arrived.

"That house is far too much work for one woman, you know," I say, when we've been haring along the lane for a while, and I am watching to see his reaction.

"I know, Beulah. I've been wanting to get a replacement for Gwen but you know how Megan is, she thinks she can manage it all herself."

"Does she?" This wasn't as Megan had described things at all. Morgan's words sprang to mind, about lies coming as natural as breathing to Megan.

"I've told her, I won't have her wearing herself out with all the work," Eli goes on, "but she doesn't want someone from the village, so what can I do?"

Why in heaven's name did Megan lie to me? Why tell me it was Eli who was against it, when all along it was herself. I hold fast to my seat with one hand as we fly around the bends in the lane, holding fast to my bonnet with the other. I want to ask Eli to please slow down but fear he will think me foolish.

"I don't know what she's got against village people," Eli is saying now, "but she seems to think they aren't good enough."

He laughs light-heartedly about it, while I am not at all amused. I am 'from the village', and I was good enough for Megan when she was desperate to find a housekeeper for her brother, and never mind not telling me of the toil it would be. And never mind pretending she was as pious as the day was long, and her with a daughter left to lodge with a whore. And she thinks the 'village people' are beneath her?

I am not a woman who is quick to anger but my anger was rising in me now. She'd lied to me, made up some excuse why she couldn't help, and why? Because now she is the high and mighty mistress of Wildwater, I am not good enough for her. The wheels of the trap hit a stone in the road and I shriek, fearing we shall be thrown overboard, but Eli is unperturbed.

"And the dairy-maid is good for nothing!" Eli exclaims, surprising me further.

"You are right about that! I caught her sleeping round the back of the dairy, you know, while the flies swam about in the cream."

"Well, we're stuck with her and all until the next hiring fair!" Eli says, glancing over at me.

"But why on earth…?"

"Megan would rather put up with her than have 'some common village girl in her dairy'."

He pulls at the reins and slows down as we approach the turn to Carregwyn. I am so confused; I am beginning to wonder if I had heard Megan correctly.

"I thought Megan said Branwen was an old friend of yours from when you worked on your uncle's farm. Do you think perhaps Branwen is taking advantage of that friendship?" I say.

Eli is shaking his head with a puzzled expression on his face.

"You must have misunderstood, Beulah. I never met Branwen before the day I hired her. Though, I must admit, I do like Branwen. She may not be much of a dairy-maid, but she is good company of an evening. Megan never stops long enough to sit and chat as we used to."

I stifle my gasp. So Megan had lied about that, too. I distinctly recalled her telling me that Eli and Branwen were old friends. It was no misunderstanding on my part. We are nearing the top of the hill and Eli turns the trap outside the gate, then turns in his seat.

"I'm sorry Megan doesn't want to take you to market. It would do her good to have a day out."

"I thought she would jump at the chance," I say, thinking Megan probably wouldn't want to be seen at market with a common spinster 'from the village'.

"You know, I go there every Friday. I could take you along with me, if you'd like."

"Oh, I couldn't possibly impose…"

"Not at all. It would be no trouble. I'd enjoy the company, to tell you the truth."

I tell him how excited Fortune will be to have a ride in a proper pony and trap.

"I'd rather you didn't bring the child along," he says and looks away from me to look down on the valley below. "You know, it's one thing to forgive your wife for deceiving you, quite another to have your nose rubbed in it."

"I'll just have to tell Fortune she can't come, then," I say, feeling sorry for the man.

We arrange to meet at the bottom of the lane that Friday. I wave as I watch him go.

The poor man. Megan has broken his heart but he's just as good as said he's forgiven her. My heart went out to him. Megan had no idea how lucky she was. And who could blame him for not wanting to see Fortune – the reminder of how badly Megan had betrayed him?

I watch until he goes out of sight, round the bend in the track. Well, I had plenty to tell Morgan, I think, opening the latch of the gate. And I didn't suppose he'd be surprised by much of it. It seems he knows his sister better than anyone; better than I thought I did.

Chapter Seven

Hey-ho, hey-ho, it's off to market they shall go.

I lie awake far into Thursday night. Eli says I have offended Beulah, my only friend in this world, with my refusal to take her to market. During the interval between then and now, I have thought long and hard. I cannot continue forever avoiding another meeting with Fortune. So, I am to be her 'aunt'. Surely, that is better than to be nothing to her at all?

This is what I tell myself as I lie staring into the darkness, listening to the wind buffeting the window panes. I was denied knowing her at all for the first six years of her life. Now, once a week, there is an opportunity to get to know her, and I must take it.

I rise before the dawn, in readiness to take Beulah to market. Now I have resolved to do so, excitement churns in my belly. The very thought of seeing Myfanwy and her daughters, again, makes me smile. Oh, it will be fun, I think, Beulah and I journeying to market with my dear little Fortune sat between us.

I shall buy her some bonny ribbons for her hair. And perhaps some bolts of cloth to make her some clothes. I'm good with a needle. Beulah told me Fortune is wearing hand-me-downs from that spiteful Mary, the

Mill. I would rather she wore rags, Beulah said. Yes, I shall make Fortune some pretty clothes of her own, and a doll to carry about with her.

I must not be afraid. It will hurt to pretend I am not her mother but it will be as nothing compared to the agony of the time when they stole her from me. This new pain will not destroy me and it will be far outweighed by the joy of being in Fortune's company.

The first light of dawn is lighting the sky above the easterly hills when I go out to fetch water from the well. The wind has died down. The air is crisp and fresh and a slight breeze rustles through the sycamore trees behind the barn. A bat flutters about the roof of the barn, looking for a place to roost for the day. Down in the orchard, I hear a song thrush begin to herald the new day.

The last of the night's stars are fading. The spell of hot weather will last a while longer yet. I will want to climb the hill to Carregwyn and surprise Beulah before the heat of the day begins. I imagine her big smile as I tell her I've changed my mind; that we're off to market with Morgan's pony and cart.

Back in the house, I place water to boil over the fire, and put oats to soak in the buttermilk for our breakfast. I go about my chores with a lightness of step. It will make my life with Eli bearable, I think, if I can spend one day a week in the company of my daughter and Beulah. It will give me something to look forward to, something to live for.

Branwen comes in, yawning loudly, and scratching her head so that I wonder if she has the lice. They are as thick as thieves, she and my husband. I hear the front door close and go to the window to look out. The air is infused with the first light of dawn. A misty haze hangs in the air and softens the edges of everything. It is that time when the day hangs pregnant with promise. Eli is harnessing the pony to the trap and steam blows from the pony's nostrils. It scrapes a hoof over the cobbles, eager to be away. The house-martins are out and about, swooping in and out of their nests beneath the eaves. If Eli is going out soon, I shall ask him if I can ride along as far as the turn to Carregwyn. It will get me there all the sooner. My heart gives a skippety-skip beat!

Branwen slurps at her bowl of oats and buttermilk. She is hunched over her bowl, a spoon in one hand, and one arm curled around her bowl as if she fears someone is about to take it away. I know nothing about her, nothing at all. I know not where she comes from; her family; her hopes, dreams. I admit to some curiosity regarding this young woman who has so captivated my husband's attention. For the life of me, I cannot see what it is that so enamours him as I watch her greedily gulping down her breakfast and wiping her mouth with the back of her hand. She is an insult to me.

I look away for the mere sight of her is enough to dampen my spirits and place a heaviness upon my heart. I will take Beulah some tea, I think, with glee. I carry a chair to the dresser and stand on it so as to reach the highest shelf. I lift down the tea caddy and am spooning out the tealeaves when Eli comes in for his breakfast.

"If you are going out soon I would like to ride along as far as the turn to Carregwyn." I tell him, wrapping up a small pouch of the tealeaves and placing it in the pocket of my dress.

"What are you going there for?" he asks, pulling out a chair and sitting down at the table.

"I've decided I will take Beulah to market, after all."

I take up Branwen's empty bowl. She is now noisily picking and sucking at her teeth.

"You're a bit late in the day. I'm taking her myself in the trap."

The spoon rattles in the empty bowl in my hand.

"I shall come along too, then." I say.

My voice trembles for I sense already that something has slipped from my grasp, something precious. I place the bowl back on the table lest I drop that, too.

"There is no room for you, Megan," he says, and leans forward over his bowl as he lifts the spoon to his mouth.

"But your trap is bigger than Morgan's cart."

"Y-e-s," he says, drawing out the word as if he is explaining to a dim-wit, "but Branwen has already asked if she can come along. Like I said, you're a little late in the day."

His spoon hovers near his lips. He pauses to look up at me and gives me a tight-lipped smile. I see the triumphant gleam in his eyes while I can only stare at him, open-mouthed but unable to speak. I want to plead it isn't fair. I want to accuse he has done this on purpose. But in the corner of my eye I see that trollop with a smirk twitching the corners of her mouth and I do not wish to give her further satisfaction by seeing me quarrel with Eli.

"Oh well, never mind. Another time. Do give my love to Beulah."

I smile as if I do not care. I can say no more lest the lump in my throat betrays me. I turn on my heel and pick up my vegetable basket as if I am just going out to the garden. I hear Branwen snort as I go out of the door and my heart shrivels with a dark hatred that makes me want to turn back round and claw that smile from her face with my fingernails. I tightly grip the handle of my basket for my hands tremble so much I fear I will drop it.

I walk down through the little gate at the bottom of the orchard and keep on walking. I walk up through the hazel spinney and keep on climbing so hard and fast that I feel my lungs will burst. I keep climbing up to that place amid the gorse where kindling is gathered for the oven. Then I sit amid the dead, broken bones of twigs that litter the ground and look down on Wildwater house, far below.

The climb has dispersed the rage that rampaged through my veins, leaving me weak and trembling. I watch my husband and his maid go haring off down the lane in the trap, their wheels leaving dust clouds in their wake. Damn them to hell, I say to myself, and immediately regret, for it is a sin to place curses on another. I cannot even weep though a maelstrom of grief storms through me.

The trap disappears from sight, taking with it all the promise of the day. I wish I did not have to return to that house, wish I could stay here above it all, forever. Down in the meadow below the house, the cow lows. Branwen has gone off without milking it; the poor thing will be ready to burst with milk. With a sigh, I get up to begin the climb down to the place I no longer want to be.

He will never let up punishing me. I never imagined he would treat me thus. All that time I kept my secret safe, while it pained me to do so, for I knew it to be a betrayal of his trust; I did not fear what he would do to me if he found out; I feared what he might do to himself. You do not know the true heart of a man until he is tested. Eli has become a stranger to me; he is so different from the kind, gentle man I married.

I am a spoiler of good men, a destroyer of men's love. I watched Morgan's love turn to hate when I got myself with child. He thought I'd made a fool of him for I'd been off laying with a ne'er do well while telling him I was merely walking the hills to get away from Mam and her constant carping. Eli hates me for he believes I did not tell him the truth so as to get his ring on my finger. Nothing I say or do will alter his mind for it does seem to be as he sees it.

The truth of the matter is not always what it seems to be. It is all a matter of intention, I believe. Injustice stems from attributing bad intention where it does not belong. I know I did not *intend* to betray Morgan or Eli. That seems all important to me while to them all that seems to count in their judgement of me is that I did betray them, whatever my intention. It is impossible to argue innocence when all the evidence points to one's guilt.

I am tired, worn out with trying to defend myself when in my heart of hearts I know I have done wrong. One wrong turn led me down a path of deception and lies, and my life is gone so far wrong there is no mending it.

I go into the dairy and fetch the stool and pail to milk the cow. I carry them down through the meadow where the cow is waiting patiently to be relieved of her burden. I am gone so far wrong, I shall never be forgiven, I say to the cow as I rest my head upon her flank. Morgan though, is to be forgiven, it seems.

The day Eli came back from giving Beulah a ride home, he told me there had been a meeting of the chapel elders which he had attended. Dafydd, the Mill, had spoken out for Morgan's good character. It was decided he should not be shunned as he had clearly been led from the righteous path by a woman of ill repute. Morgan has been forgiven, yet if they had known Fortune was mine and not his, they would have cast me out.

"All the sins of the world have been placed at the doors of women, since the time of Eve," I say to the cow, who calmly chews the cud while I bring forth her milk, sat there on the edge of the meadow under the shade of a hawthorn tree, the hems of my skirts stained yellow by the buttercups.

They will all be well on their way to market by now, riding along with the wind in their hair, their laughter trailing behind them. I feel a pang of jealousy at the thought of Beulah riding along with them, laughing and joking with Branwen, who she had not one good word to say about just days before. It pains me to think of my little girl chattering away with that dairy maid who would gladly see me destroyed.

Rage begins to swell up in me again as I think it is me that should be riding along with Fortune, not that dairy maid. Branwen should be here milking this cow, not me. The cow kicks over the bucket of milk and I watch it seep away through the grass and flowers into the ground. The cow was disturbed by my feelings. It was my own fault. I should have known better. I have brought it all, every bit of it, upon myself.

"It was just like the old days!" Branwen says to Eli.

She nudges him in the ribs with her elbow, and bumps into the door frame as she stumbles through the kitchen door. She goes to the kitchen table, drags out a chair and sits upon it so heavily it groans beneath her.

"I could eat your horse, Eli," she says, casting her eyes towards the pot that hangs over the fire.

I make no move to get up and fetch the pot to the table. I am sat in the chair near the fire, stitching repairs to the frayed hem of a skirt. If she is hungry she will have to fetch it herself, for I will not wait on her.

They have brought a smell into the kitchen with them; a smell that is at once familiar and sets my mind to reeling backwards. For a moment, I am unsure where I know it from. Then I remember, as if it were yesterday; Da coming home from evenings spent at the tavern. The house would reek of the smell of ale. It would waft up the stairs to the chamber where Morgan and I lay, waiting for the fighting to begin between our Mam and Da.

Now you know what I had to put up with, I hear Mam say as if she is sat right there beside me, and I prick my finger with the needle. As I stare at the spot of blood that swells up and spills onto my mending, I think my life is an endless going round of circles that keep whirling me back to places I no longer wish to be.

Da's drinking and cavorting with the women of the tavern turned our Mam into a bitter, malicious, old woman. Upon my head she did wreak all her frustrations and anger. I will not be like you, I think, as I get up with a sigh and go to the sink to rinse the blood from my mending. As I soak a cloth in the water bucket and rub at the stain, I listen to Eli and Branwen, reminiscing over their day's cavorting. They have not so much as said hello to me.

"I haven't enjoyed such merriment since that day we went to the horse fair in Cardigan. You remember, Eli? We stayed so late, the dawn was breaking as we walked into your Uncle's yard," Branwen is saying, her voice full of laughter.

"Aye! We got to drinking with those horse traders from across the water! And you entertained them by trying to jig to the music from their fiddles."

"Oh, yes! That's right! I ended up on the floor of the tavern, my skirts soaked from the spilled ale and my hair full of sawdust and dirt!"

She says this as if it is a matter of some pride to her. I wring the water from my mending as though it was Branwen's throat between my hands.

"I had to sneak you in round the back when we returned, lest my Uncle see you and fire you on the spot."

I turn from the sink and see Eli smiling at her with the fondness he used to reserve for me. I hang the wet skirt to dry over the chair by the fire. I stand for a moment, with my back to them, frozen by indecision. I cannot bear to hear another word but do not want to create a scene.

"Beulah's not a bad old girl, is she? There's more fun in her than I expected," Branwen says, and I have heard enough. I do not look at either of them but quietly pick up my mending basket and slip through to the parlour.

My mind is a whirl of confusion, for I do not understand why my husband must condemn me for my past lack of piety, yet does feel fondness and admiration for that wanton trollop sat beside him. The injustice is like a hot iron branding my heart. I do hate him! I think, and throw the mending basket down on the parlour floor. Needles, pins, and scraps of fabric go scattering across the flag-stone floor.

Not once did I stoop so low as to drink in taverns with men, I think, hitching up my skirts and getting down on my hands and knees to right the mess I have made. I can hear them still, through the closed door, out there in the kitchen. Eli says he will fetch the pot from the fire himself, in answer to Branwen's question if they were ever going to eat tonight. *You* shouldn't have to do it, she says, where has Megan got to?

I have to use my fingernails to retrieve pins and needles from where they have fallen into the cracks between the flagstones. My hair falls over my face and I toss it back over my shoulder. How dare she expect me to come and dish up her supper for her? I would like to go out there and tip it over her head. My husband is a cruel and unjust hypocrite. I sit back on my haunches. The portrait of Eli's parents is above me. Their faces look down with disdain on my dishevelled self. I'm a sight better than that one he is laughing with out there, I think with defiance. Would they have rather he'd married her? I think not.

Words build and build inside me. The words I would say to Eli if I had only the courage. You are a hypocrite, I would say to him. There is one rule for yourself and quite another for me. You go to chapel every Sunday and people think you a great and pious man, yet you are not. You would punish me to the end of my days for laying with another man. Yet while I was doing that, what were you doing? Drinking and plenty more with that dairy maid. Yet you do not condemn her as you condemn me. I wish you had married her. I wish you had never come back here wishing to marry me.

I get up from the floor and pick up my mending basket. The evening sun has moved round and streams through the parlour window. Soon, the sun will fall behind the barn and the parlour room will grow cold, even though it is summer. No evening fire has been lit in here since Gwen's departure and Branwen's arrival, for Eli and I no longer spend our evenings here together.

I stare at the chair where I sat when he hit me to the floor. If he loved me he would not treat me thus. If he loved me he would try with all his might not to condemn me.

From behind the door to the kitchen comes the sound of spoons scraping the bottoms of bowls. I will not enter there until they are gone out again. She has yet to do the evening's milking of the cow. It is a great pity the cow kicked over the morning's milk for it will mean less work in the dairy for her to catch up with.

I reach into the pocket of my dress for a handkerchief and my hand comes upon the little pouch of tea I wrapped up for Beulah, this morning. I will go to her before next Friday, and impress on her that I am more than willing to take her to market myself, that she has no need to go with Eli. She is my only friend in this world.

"It is no surprise that ne'er-do-well upped and left you, Megan, for you are quite the scold," Eli says, rendering me speechless. "He had a lucky escape. Unfortunately, his gain is my misfortune."

I feel a hot flush of humiliation burn my cheeks. I could only think myself grateful that Branwen was not there to witness my humiliation. We are standing outside the outhouse where I had gone to fetch peat for the fire. I had merely complained that, once again, my stomach had been turned, this morning, at finding a fly deep within the butter.

"Did you tell Beulah I will take her to market next Friday?" I ask him, before he strides off again.

He makes a sigh of impatience. "Yes, Megan, I told her you'd changed your mind, yet again."

"And, what did she say?"

"She wondered why you would think she'd prefer to ride in Morgan's old rickety cart when she can go with me in the trap."

"But surely, you won't be going every Friday..."

"We've arranged to pick her up every week, as it happens."

In my stupidity, I don't realize he refers to him and Branwen when he says 'we'.

"Oh, good. I haven't been to market in such a long while."

"I thought I'd explained, Megan, there isn't room for you and all."

My mouth falls open but I close it again for I cannot speak, and it does not matter for he is already striding off. So, I am to be shut out, left behind to do all the work while my husband goes off cavorting with other women in the taverns of Dinasffraint. I can just hear Mam's laughter for that is what Da did to her. She despised him for it and despised me because I reminded her of him. History does repeat itself with astounding cruelty.

I go into the outhouse and fill my basket with slabs of peat. I carry the basket across the cobblestoned yard; it is still damp and slippery from the morning dew. Weeds are flourishing in the gaps between the cobbles; weeds that Gwen somehow always managed to find time to pull no sooner than they appeared. There is groundsel, nettles, and the dandelions and forget-me-nots all gone to seed. They should have been pulled up before they went to seed, for now there will be all the more to pull next year. That is what happens if you allow contaminating weeds to flourish. They take hold, and spread, until there is no controlling them.

You have to keep on top of things. That's what I told Beulah when she first came to Carregwyn. Just keep on top of things. Don't put off till tomorrow what you can do today. Get the hardest work done early in the day, while you are fresh from sleep, before you begin to tire. Or else, before you know it, it all becomes too much and you feel you are suffocating under the weight of it all. That's what I said to Beulah, when she first came to Carregwyn. That's what I said to Beulah.

And I said to Beulah, get Morgan to take you up on the hill to where all the wild flowers grow. Make sure he takes you, I said, for it will ease your mind and body so the work comes easier. Make sure to take her, Morgan, I said, when the Heartsease is in flower, for then she will come to love this place as much as I. Didn't stop you leaving, he said. I had promised to marry Eli, you see, and I thought I would be happy here.

I carry the basket of peat in through the house; through the hallway, through the parlour, and out into the kitchen. I bank up the fire with the peat, in readiness for cooking our food for today and tomorrow. For tomorrow is Sunday, a day of rest, a day for worshipping the God that knows no mercy. A day for standing in the Chapel and pretending I am someone and something I am not. For if I don't they will condemn me too and then where will I be? I'll be in the watery grave with Sian, that other young woman who was duped by Iago's charms into giving him what he wanted. I'd rather be with Sian than anyone else right now, for she was the only one who would understand what it is to be me. There is no greater loneliness in this world than when surrounded by people who do not care if you live or die.

I turn to the mound of vegetables lying on the table, which I have gathered earlier this morning. I take a knife from the drawer and then put it back again. I cannot do it. I cannot do any of it anymore.

Chapter Eight

Mary, Mary, so contrary, must a-snuffling go.

The sound of a horse's hooves on cobble-stones is a rich and wholesome sound, not one you would imagine could strike the listener with dread. Yet dread is what I feel, for it means we have an unwanted visitor. There is not a soul in the world who I wish to see at this moment. I turn away from the table and the mound of vegetables I cannot face. I compose my face into something resembling sociability. I lift my shoulders and take a deep breath. The horse has come to a halt and I listen to footsteps cross the cobblestones to the open kitchen door.

Too late, I remember my skirts are hemmed with dirt from my rooting around in the garden, and I do not recall having brushed my hair this morning. I do not even know if my face is clean. I think I shall just go and check in the mirror when Mary's frame appears in the doorway. Of all the people in all the world, she lies at the bottom of the list of people I may wish to meet again in this life.

She waits not for invitation to enter but walks straight in and stands in the middle of my kitchen. She pulls off her riding gloves, and all the while her eyes are darting into every nook and cranny. Then she sniffs and pulls the sides of her mouth down, as if she has smelt something rotten. Her gaze wanders over me from head to toe, and by the set of her mouth, she is not impressed by what she sees.

I push my dishevelled hair from my face and apologise.

"I was not expecting visitors," I say by way of explanation, smoothing down the creases in my skirts. My pinafore is streaked with dirt.

"You are not on your hill now, Megan," she says, going to sit at the table and thinking better of it when she sees it is covered with vegetables and dirt.

"I have just this minute brought those from the garden. The table shall be clear in a moment, then I shall make us some tea."

I pray she will say she has no time to stay but instead she picks up a chair, moves it away from the table, and sits down.

"That would be nice," says she, folding her hands in her lap.

With a wide sweep of my arm, I swipe the vegetables from the table and back into the basket. I notice my hands are trembling when I wipe down the table with a wet cloth. Under her watchful gaze, I get a chair to stand on and climb up to reach down the tea caddy. The hand that scoops tea into the pot is so unsteady that I spill some on the dresser top. I glance over to see if she has noticed but she is now surveying the cobwebs lacing the overhead beams. I scrape the spilled tea back into the caddy.

"So what brings you here?" I ask as I pour boiling water from the kettle into the pot.

I am unable to bear the suspense any longer for she will not have, has never, come to me out of friendly neighbourliness. Whatever mischief she has come to cause me, I want it to be over and done with.

"I wondered how you were managing, now Gwen has upped and gone. Things have gone downhill since she left, I must say."

Must you? I think. Must you really have to say that? I push her tea towards her. I dare not pick it up for fear the cup will rattle about in the saucer, or that I will give in to the temptation to pour it in her lap.

"There is too much work for one woman," I say and take a sip of tea for my mouth is so dry I fear my tongue will stick to the roof of my mouth.

Mary makes a clicking sound with her viperous tongue.

"Really, Megan, you are no stranger to hard work. And you do have the dairy maid. As I recall, you did everything up on that hill of yours. There is no excuse for lax standards."

"Carregwyn was a far smaller house."

"Yes, but you no longer have the dairy work to do."

"No, but.." I fall silent. It is true, what she says. I don't know why there are not enough hours in the day anymore.

She looks me up and down again.

"I don't want to appear rude, but you really must make more of an effort, Megan. What your new husband must think, I really can't imagine. You cannot walk around looking like an urchin when you are a farmer's wife, my dear."

I open my mouth to speak but she does not wait for me to answer.

"One urchin in your family is more than enough, I think, don't you?"

"What do you mean by that?" I ask, my temper rising now for I know she is referring to my Fortune.

"Poor Eli must be wondering what sort of family he's married into."

I am wondering how she dares to come here and speak to me thus when I realise Eli is standing in the doorway.

"Aye! I've had plenty to pause and wonder about of late, Mary. How are you, girl?"

It hurts like a cut from his scythe. Down, the pain travels, settling deep in the heart of me. I feel tears come to my eyes to hear him agree with Mary against me.

"I was just telling Megan, she's not up on her hill now, though you'd never think it to look at her."

Mary laughs as she says this, as if it is nothing but harmless teasing. I am suddenly made deeply aware of how I look when Eli looks over at me with an expression that says he is ashamed of me.

"I've been gardening. I was just about to go and change when Mary arrived."

"You can bring the girl down from the hill, but you can't take the hill out of the girl." Eli laughs too, as he says this.

"Megan is very set in her ways, aren't you Megan?" He says to me, then turns to Mary. "I think Megan's had a bit of a shock since Gwen left. She thought being a farmer's wife was the life of a lady." Then he turns back to me. "Didn't you, Megan?"

"No, I merely...I'm not...Gwen did such a lot..."

"Spoilt is what you've become," Mary says. "I'll wager you didn't do a thing while there was Gwen to do it all for you."

"That's right enough!" Eli says, rolling his eyes to the ceiling.

"Gwen used to tell me she didn't need my help!" I say in my defence.

"And you didn't stop to argue, I'll wager!" Eli scoffs.

"I didn't like to step on her toes..."

117

They both laugh heartily at this, as if this is something I made up just so as to let myself off.

I glare at Eli. "You told me, yourself! Make the most of it, you said, for there will be plenty to do when the children start to arrive."

I regret the words the minute they are out of my mouth for Eli blushes to the roots of his hair. I should not have said it, I have upset him now.

"Speaking of children; how is your brother's bastard?" Mary asks with a bluntness which knocks the breath out of me.

I glance over to where Eli has gone to stand at the window with his back turned to us. I can see only his profile but I know by the tick at his temple that his anger is up.

"I really have no idea. I haven't been there since Morgan's shearing," I say.

She looks at me then with a stare so hard and challenging that my gut clenches with fear. She knows, or thinks she knows, but has not the evidence to say so directly. Try as I might, I cannot hold her gaze and have to look away, sealing my guilt in her eyes.

She picks up her gloves from where she has placed them on the table. She makes a big fuss over pulling them on. Then she looks at me again and her look tells me she hasn't finished with me, she will have her day, but not yet.

"I shall be on my way," she says, getting to her feet.

"You're welcome to stay and eat with us," Eli says turning round and without looking to me for acknowledgement.

"That's very kind of you, Eli, but the life of a miller's wife is no different from any other. We all have our weight to pull."

"Yes, indeed," Eli says, walking with her to the door. "I've got to return to my work so I'll walk to your horse with you."

I know she has three daughters helping at home, all over the age of twelve. Anger surges up in me then and gives lash to my tongue.

"Surely, you've got all the time in the world with your girls helping you at home, Mary! You wouldn't want to go spoiling them, after all!"

My bold courage shrinks back inside me when I see her turn at the door and look at me with venom. She ignores my remark and changes the subject.

"By the way, Megan," she says, with menace in her voice, "do you have a message for Gwen, perhaps? We are going to write to each other. I'm looking forward to all her news!"

She looks me straight in the eye but does not wait for any reply.

"Such a shame Gwen had to leave. Half her life she'd been here…" I hear Mary saying to Eli as they go out of sight.

I have to sit down for I am shaking. To think of those two keeping in touch; Mary digging and digging, like the pig in the sty, until she'd rooted out the real reason for Gwen's departure. Gwen would gladly tell her and the rest of the parish, too, if I were the only one to be hurt by such gossip. Would she keep quiet, for Eli's sake, or decide the world needed to know how he believed me to have tricked him?

I was pondering these unanswerable questions when Eli's accusing voice broke into my thoughts. I had not heard him return, so deep I had been in thought.

"How dare you speak to our neighbours like that!" He is white-lipped and shaking with rage but I spring to my defence.

"How dare I? How dare she come here, only to insult me?!"

"What do you expect, Megan? Look at yourself. And you dare to criticize Branwen for her slovenly ways!" He curls his lip and snorts.

"Branwen does not have to dig vegetables from the garden. How am I to do that and not get dirty?"

He does not know what to say to that and glares at me.

"You will treat our neighbours with the respect they deserve," he says through clenched teeth.

"And why should I do that when Mary does not treat me with respect?"

"I'm sure you don't need me to remind you, Megan. You are worthy of no one's respect."

He is too much to bear. He has only one mission and that is to cause me pain, to hurt me as long as I live and breathe. There is an old saying; that we remain as God made us from cradle to grave. If that is true, then there has always been this cruel streak in Eli, and Iago unleashed it, like a spell, with his evil words.

They say it takes only one rotten apple to turn all others around it. Before she threw herself in the Wildwater, Sian rightly said the preacher was tearing her out like a weed from his garden of Eden, lest she contaminate the rest. He would do the same with me if the truth came out. He would publicly shame and name me as the rotten apple among the rest.

Yet, I never did a thing but love. Why was it so wrong to love a man as I loved Iago? I do not believe the wrong was in the loving but in what he did with that love; he used my love for his own ends then threw it back at me as if it were a thing of no value. There was the wrong, and that wrong almost destroyed me, and continues to tear my life apart at the seams.

Why does my husband not see the truth for what it is? Why does he choose to punish me when surely the blame lies with Iago? Because we are either angels or whores, we women, in the eyes of men. There is no place in their hearts, minds, or marriage bed, for fallible women; for women who give them what they ask for before God himself says they can have it.

The voices of Eli and Branwen in idle chatter, drifting across the yard, stir me from my reverie. I look to the clock ticking away on the wall and see it is supper time. The vegetables are still in their basket. The fire is all but out. I am as Eli left me; dirty, dishevelled, slovenly. There is no supper ready to eat. The chores have gone undone. I cannot face them and their denigration; my husband and his dairy-maid. I rush out in the other direction, through the parlour door, out into the hallway, out through the front door, leaving it open behind me.

Chapter Nine

Grind, grind, the miller's stones do turn alike the
wheels of fate.

My wife is sewing a new patchwork quilt. She is sat in
the chair across from me, in front of the kitchen fire. An
array of baskets lies on the floor at her feet. One basket
contains small pieces cut from the newspapers which she
insists on my bringing back with me whenever I travel to
town. Within their tainted pages she finds meat enough
to assuage her hunger for salacious gossip.

Another basket contains small scraps and
fragments of fabric, cut from outworn or outgrown
clothing. I recognise some as coming from a dress our
little Angharad wore when a small child. And there are
remnants of a green woollen jacket I wore when we were
first married. Over the years, the jacket grew tighter until
I could no longer do up the buttons.

There are scraps too of garments which my wife
has long outgrown; fragments of the pretty sprigged
dresses she wore when she first came here to the mill.
Mary wears sombre greys or blacks now, and is no
longer the slip of a woman she was when I first met her.
These past twenty years of our lives are represented in

the growing quilt that lies on Mary's lap; cut up and rearranged into something far prettier than our lives together have been.

I was forty, and Mary twenty eight, when she first came as a general maid to work here at the mill. My Mam and Da, God rest their souls, had passed to the other side, leaving me to manage the mill alone. I'd given up all thoughts of marrying. A miller's days are long, and the miller works when everyone else is resting. So, I'd never had much time to go a-courting. Then along came Mary with her quiet determination to marry. Until death us do part, I am promised to love and cherish the wife sat across the fire from me. It is my cross to bear.

She bites a length of thread from the reel.

"You should have seen her, Dafydd. No better than a common slut. Eli himself said as much."

"Eli said that?"

I didn't believe it, Mary has always been one to exaggerate to get her point across. She licks the end of the thread to wet it.

"He said he'd had plenty of cause to wonder what sort of family he'd married into. And I could see by his face, he was ashamed of the sight of her."

I hoped that wasn't true. Megan has had more than her fair share of trouble. Mary squints her eyes to thread her needle, pulls the thread through, and ties a knot in the end.

"Filthy she was; dirt on her face, her skirts hemmed with mud, and her hair looked like it hadn't been brushed since heaven knows when. She looked no better than those peasant women on the common. And as for that brother of hers…."

"It can't be easy for Megan since Gwen left," I interrupt, hoping to stem my wife's rising anger.

Mary holds the needle between her teeth and reaches down, with a grunt, to the basket at her feet. "Can't be easy, indeed! She has an easier life than most of us, and it's not like she isn't used to work, is it, coming from that hill of hers? Eli says she was expecting the life of a lady once she married him! Who does she think she is?"

She folds a scrap of fabric around a piece of paper, and takes the needle from between her teeth. I can bear to hear no more. I cannot abide listening to my wife berating Megan this way. I've always had a soft spot for Megan, since she was a born. Her mother was a tyrant and worked that girl from morn 'til night from the day her husband died.

"What *have* you got against her?" I say more sharply than I mean to. "You have never liked her and I cannot for the life of me understand why."

"I have nothing against her!" is my wife's reply, contradicting all she has said against Megan for these past twenty minutes or more. It is impossible to reason with someone who denies their own words.

"Good. I am glad to hear it, for she has never done anything against you."

"That's where you are wrong, husband!" She says, stabbing her needle in my direction. "Eli had to apologize for her this very day, as it happens, for she spoke to me with such insolence."

Good for you, Megan, I think. It was high time she stood up for herself and I'll wager my wife provoked her somewhat.

"Eli apologised for her? You would not like it if I went apologising for you."

Mary stabs her needle through the fabric scrap. "I would not mind in the least if I gave you reason, which I never have done."

In truth, she would batter me into next week with a barrage of angry words if I ever did such a thing.

"She won't do it again in a hurry. I knocked the wind from her bellows! I told her Gwen is going to write to me. That frightened her!"

My wife's face is lit with glee at this prospect.

"What makes you believe that would frighten her?"

"Because there's more there than meets the eye, that's why," she says, nodding her head up and down, "and I shall get to the bottom of it."

"It is none of your concern," I say, with a heavy weariness descending upon me, but my wife carries on, disregarding my words of caution.

She stops her sewing, laying it down in her lap and her eyes and mouth narrow with spite. "I don't think it's a coincidence, do you? That Gwen upped and left when she did? I smell a rat and I know where it lives and all. Up at Carregwyn! That urchin is the image of Megan, if you ask me. And as for that story about Morgan being the father!"

She snorts with derision before going on. "Him so shy he could hardly speak to a woman let alone do anything else. And now, all of a sudden, we're supposed to believe he fathered a child with some trollop or other!"

I am worn out. All day, I have been lugging sacks of grain and tipping them into the hopper, then filling and stacking sacks of flour below. God granted me three sweet and kind daughters, for which I am grateful, but I am growing old and weary and have no son to help me.

"You want to stop right there, Mary. You're heading for dangerous waters. I wouldn't say any more, if I were you."

"Tosh! You never could see a thing even if it was right under your nose."

She picks up her sewing again. I see a lot more than she thinks I do. I've known for years about Megan's secret, though they don't know I know it. I didn't know what they'd done with the baby, mind, but feared the worst; hadn't put it past old Esther to have drowned it in the washing pool. They must have taken it from Megan

127

and boarded it with one of those women who take in such babes. Esther was a heartless old devil. Megan was never the same again, I know that.

Why Morgan has brought the child home now, I don't know, but I suppose he must have had good reason. Poor Megan, is all I can say, to have the little one living so near and having to pretend she isn't hers.

"I wager Eli knows it is Megan's," Mary is saying now, her mouth twisting with a satisfied smile, "for he's cooled towards her, I'll tell you that. They're not the happy, young newly-weds they were a few weeks ago!"

Stab, stab, her needle goes, as she stabs Megan in the back. If what Mary says is true, then Megan can't have told Eli before the wedding. Surely to God, she wouldn't have been fool enough to tell him after it was too late? Some are born with no conscience, and then others, like Megan, are born with more than is good for them. She'd have found it hard keeping that a secret from Eli.

"You're jumping to a lot of conclusions with no evidence at all. I've told you once, Mary, I'll not tell you again, leave well alone. You don't know what you're speaking about."

"That's just like you, isn't it? You've always been soft on that Megan. Don't think I haven't noticed. You've never had a bad word to say about her."

"Why in hell would I? Why would I say a bad word about anyone?"

I have heard enough. I have never understood my wife and never will. I rarely raise my voice to her but she is meddling too deep. I can see I've upset her by raising my voice to her, and I'm sorry for it, but she needs to learn to mind her own business.

"What you're talking about," I say more quietly now, "is the kind of thing that ruins lives. Do you really want to do that to someone who has never done you any harm?"

"If what I suspect is true, she doesn't deserve to live among us, she is a sinner."

I have gone too far. She is on her high horse now, her face pinched and closed to me because I have dared to go against her on this.

"I'm asking you," I say, "let it drop, Mary, for I fear you may do irrevocable harm."

"The innocent have nothing to fear from the uncovering of the truth, Dafydd. If I am wrong, then no harm will be done."

"Dirt once thrown has a habit of sticking, Mary."

She shrugs and picks up her sewing again. I am quiet for some moments, pondering how best to keep Megan's secret safe from my wife's meddling.

"Only those without sin should go throwing stones at others, Mary," I say, knowing there will not be an easy time between us again once the words are spoken.

She stares at me, mouth open, and then snaps her mouth shut with indignation. But she says nothing for she knows to what I refer. I have paid the price, these past twenty years for getting her with child. I paid the price by marrying her, even though I never loved her. She knows it, and I know it, and it has never been spoken about since the day we took our vows in the chapel. Yet, she was happy to see Sian end up in the water, and would gleefully see Megan shamed and cast out when she would have ended up the same if I had not done my duty.

My wife gets up from her chair, folds the quilt, and places it in the basket at her feet. Then she leaves the room with as much dignity as she can muster. There are some who look for and find fault in everyone around them, for in so doing they avoid facing up to their own shortcomings. If my wife loathes Megan for getting herself pregnant, it is only because Megan is a living reminder to her of what she did herself.

Never before have I dared to force my wife to face up to her own faults, and I know I shall not be forgiven for it. I may have nipped her meddling in the bud, or I may have made her more determined. Sometimes a man must take the only course he can with no more than hope to guide him. I pray, for Megan's sake, the course I have taken was the right one.

Chapter Ten

Beulah gets more than she bargained for in a God-forsaken inn.

"So long as I live, I shall not go with those two again," I tell Morgan, when I finally arrive back from market. "Standing there, waiting on the side of the road for hours I was, and with a mountain of chores waiting for me when I got home."

I throw my basket into the corner by the door and roll up the sleeves of my dress.

"And I don't suppose you two have done a thing but wait for me to come home and wait on you."

I bustle out to the scullery to fill a kettle from the water pail while those two stand there and gawp at me.

"I did churn the butter and got peat in for the fire," Fortune pipes up.

"Thank you, Fortune." I ruffle her hair and look at Morgan to see what he has to say for myself.

"I've been busy," says he.

"Da's hay is nearly ready for cutting!" Fortune says.

"I'll have a harvest feast to prepare and all then, will I?"

Morgan avoids my stare and I think I shall not be able to count on his hoity-toity sister to help me.

"Megan got a new housekeeper yet?" He asks, as if reading my mind.

"That's another story! Remind me to tell you what Eli told me the other day. I haven't had a chance to tell you, yet. You need to set that sister of yours straight on a few things."

"But she was a help to you, today, wasn't she?"

"Your sister did not come! She had others things she preferred to do than to accompany us to market."

"I thought she'd jump at the chance to go with you. She used to love her trips to market."

Morgan looks puzzled, as well he might, for he does not yet know that his sister now regards herself as too good for the likes of us.

"I've got a bit of news to tell you," Morgan says, clearing his throat and shuffling his feet like he does when he is about to tell me something I will not want to hear. I look at him warily, waiting to hear whatever next.

"I caught sight of the wool-pickers up on top of the mountain, earlier."

I do not know why he is telling me this as if I will have a care about who is roaming his mountain. I look at him with a blank stare and shrug. He clears his throat again. He has his cap in his hands and appears to be wringing it to death.

"Well, they'll all want feeding. They come every year and sleep in our barn at night. The neighbours all come for the singing and that...and Megan always made a big pot of broth and extra bread..."

"God help me!" I say and close my eyes.

"You'll love it Beulah, it'll be a bit of merriment for you."

"Merriment? You are the first I've ever heard call extra work merriment! How am I to make extra bread at this time of the day? Do tell me that, Morgan!"

I am close to tears, already worn out from standing on my feet all day.

"I'll go round the neighbours now to let them know they've arrived. I'll tell them to each bring some bread with them, and all. Then you'll only have the pot of broth to make..."

"Only the pot of broth? And for how many will I be doing that?"

He has that look on his face, like his dog when it has stolen food.

"Well, with the wool-pickers – a couple of dozen? Fortune will help you, won't you Fortune?"

Fortune has run to the corner and picked up my basket, and is now stood in front of me with a wide, eager smile on her face. It makes me laugh out loud.

"Go on, then! Fill it to the brim with carrots and potatoes, and put some turnips in there and all. Pick a nice big bunch of parsley, too."

Fortune runs out the scullery door, shouting at the top of her voice.

"The wool-pickers are here! The wool-pickers are here!"

Morgan crosses the floor towards me. Then he plants a kiss upon my lips.

"I love you, Beulah," he says, and then he pulls his cap on his head and is gone before I have time to catch my breath.

I can think of nothing else but that kiss and his words as I go about preparing for the evening. In a daze, I am, when I go down to the gorge with the yoke and pails, to fetch the extra water we will need. Does it mean what I think it means? That he loves me like a man loves a wife, and not like a sister? I am shocked to find myself smiling at the thought. Have you taken leave of your senses? I ask myself.

Just today, I'd been thinking of handing in my notice, for it is all too much for me, the toil that is living here. Now, I am grinning all over my face at the thought he might marry me. I've always longed for some babes of my own to cwtch. I'm not too old, yet. An image flashes into my mind; Morgan and I are standing over a crib, smiling down at the babe lying there.

You are off your head, Beulah, I say out loud, banishing the image from my mind. I am back at the house with the pails of water, not having noticed the gruelling climb back up the hill. I fill the big pot and place it over the fire, with my mind flying away on flights of fancy, against my will. One child has become a houseful now; they're running in and out of the house, filling the rooms with laughter.

It would be nice for Fortune to have brothers and sisters, I think, as she comes back in the kitchen, dragging the basketful of vegetables behind her.

"It was too heavy for me to carry!" she says, huffing and puffing from her exertions.

"You are an angel!" I tell her and hug her too me. "What would I do without you?"

We sit together at the table, peeling and chopping the vegetables for the pot. Fortune chatters away, telling how Da says this, and Da says that and what they had done together today while I was away. Every time she calls him Da, it makes me feel uncomfortable. It is not right to deceive the little one, I think. It is not right she will not know her own mother is living down the hill. But what is done is done, and I don't see how it can be undone without harming this little one; bad enough that we have lied to her, worse still if she were to find out now that we had.

Now I am sat down at last, I realise just how much my feet do ache. Oh, that pair living down there with Megan, they have shocked me to the core this day. Branwen stuck around just long enough to help me find a space to lay out my cheeses and butter for sale. I kept the butter pats in a pail of cold water else they'd have melted away in no time; such was the heat there in the market place with no shade from the blazing sun.

"Right, I'm off," says she, looking about the square to see which direction Eli had took.

I watch her go, shoving her way, this way and that through the crowds, without so much as an excuse me. I had no idea how they planned to spend the day. If I had known, I would never have accepted a ride with them.

So there I was, stuck to that dusty spot in the blazing heat, for I knew not one person there who I could ask to watch over my wares so that I could go and find refreshment. My bonnet provided some shade for my face but my head poured sweat beneath it. By mid-morning I felt weary to my bones and my mouth was parched with thirst. A cold and clammy sweat had broken out on my brow and at the back of my neck. I was certain that if I did not sit down I would surely faint. Why had Morgan not thought to tell me to bring a milking stool along?

"Here! Come and sit by here for a bit!" For a moment, I do not realise that the knitting woman sat across from me is speaking to me. She gets to her feet and jerks her head at the stool she has just vacated. "You look worn out, you do, come on!"

I glance back at my wares, not sure if I should take my eyes off them for I knew there were thieves aplenty in the towns on a market day.

"Don't worry about those. I've got my eye on them," the woman says, and I gladly lower myself onto her stool.

"There. You looked like you were going to faint clean away. I used to get like that when I was carrying my girls," she says.

I laugh. "Well, there's no chance of that with me. I'm a widow."

She looks down at me with a sympathetic smile that deepens the dimples in her round, red cheeks.

"Myfanwy's my name. You're new around these parts. Have you come far?"

My answer causes her face to light up.

"You'd know Megan, then! Megan Jones! Oh, tell me she's alright, for I haven't seen her for years, and have often wondered what happened to her."

"She's Megan Jenkins, now," I say, shifting my weight on the stool, and stretching my aching legs in front of me.

"She married, then! Thank the Lord. When her young man did disappear like that, I thought he had done the dirty on her. He was a farm manager or something like that, as I recall. When we never saw hide nor hair of her again, I feared the worst if I'm honest."

She leans down close to me and whispers into my ear. "I feared he had left her in the family way, you know, for she was so a-feared when she had heard nothing from him," she says, then straightens and looks around her to assure herself no one was close enough to overhear.

"But I was wrong, I'm sure, for she was a good, decent girl. It was just that she was in such a panic, you know, and it made me wonder, that's all."

So this must be the man that left Megan in the lurch.

"You knew Megan well, then?"

"Oh! We were the best of friends, we were. Hit it off from the first day she came here to sell her wares. I've often thought about her. One week she was here as always, and then she was gone and we never heard from her since."

I don't know what I should tell her and so I say nothing. Why would Megan refuse to take me to market when it was a chance for her to meet up with Myfanwy again?

"Tell her I've missed her. My girls are all married off, now, their hands full with children of their own. I'd love to see Megan again, I would. They all loved her here in the market, you know."

"Yes, I will tell her when I see her again," I say, my mind wandering, lost in puzzlement.

"I'm so relieved to hear she married and got out from under the thumb of that mother of hers. Old devil she is, if you ask me. Megan was very unhappy at home, you know."

"Her mother died at the start of the year."

"Well, good riddance. I know one shouldn't speak ill of the dead but, well, I speak as I find I do. You ask Megan! I'm plain speaking I am!"

She chuckles. I think she does not know the half of it; does not know that Esther took Megan's own babe from her and turned her brother against her.

"You two will have to meet up. You've got a lot of catching up to do."

"Oh, I would love that, I would. Tell her to come and see her old Myfanwy!"

By mid-afternoon I had sold out. Myfanwy was leaving to help one of her daughters with her children, and I picked up my empty basket and pail, and went in search of Branwen and Eli. I had not thought to ask them what time we should meet, for I had not known they were going to abandon me. Now, I had no idea where they might be. I wandered around the hot and dusty market square, where most of the traders were already packing up to leave as the crowds thinned out. Eli and Branwen were nowhere to be seen.

Hungry and thirsty, I went over to the coaching inn on the edge of the market square. I fancied a meat pie with a little ale to wash it down; something I'd not enjoyed for a long time, not since my poor, late husband treated me to such on a rare day out at market. I did not like to enter such a place alone but had no choice. As I neared the open doorway, the noise of loud chatter and laughter came to greet me. Inside, the noise was deafening. The room was packed full with jostling people. I passed by a man carrying two jugs of ale aloft to keep them from being spilled in the commotion. He winked and leered at me and from then on I kept my eyes downcast as I sought out a place to sit at one of the trestle tables.

Mercifully, I found a small space and squeezed in between an old woman and a young boy. The old woman sat in front of her empty plate, puffing away on the stub of a clay pipe. Though the smoke from her pipe made my eyes water, I was thankful not to find myself sat between two leering, drunken men.

I waited for the serving wench to come over and take my order. As she weaved her way through the crowd, she was jostled and poked and groped like a cow for sale at the market. When she reached me I had to shout my order to her to be heard above the noise of shouting, laughter, and clattering plates.

The man sat across the table from me, who had done nothing but grin and leer at me since I sat down, got up and stumbled away, and was quickly replaced by another. This one pulled his young companion onto his lap and proceeded to nibble at her ear lobes and grope her breasts, and I quickly look away. Never again would I enter this god-forsaken place on a market day.

After some time of sitting and waiting and staring into my lap, my food arrives with a jug of ale. I drink greedily from the jug, for my mouth is too dry to eat without. I am biting into my meat pie when I hear a laugh I recognise. Looking over to the open door, I see Branwen stumble inside, laughing like a horse. Eli is behind her and he too is unsteady on his feet. The two of them push their way inside, oblivious to my frantic waving to gain their attention.

They cast their eyes about, looking for a place to sit, and I am shocked to see Branwen rest her head on Eli's shoulder. I stop waving and hurriedly finish eating my pie. By the time I am finished and have drunk down the last of my ale, I have lost sight of them. Reluctantly, I give up my seat, and go in search of them. I find them sat on a bench inside the door. Branwen is leaning against the window frame behind her, head tipped back and open-mouthed, clearly the worse for wear. Eli sits with his elbows on his knees, his hands dangling loose between them.

"I've been looking all over for you two. I think it's time to make tracks for home, don't you?"

Eli squints up at me, and Branwen straightens herself.

"Beulah, dear old Beulah," Eli says, slurring his words, and I bristle for I'll wager I am younger than he. "Come and take some ale with us! Wench! Wench!" he shouts across the room.

"I think there's been enough ale for one day, don't you?" I say, glancing at Branwen who is now slumped against his arm.

"Now, now, Beulah, no need to get all hoity-toity! There's no harm in a bit of merriment now and then."

"I have chores waiting to be done at home."

"Chores! Chores! You women and your chores! What would you ever have to enjoy complaining about if it were not for your chores?"

Branwen laughs at this.

"I don't know what you're laughing at, madam. There is a dairy waiting your return and god knows, looking at the state of you, I pity the cow that will be milked by you this night."

Her laughter turns to a sour smile and she loudly hiccups.

"Walk home if you don't like waiting," she says, knowing very well it is too far a journey to walk.

"I will be waiting by the side of the road where you left the trap," I say to Eli, and do not wait for a reply.

They kept me waiting there for another hour or more, and I vowed I would never ride to market with them again. It's a queer business, the way things lie, down at Wildwater. I don't understand or know Megan, at all. And as for Eli, I've seen another side of him that I wouldn't have believed if I hadn't seen it with my own eyes; him so big in the chapel, and all, drinking in the taverns with that strumpet of a dairy maid. I'd like to see the faces on that chapel lot if they had seen him. I'm looking forward to seeing Morgan's face when I tell him.

"I don't understand why Megan hasn't come," Morgan says "I told Eli days ago, to tell Megan the wool-pickers are here."

"Perhaps she'll come tonight, before they all leave, tomorrow," I say, and think to myself; wouldn't that be just like her, to turn up for the merriment when it will be too late to offer one scrap of help to me when I have had to cook for them all, every night this week.

I have not had a chance yet to tell Morgan about the day at market. It will have to keep until the wool-pickers have gone. I want to tell Megan, too, that I have met her old friend. I hope it will persuade her to take me to market from now on. If she will not, then I shall have to learn to drive that pony and cart and I would rather pull out my toe-nails.

But Megan does not come. Eli and Branwen come alone. Eli seems embarrassed to have to make excuses, yet again, for Megan.

"I tried to persuade her," he says, "but you know how she is, these days. She seems to think it is unseemly for a farmer's wife to be out merrymaking."

I bite my tongue. Is it any wonder her husband looks for his fun elsewhere when she persists in

143

behaving as though she is too good for the rest of us? And with the evidence of her murky and recent past singing right here in our barn, who does she think she is?

Still, I have yet to forgive Eli and that strumpet, for the merry-go-round of market day, and so I avoid their company in our barn, though Branwen made to sit with me as soon as she arrived. I got up on the pretext of stirring the broth over the brazier which Morgan had set up to keep it warm. Then I sat elsewhere.

When I saw her gesturing to Fortune to sit beside her, I called to Fortune to come and sit and sing with me. I don't want the likes of Branwen anywhere near our little Fortune.

Chapter Eleven

The wool pickers come, the wool pickers go, and a-singing shall the dairy maid go.

"We would have told you if you'd been here but you were nowhere to be found," Eli is telling me the next morning.

Branwen is sitting next to him, reminiscing, while chomping on an oatcake, about the fun they'd had the evening before. It transpires that while I was hiding away in shame at having failed to prepare any supper, Eli and Branwen had gone up to Carregwyn without me. I'll wager they did not look long for me before leaving. It seems the wool-pickers have been up there all week and the previous evening had been their last night before their long journey home to the coast.

How I would have loved to have seen them and joined in with their singing. It would have served to raise my spirits. How much better it would have been than walking along the Wildwater until it grew dark, lonely and filled with foreboding that Mary, the mill, will not rest until she sees me undone. My fear is like a black thing lurking in the corners of my mind, and following me like a shadow.

"When did they arrive? Did you know they had been there all week?" I say to Eli.

"Morgan did mention something."

He snaps an oatcake in half and dips it in his porridge.

"And you didn't think to tell me?"

He rolls his eyes, and lets out a long, heavy sigh.

"I think I am about to get another lecture," he says to Branwen.

"So when did you see Morgan?"

"He was at the blacksmiths a few days ago, getting that old nag of his reshod."

Branwen snorts with amusement at this unfair slight against Morgan's pony.

"And he told you to tell me the wool-pickers had arrived but you didn't think to let me know?"

He shrugs as if it is of no importance.

"So who else was there? Was I the only one in the parish to have missed them?"

"Quite possibly, Megan, but you cannot blame me if you were not here when we left."

"I would have been here if I had known you were planning to go," I say, and get up from my place at the table, too upset to eat my breakfast.

"Was Beulah alright? I would have helped her prepare food for them if I had only known they'd arrived," I take my bowl to the sink, and stand looking out of the window.

"I realise you like to think Beulah cannot manage without you, but Beulah is quite capable of managing on her own, Megan. In fact, she seems a damned sight more capable than you from where I'm sitting."

How he loves to humiliate me. I have the feeling that I have been squeezed into some far flung corner and Eli is pushing me further in and I have not the strength or wits to get round him.

I am brimming over with questions I could not ask. Did Fortune seem well and happy? Did she enjoy the singing? As if he could read my train of thought, Eli says;

"That child took a real shine to Branwen, didn't leave her side all night."

"I'd have rathered she had not. What a little chatterbox she is!" Branwen says.

"Branwen and Beulah are the best of friends now, aren't you Branwen?" Eli is saying, "Singing together well into the night they were."

I turn round from the window and see Eli is watching me to see my reaction.

"Aye, I like Beulah!" Branwen says, and casts a cool glance in my direction. "Plain speaking, Beulah is, not too good for the rest of us, like some I won't mention."

"It is not difficult to feel one's self better than the likes of you!" I snap back at her.

"Who does she think she is, talking to me like that?" She asks Eli, but I do not wait for his answer.

"I'm his wife, and you'd do well to remember it."

"Well, deary, it's something *he* spends most of his time trying to forget!"

She jerks her thumb at Eli and looks triumphant. I look to Eli, praying he will deny what she says.

"You are sadly right about that, Branwen," he says, rising from his seat.

Branwen lets out a loud cackle of amusement. I am no match for either one of them and together they beat me to the ground with their cruel words.

I must rise above it and prove myself a capable and worthy wife. It is the only thing I can do to show that strumpet her place in the order of things. In giving them no reason for complaint or criticism, I shall thwart them. In this frame of mind, I set upon cleaning the house from top to bottom. I begin by changing the bed-linen. I open all the windows. I drag the sheets from the beds and roll them up and throw them out of the windows. They fly through the air and land with a muffled whoosh on the cobblestones below.

I sweep the dust from the bedroom floors and plump up the pillows. I empty and rinse the chamber pots and carry fresh water upstairs to the wash bowls. I sweep the dust from the landing, all the way down the front stairs. I sweep it all out the front door to be carried away on the summer's breeze. And all the while I am sweeping, I am muttering all the things I wish I had said to that strumpet up there in the dairy.

Just in time, I remember to put broth to boil over the fire, for it would never do for them to come in at the middle of day and find there is nothing to eat, yet again. That would be to invite their scorn. While the broth boils, I continue to sweep, through the parlour, through the kitchen, and out of the kitchen door I go, with the sweat running in rivulets between my breasts and down my back. Then I set to scrubbing the floors.

I can barely stand or sit down, for my back feels it will snap if I do, when they come in for their mid-day meal, but I stand at the table where the pot of broth is sitting waiting, and smile. I continue to smile as if I have not a care in this world, as I ladle broth into their bowls and cut large chunks of bread. My smile must disarm them for they both glance at me from time to time but do not say a word. They are silent all through their meal and I go on smiling as though I am the happiest soul in the world. It is very satisfying.

The moment they are gone, I go back out to the front hallway, for on passing Eli's study this morning it occurred to me that Gwen must have cleaned in there from time to time. I have never been in this room before. It is where Eli keeps his farm accounts and such, and he has never invited me in. I think how it will surprise him to find it all cleaned the next time he enters here. Yet, I feel like an intruder as I open the door on my husband's private space.

The air in here has a musty smell, like an old cupboard that has not been opened and aired for years. There is a large table in front of the window and it is strewn with ledgers and loose papers. Loose papers lie all over the floor, too. A high backed chair sits behind this table and I imagine Eli sat here with his back to the light streaming through the window. An oil lamp sits on the table, to the left of his chair. A ledger lies open. It is filled with columns and figures, outgoings and incomings. I open another ledger which sits beside it. This shows the wages paid to his men.

On the floor beside his chair is a large, mahogany box with a key left in its lock. I get down on my knees, turn the key, and lift the lid. I gasp when I see the contents; more money than I have seen in my life. It must be here he keeps the money to pay the wages of his men. I hear the sound of the yard gate opening and closing. I slam the lid shut on the box and turn the key. A sharp pain shoots through my back as I get to my feet too quickly and I have to pause for a moment before I am able to walk.

Back out in the kitchen, I arrange my face to assume a picture of innocence. When the expected shadow crosses the doorway, I expect it to be Eli so am somewhat taken aback to see that it is our good neighbour, Dafydd, from the mill. He is a far more welcome sight than his wife, I think, until I remember my conviction, on the day of Morgan's shearing, that Dafydd knows Fortune's true identity.

Whether it is this thought or the exertions of the morning, I am suddenly taken to feel quite giddy and grope for a chair to sit down. Dafydd rushes over and takes my elbow, gently lowering me onto the chair.

"There, there, Megan, cariad, sit yourself down here," says he.

They are the first kind words I have heard in too long and they have the effect of making me want to weep.

"I fear you have ruined that dress, little Meg," he says, which only makes me want to weep all the more, for 'little Meg' is what Eli used to call me before he hated me. I look down at my dress with dismay. It is a best one which I put on this morning, on rising, thinking I would not be caught out in a workaday dress by the likes of Mary, again. Eli bought it for me, at no little expense, before we married. I had quite forgotten what I was wearing when I took to cleaning the house.

The dress is quite ruined. The skirt, from the knees down, is caked with dirt from my kneeling to scrub the dirty floors. The sleeves, beyond the elbows, are water-stained from the dirty water. I have somehow managed to tear the bodice, also. What must they have thought of me when they came in for their meal? The silence I attributed to my having outdone them must have been one of shock at the sight of me. I am a pitiful, stupid wretch.

I do not know I have spoken aloud until Dafydd replies. "You are nothing of the sort, Meg. Do you want to go and change? I think I can manage to make us a strong cup of tea. You run along, I know where everything is. I took many a cup of tea here with Gwen in the past."

I make my way up the front stairs and into my chamber. I tear off the spoiled dress and look into the glass. My face is smeared with dirt and all. I wash at the basin and put on a clean dress. I brush my hair and tie it up with a ribbon. I look almost like my old self again. I wonder if Dafydd has come to scold me for my rudeness to Mary. But no, he spoke kindly as he has always done. Perhaps he has come to tell me that he knows who Fortune is. This thought makes me cringe inside and it is with some trepidation that I go back downstairs to join him.

A pot of tea awaits, steaming on the table. My heart swells with fondness for this man pouring milk into teacups as though he has done it every day of his life. Dafydd has always been so kind to me.

"There, now. You drink this and you'll feel a lot better," he says, tipping a small measure from his flask into each of our cups. It reminds me of that night when they'd found Sian's body in the Wildwater, when Mam scolded Dafydd for lacing Morgan's milk with alcohol.

I take a sip of the sweet, pungent smelling tea. As the heat of the brandy hits my chest, I cough. "I've never been fond of tea but I think I could get to like it the way you make it, Dafydd."

He laughs at that. "Aye, well, don't get to like it too much, Meg, else the elders will be after me for corrupting a young woman to drink."

"I was surprised to hear you didn't want to come to the singing with the wool-picking girls," he goes on, "you used to enjoy it so much as I remember."

So that is what Eli told them, that I hadn't wanted to come. I do not want to tell Dafydd that Eli lied, so I say nothing. He strokes the white stubble on his chin between his fingers and thumb. There is more he wants to say to me, I think, but he doesn't know how to say it. I do not know what I will say to him if he speaks of Fortune. I gulp down the rest of the tea and find it quells my nervousness.

"Here, have a bit more," Dafydd says, pouring me another cup and lacing it from his flask. I do not loudly protest.

"My Da had a liking for this stuff, didn't he?" I say.

"Your Mam, too, in her day!" he says, and I splutter my tea with surprise.

"Mam! I don't believe it!"

153

"I knew your Mam long before she converted, Megan. She was wilder than your Da in her youth. He didn't frequent the taverns alone in those days."

This revelation is so shocking, it renders me speechless. I try to square this new knowledge with the Mam I had known all my life and the two did not fit together.

"You know she was already carrying you when she married your Da, don't you?" Dafydd goes on.

I gape at him, unable to believe what I'm hearing.

"But then, why? Why was she so against Sian and …." I was going to say me, why was she so without sympathy for me if she had been in the same predicament herself?

"The reformed sinner is the least forgiving of other people's sins, Megan," he says, gazing into the bottom of his teacup.

"But she…she stole…" I bite my lip to silence myself from saying that my own Mam had so little sympathy for me that she stole my babe from me.

"…stole Fortune from you, I know, cariad," he says, and I see the dear man's eyes are moist with tears.

I swallow hard and avert my eyes from his, looking down into my lap. "How long have you known?"

"I wasn't certain, you understand, or I'd have said something before it was too late. I couldn't go asking you if you were with child in case you were not. I hoped if you were, you'd come to me, for I let you know that I had nothing but sympathy for little Sian."

I do not say that I was afraid to tell even him, for fear he would turn his back on me too, thinking I was older than Sian and so should have known better.

"Remember that night when the wool-pickers were here afore? Just weeks after Morgan dragged Sian from the Wildwater? I suspected it then, when Eleanor was singing that ballad about a girl abandoned with child. I looked at you and saw the look on your face and I thought, oh no, not our little Meg, too."

My eyes fill with tears and I feel a sob rise in my throat.

"I saw you with that young man once, too, in the market at Dinasffraint. Eli's manager, the one he had to sack for stealing his profits."

I gasp at this. I never imagined we'd ever been seen. Dafydd says why don't I walk down the garden with him, in case of prying ears? I follow him down to the vegetable patch and we stand there as if we are discussing this year's crop.

"So Mary knows, then. She implied as much," I say.

"That's why I came. Mary suspects that Fortune isn't Morgan's child but she doesn't know for sure. I can assure you; it will never come from me. But you know how she is; she won't rest until she's uncovered the truth, one way or another. I wanted to warn you, in case she should say something to Eli."

"Eli knows," I say, bending down and pulling a weed from among the carrots. I look up at Dafydd. "I didn't tell him, though I had intended to, and it would have been better if I had before he got to hear it the way he did. He ran into Iago, the man you saw me with at market, and it was Iago told him out of spite." I toss the weed over the picket fence and straighten. "Eli hates me now," I say, choking on the lump in my throat.

Dafydd places his hand on my shoulder. "I'm very sorry for you, Meg," he says, making the tears spill from my eyes. "He'll come to forgive it in time, cariad, it's just his pride that is wounded, that's all."

I lean down and pull up a stem of grass and chew on it.

"No, Dafydd, you are wrong. He thinks I have tricked him into marrying me and he is quite set on punishing me for that to the end of my days."

"Not if I have anything to say about it," he says, swatting away a bee that is buzzing near his head.

"Please don't say anything to him. He will be furious with me if he were to find out I have told you. He doesn't want people knowing about it and laughing at him behind his back."

"It's you that should be his concern," Dafydd says, kicking the ground.

We walk back up the garden path and I see all the sheets out on the cobblestones from the morning.

"Oh, Lord, I forgot about those," I say, rushing to gather them up in my arms.

Dafydd takes his leave, telling me to promise to come to him if there is anything I need. He is the closest thing I ever got to a Da since my own one died, and I feel quite bereft at the sight of him walking away.

Chapter Twelve

Push a pig into a poke and the pig shall surely squeal.

My mind reels from the things Dafydd has told me. Hypocrisy will now be added to the list of Mam's wrongs against me. And my husband is a liar, telling them all I hadn't wanted to go when he knew very well I'd been given no choice. It is a mean trick he has played on me and one I shall not forget. But I am uplifted by Dafydd's visit, for though I cannot tell him of my husband's cruelties it helps me to know there is at least one who is not against me.

I stink like a pig from my day's exertions and decide to go down to the Wildwater to bathe; down below the farm where the river widens and shallows and is tamed. I carry a linen sheet and a bottle of rosewater to rinse my hair. I lay them on the river bank and strip down to my undergarments. Despite the run of hot weather, the water is icy cold. The stones beneath my feet are slippery with weed but I wade in deeper, gasping as the water reaches up to my waist.

Alder trees overhang the river, breaking the sunlight into sparkling pools on the river's surface. Insects spin in dizzying circles just above the surface. I gasp in wonder as a kingfisher darts past me in a blaze of colour. The only sounds are the water gently flowing, a fish leaping here and there with a plop, leaving circles in the water, and the warbling of a bird further downriver. I lower myself in the river until it is over my shoulders and lean back to let the water ripple through my hair.

It would not be a bad death, I think, to be carried away beneath the water in such a beautiful place as this. It would be a peaceful end. I have little to live for and yet, I do not want to die. If only life was as simple and free from pain as it is for the fish and the birds. But it is not, and I must learn to fight for what is mine or I will surely not endure.

I stay in the water until my head aches from the cold. I climb out onto the bank where the sun blazes and warms my chilled bones. I rinse my hair with the rose water I made from last year's roses. It will soon be the time for making more. I lie in the sun until my undergarments are dry on me, then I put on my dress and pick up my sheet, and prepare to return to the house.

Along the flower-bejewelled paths I walk, breathing in the sweet scents of meadowsweet and honeysuckle. I gather a small bunch of yellow vetch, ox-eye daisies and dog roses, and fill my mouth with wild strawberries as I walk, their bitter-sweet flavour bursting on my tongue. When I reach the gate to the bottom meadow, where the cow grazes and flicks her tail against the flies that plague her all summer long, a movement catches my eye beneath the sycamore tree at the bottom of the field. Branwen is stood with her back against the trunk and Eli leans over her, his two hands against the tree, either side of her. She is looking up at him with love in her eyes. He leans in closer, his face hovers over hers. I do not want or need to see anymore. I scuttle back to the house, unseen.

It is the image of a neat and clean farmer's wife which greets them when they come home; quite the contrast from the image which met them at mid-day. My hair has dried and is a sweet-smelling, gleaming cascade, tumbling down my back. Eli glances at me, and then takes a more interested second look at my improved appearance. It is gratifying to note the scowl that crosses Branwen's face at seeing me so transformed, and I smile.

On my return, I had seethed with a cold rage, but the sight I saw down in the meadow has curiously strengthened me for I feel no obligation now to do my husband's bidding. He has broken a marriage vow and so I shall break one of my own and no longer acquiesce to obey him in all things. My life will be easier for it.

I wait until they are seated at the table before breaking my news.

"I am going to the village tomorrow to hire a house-maid," I say to Eli.

I watch surprise register on his face, and that surprise quickly turns to anger, flooding his face with colour and blackening his eyes.

"I shall be the one to decide if we need a housemaid or not," he says.

"You are obviously far too busy wandering around the meadows, so I have taken the task upon myself."

He looks at me sharply. There is colour too in Branwen's pasty cheeks. I can see by Eli's face that he knows I have seen them together for he flushes a deeper red. He continues to eat in silence and I think I have him beaten.

"And with what will you pay her?" He asks without looking up from his plate.

Oh, I think I do hate him for lording it over me just like mine own brother did before I came here. At every turn he does outplay me for it is he who holds the purse strings, not I. But I hold the trump card at the end of the day, though it hurts me to have to use it against him.

"That is your concern, Eli. Perhaps you would rather we all go to the chapel this Sunday and own up to our numerous sins. I am quite ready to own mine for they cannot punish me more than you have been doing of late."

I have struck him a cruel blow. He stares at me for so long, I fear he is going to strike me, but he gets up from the table, knocking over his chair, and strides out into the evening. Branwen does not loiter, but rises from her chair and hurries out with her eyes downcast. She knows who is the mistress, now.

I pick up and right the overturned chair. Those who cast stones at others should be careful those stones do not rebound.

The village lies a mile below Dafydd's mill. It is no more than a scattering of low, thatched cottages with hens pecking about in the dust. There are no boundary fences across the fronts of the cottages; the dirt road goes right up to their front doors. Many of the doors are flung open to the summer's breeze, allowing passers-by, like myself, a view into the bracken-strewn mud floors inside; though there is little to see, for the interiors are so dark compared with the bright sunshine outside.

It is but months, yet seems a lifetime ago, since I came here to ask Beulah if she would take up the post of housekeeper for Morgan. There was just the one room downstairs, with a hearth, and a table and two chairs, nothing else. A rickety ladder led up to the straw mattress in the loft. Beulah was able to wrap the total of her belongings inside a shawl. Her most prized possessions were her knitting needles which provided her only source of income.

Yet, I think she was happier here than she is with the endless toil of Carregwyn. A simple life is not a bad life so long as one has enough to eat. I have never known hunger, not once in my life, but there are many here who have. Many who had nought but what they could grow for themselves have died in the famines which strike from time to time. How terrible it must be to see one's children waste away from hunger. Good weather and good harvests are the only thing keeping many from death's door.

A wheelwright's place lies at one end of the village, with an array of wooden wheels stacked against the wall outside. At the other end is the blacksmith's forge. It is an open fronted building with a slated roof canopy overhanging the forge. Behind this is a large field where the horses wait to be shod. The heat and smell of the glowing, hell-hot pit waft towards me up the street. The singeing smell catches in my throat and makes me cough.

Twm, the Oaks, is straining to hold onto the reins of his cart horse while the blacksmith leans over and nails the new shoe to the horse's hoof. On hearing me cough, the blacksmith glances at me over his shoulder, and Twm, pulling hard on the horse's reins, smiles and greets me.

"What brings you into the village, girl?" He asks, giving the horse a sharp smack on its nose as it pulls to try to free itself.

"I'm hoping to find someone who will come as house-maid for me," I say, keeping a safe distance from the massive horse.

"I heard Gwen had left. Gone to live with her sister, hasn't she? I'll wager you're missing her."

I shield my eyes against the dust being kicked up by the horse.

"Aye, it's a big house for one woman to manage."

"Well, there was Kitty's niece who was looking for work but she's gone to be a maid up at the landlord's place." He lifts his cap and scratches his head, looking down at the ground. "I can't think who else there might be. So many have left, you see. Married or gone to the town where there's more chance of finding employment. It's a pity you didn't look when the hiring fair was in town, you'd have found plenty there. There won't be another until next spring."

"I have a granddaughter living ten miles away," says the blacksmith, straightening up and stretching his back. "She's fourteen now and they'd be glad to see her away and working. I'll ask next time I see them. The wife and I go over there once a month to visit the daughter and her family."

The blacksmith grabs another handful of nails from the pouch that hangs from his belt. 'Hold her steady, Twm', he says, grabbing another of the horse's hooves.

Another month will be the death of me, I think. "When will that likely be?" I shout over the noise.

"We were there last week so we'll be going again in a few weeks."

"I was hoping to find someone sooner than that," I say, thinking of the mountain of bed linen waiting to be washed since I stripped the beds. The very thought of beginning the task makes my shoulders droop with weariness.

"Old Angharad, the midwife, has a granddaughter staying with her since she took ill. Maybe she'll be able to spare her for a few hours a week until you find someone more permanent. I'll ask her if you like. I'm passing her place on my way home. I'll let you know what she says when I come to chapel next Sunday."

The horse rears up and almost knocks Twm off his feet.

"Yes, thank you, Twm. I'll be getting along."

"Hang on!" Twm shouts. "What about one of the miller's daughters? He has three there at home. I'm sure Mary would be only too glad to get one of them from under her feet."

"Yes, perhaps, Twm, I'll ask her," I say, knowing I shall do no such thing. Mary would send one of her daughter's to hell before she'd allow them to be any help to me.

I make my way home along the dirt road. I don't know why I imagined the village would be brim full with girls looking for work. I had only imagined what I hoped for. How pleased Eli would be that I had found not one to bring home with me.

Thunder flies torment me all the walk home, buzzing about my head, undeterred by my flailing arms as I try to swat them away. On the horizon I see there are tall columns of yellow-grey clouds gathering, portending a thunderstorm. The heat is the prickly, airless heat before the weather breaks. There is no point in washing bed-linen if I cannot hang the sheets out on the bushes to dry so they will have to wait, and I am greatly relieved for I truly cannot face the task.

As I near the house, I hear loud shouting in the distance. I carry on walking until I am close enough to identify its source. It is Eli who is shouting, screaming, more like. It is coming from the hill above the house. I turn a bend in the track and the hill comes into sight. I can see Eli rounding up some sheep with his dog. It is a good dog and I have never heard Eli raise his voice to it before. I watch the dog do as he commands, going out beyond the sheep and bringing them slowly down the hill. Though the dog appears to be doing his bidding, Eli is screaming at him. I watch Eli stride over to the dog and strike him with his shepherd's crook. The dog begins to yelp and howl with pain. Eli strikes the poor dog again and again and the dog is silenced. I have to look away, unable to bear to see anymore.

I hurry back to the house, thinking of the poor, loyal animal receiving such a beating. Like a madman, Eli had beaten him for no reason I could see but knew instinctively. Unable to stop me going to the village, lest I carry out my threat to confess all in the chapel, he used that poor dog as an outlet for his malicious anger.

I believe I will never respect my husband again after this moment. His actions were those of a coward, for coward it is that takes out their anger on a defenceless animal. I never imagined my husband capable of such callous cruelty. His poor dog has paid the price for my outspokenness and for that I will never forgive Eli. I would have preferred he had beaten me.

I leave a supper of bread and cheese out on the table and go to my room until I hear their voices coming towards the house. I do not want to see Eli for fear of what I might say or do. When they have entered, I go down and sneak out the front door, and go out to the barn where I know his dog sleeps.

At first, I think the dog is dead for it does not make any movement on my approach. Only as I kneel down beside him, do I hear his whimpering, and he opens one eye and looks up at me with such beseeching that I feel my own fill with tears.

"He will never lay a hand on you again, not as long as I live and breathe," I whisper.

I lay my hand on him to gently stroke him but even this causes him to whimper with pain. There is a bucket of water in the corner of the barn and I fetch this.

"Are you thirsty?" I ask him and he twitches the end of his tail.

He is unable to raise himself to drink, so I scoop up water with my hands and the dog laps from my hand, still lying on his side. This dog has followed Eli everywhere, always eager and willing to do his bidding. I lay my hand gently on the dog's head.

"And this is how your master repays you for the years of your love and loyalty. It is unjust."

I begin to get cramp in my legs from kneeling there on the cobbled floor of the barn. I readjust myself to a seating position and there I remain with my hand resting on the dog's head until it is growing dark. By the twilight, I fetch a blanket from the house and take it back to the barn and place it over the dog.

"I will be back in the morning," I say, and go up to my room with a heavy heart, not knowing if the poor animal will live or die.

My husband and his dairy-maid have not yet retired for I hear their muffled conversation drifting up from down below. Thunder rumbles away in the distance. I lie staring into the darkness, reliving the scene I witnessed between Eli and is poor dog. I do not realise

I have fallen asleep until I am woken by a series of flashes of lightening. Thunderclaps crash, closely followed by another flash that momentarily lights up the whole room. The storm is directly over us now.

I have always hated thunderstorms for they can do so much damage. As I lie there in my bed, counting the seconds between each thunderclap and flash, I remember how, as a child, I was frightened by the story of a neighbouring farmer being struck by lightning as he ploughed his field. And of another who was lifted clean from his chair by a thunder bolt that came down the chimney and rolled out of the open door.

There is a loud crack from outside and I jump from my bed and go to the window to look out. I cannot see a thing in the blackness but can hear the poor dog howling in the barn. The storm has passed over and the lightning flickers away in the distance. I fumble around in the darkness until my hand alights on the candle. I light it and go down to the kitchen, intending to light the oil lamp there and go across to comfort the poor, frightened dog.

As I light the oil lamp by the light from the fire, I hear a noise from Branwen's room above. It is a slow, rhythmical thumping sound and I cannot think at first what it is. Then I hear her cry out, 'Oh, yes! Oh, yes! Eli! Eli! Yes!' and her cries are mingled with his. 'Ah, ah!' he goes and the thumping of the bedhead against the wall grows faster.

I put my hands over my ears but still I can hear them rutting. How could he do this? It is the ultimate humiliation, to be thrown over for that dumpling of a girl. I cannot bear to listen, for the sound of them only serves to remind me of my own unfulfilled desire. Eli gives out one last anguished cry, then groans like a man in pain, while she sighs away like a cat that has just polished off the cream.

How long has this been going on? Every night since my husband left my bed and I slept in ignorance? Is this what they were doing while he was on his uncle's farm? And he dares to punish me for doing no more than he has done? I think back to our wedding night, when the elders all sat on chairs around the margins of the room, their faces set in condemnation because Eli had *dancing* and *cider* on our wedding night.

How fortunate I had thought myself to be married to a man who was bold enough to embrace more liberal ways than those taught in our chapel. He is a cut above all the rest, I thought, for he seemed to treat me as his equal in all matters other than those concerning money. But he is no better than those with their sermonising and their condemning while thinking themselves entitled to beat their wives, and their children too, if they dared to disobey them.

But no, he is no better than the rest, for there is one rule for Eli but quite another for his wife. Eli is a married man who goes to the chapel every Sunday, yet he lays with a servant girl while condemning me for something I did when not even married. And does he condemn the servant girl for doing the same? Oh, no, for she is not his WIFE!

God does not help all us women who wrongly believe that marriage is an escape from the drudgery and loneliness of spinsterly servant-hood. I wish I had never married. I wish I had stayed with Morgan; for all his faults and attempts to control me, he is a better man than my husband shall ever be. Oh, Morgan! I weep to think of all I have lost. If only he had listened to his own conscience and not gone along with Mam; I would be in some far flung place with Fortune, now, as I had wished, and not married to a man who is incapable of loving a woman who is flawed in any way.

The bed creaks in the room above me and I hear my husband's feet upon the floorboards. I listen to the floorboards creak as he creeps back to his chamber, never knowing that his wife is in the room below, listening and knowing.

On one of my visits to Dinasffraint, when I went there selling my butter and cheeses, I was witness to an unforgettable spectacle. Two women were fighting like barn cats, out in the street for all to see. As they tumbled about in the dirt, pulling chunks of hair from each other's heads and drawing blood with their fingernails, Myfanwy explained.

"They're fighting because that one's husband," she points at the dark haired woman who was sat atop the other, "has been laying with the other."

Why any two women would fight over such a man who was not worth the having, I could not fathom. And I feel no differently now. Branwen is more than welcome to have my husband now, for he is as nothing to me.

I make a bed of straw next to the dog and spend the rest of the night in the barn, wrapped up in the blanket beside him. Rain pelts down upon the roof and the wind howls through the gaps in the weather-boarding. I hear the sound of rats scuttling about the floor and draw my feet up close to my body. The poor dog whimpers in his sleep.

When the dawn creeps through the cracks in the barn door, I get up and stretch my aching limbs. I lay the blanket over the still sleeping dog and walk out into the yard. At first, I cannot fathom what is different. It is something about the light, I think. Then I see the expanse of sky where the beautiful, old sycamore tree used to be. I walk round the back of the barn. The sycamore lies on the ground, mercifully fallen away from the barn. It is split down the middle, torn asunder, as surely as my own marriage.

Chapter Thirteen

Wild imaginings.

I bide my time, and in the meanwhile, I share my food with the dog. He improves each day but whimpers when he has to get up and go out to relieve himself. And me, I do not whimper once, but stitch and stitch the evenings away, while the clock ticks and whirrs; counting the hours nearer the day when I shall no longer have to suffer my husband's humiliations. I no longer eat with them, but leave their food upon the table and shut myself away inside the parlour.

I wait for three whole days and nights before I confront my husband. Branwen is down in the meadow, milking the cow. My husband is out in the stable rubbing melted beeswax onto the pony's reins and saddle. I stand just inside the doorway, looking down at his head bent over his task, where he is sat on a bench against the wall.

"I was awake for hours on the night of the storm," I say, with my blood pounding in my ears.

"Oh, yes?" he replies without looking up from his task.

"I went down to the kitchen to fetch an oil lamp to go out and comfort that poor dog that you beat half to death the other day." My rage is rising in me now, tightening my throat so that my voice rises.

He continues to rub the wax into the saddle sat on his lap. His hand goes round and round in circles.

"I don't know what you're talking about. I have not laid a hand on him."

I gasp. "You are a liar! I saw you myself, up there on the hill!"

His face flushes with guilt but still he denies it.

"You should not let your imagination run away with you, Megan."

"I imagined nothing!"

He whistles then, to call the dog and it comes running to sit at his side.

"Good lad," he says, patting the dog's head. "You see, Megan? The dog is quite alright. You must have been seeing things."

"If the dog is alright now, it is only because I have nursed him these past few days. He could not walk after what you did to him! How could you be so cruel?"

"Megan seems to have taken leave of her senses," he says to the dog, and takes up his rag again.

"And I suppose you will also deny what I heard from the kitchen on the night of the storm?"

"Hearing and seeing things? Oh dear, Megan."

"I heard you up in that dairy-maid's room! I heard what you were doing!"

I am shouting at him now, and shaking with rage at his denial.

"The dairy-maid's room? Ha! Really, Megan, I have heard quite enough. Your ridiculous jealousy has quite made you lose your mind."

"Jealousy? You fancy that I am jealous? She can have you for all that I care. You are not worth the having!"

Spittle flies from my mouth and I think I must try to compose myself for I am quite overcome with rage. He places the saddle on the ground and gets to his feet. I shrink against the frame of the door, thinking he is going to strike me. But he gazes down at me with a look of abject disappointment.

"Please try to control yourself, Megan, for you are behaving like a mad woman. Let me impress upon you, the things you accuse me of are nothing but the flowers of your wild imaginings. If I had known you were feeble in mind…well, there are too many reasons why I would not have married you, if I had only known. Your brother must be laughing to know I have relieved him of such a burden, for it is clear that you are quite soft in the head."

He pushes past me and I follow after him.

"I know what I saw and what I heard. You are a coward to deny it."

He stops and turns round.

"There are places for women like you, Megan," he says, and there is menace in the quiet way he says it.

He leaves me standing on the cobblestones, and my blood runs cold with fear, for I am remembering a conversation I once had in the market place with Myfanwy.

"He sent his wife to one of those places, for lunatics, you know," she says of a wealthy gentleman who comes each week to buy cheese from me. "She took to wandering that big, old house of theirs with a carving knife, so they say. It was after their eldest girl died of the whooping cough when she were just five years old."

"What kind of place?" I wanted to know.

"The kind with bars on the windows and where they throw you in, then throw away the key," Myfanwy said with a sage nod of her head.

I run after Eli. "I saw you kissing her down in the meadow, too!" I shout after him, adding weight to my accusations, or so I believed.

He stops and waits for me to catch up.

"When was this, Megan?" he asks with a puzzled expression.

I am not sure of the day or date. I cannot remember exactly which day it was.

"When I was coming back from the river....a week or more, perhaps?"

"Your delusions are no recent thing, then. How long have you been doing this, Megan?" he says, as if it is I who is in the wrong.

In and out, in and out, my needle goes. He has taken my words, and twisted and turned them to make a mockery of me. Over and over in my mind I go, reliving the scenes he says I never saw or heard. Down, down, down comes the stick upon the poor dog's back. Thump, thump, thump goes the bed against the chamber wall. It happened, it happened, it happened. I'm sure, I'm sure it did.

What is truth if it is not what we witness with our own eyes and ears? Where is truth; if a man can simply deny to make the truth a lie? Where justice; if a man can say the truth does not exist outside another's imaginings? He has only to say these things are not, to make it true, even though it is a lie.

I see now, the way the wind blows and it is an icy, brutal blast that chills me to my marrow. Like his dog out there, I must come to heel; I must remain loyal and faithful and never judge him no matter what he does. For he is my master and can do what he likes. And should I displease him, he can dispose of me with ease, for he has money and I have nothing.

"That's what the rich can do with their money," Myfanwy went on to say. "They can pay someone else to hide away their secrets and their shame."

"For how long will she have to stay in such a place?" I ask.

"Oh, she'll not see the light of day again, I'd say."

I looked at her, aghast.

"Tut, look at your face! Worse things than that happen. They say the innkeeper got his wife put away after he found her with the groom."

Myfanwy knew all there was to know about the ways of men.

I have taken to listening, pressed up against closed doors.

"You could afford to do it, with all that money you got from the sale of your uncle's farm, you wouldn't miss the cost of it," I hear Branwen say one evening when they are sat eating their supper.

I do not know, of course I don't, if she is talking about putting me away. But what if that is what she is speaking of? I do not doubt she is capable of thinking such, for I know she would be happier if I were not here. She'd have him all to herself then, which is all she's ever wanted.

I go up to the dairy to fetch a block of butter. They are standing in the doorway. On my approach, Eli says some aside to her, and she guffaws like a whinnying horse. I wait for them to stand aside and do not look at them. I fetch the block of butter and she stands in my way, so that I have to push past her to get out.

I watch from the kitchen window, until I see Eli return to the fields. I go up to the dairy where she is stood turning the handle on the cheese press. Whey bubbles out of the bottom. That is what she'd like to do to me, I think, she would like to squeeze me 'til I am dry and empty as a husk of wheat.

I stand leaning against the door jamb, watching her. She doesn't like being watched. I can tell by the way her cheeks are twitching.

"Why do you think Eli never married you when he was on his uncle's farm?" I say, as bold as you like, and her face is a picture of surprise.

She shrugs as if it doesn't matter to her but I know that it does.

"I'll tell you why. Because he thinks you are a whore, that's why. Men like Eli don't marry whores."

"You want to wash out your mouth," she says "I'll tell Eli what you said."

"I'll wager you think he'd marry you, if I was out of the way."

A mottled, red patch flushes her neck.

"You are a fool. He will never marry you for the same reasons he wishes he hadn't married me. Because men like Eli only want to marry women who are as pure and unsullied as a fresh fall of snow."

181

I have disturbed her now. I can see she is thinking hard on this, though she does not want to.

"Was there something you wanted, for I've a lot to do?" she says.

"I don't want anything, Branwen. It is you that is doing all the wanting and I pity you for it."

"You got no reason to go pitying me!" She says, bridling.

"Oh but I do, because you have paved yourself a road to hell already, alongside him out there," I jerk my head in the direction that Eli took.

"If you go riding with the devil, then the devil will take you, Branwen. You've enjoyed your sport of helping my husband to punish and humiliate me. Everything comes at a cost in this life. You've had a lot of amusement at my expense. You'll pay a high price for that one day."

"Are you threatening me?" she says, placing her hands on her hips.

"It's not me you should fear, Branwen," I say and leave her to chew her cud on that.

Her voice carries after me as I walk back down to the house.

"There's madhouses for women like you!" she shouts.

This I know; wishing a thing to be so can make that wish come true, for to persist in telling a person they are insane will surely make them so. I see that I am trapped, for not only has my husband driven me into a corner but has closed and bolted the door behind me. How to unlock the door when another holds the key? How powerless are the ignorant! I have no room, or place, to turn. If what my husband says of me were true – that I am given to the imaginings of a mad woman, then he has all the excuse he needs to have me put away. Who in this parish could condemn him if he did, especially if he told them everything else I have done?

Worse still to contemplate, being as sure as I am of what I saw and heard, then my husband is more callous and cruel than I imagined. What crueller trick to play than to accuse and attempt to convince me I am mad, for the purposes of keeping his guilty secrets safe? It is worse than callous cruelty, it is evil to do such a thing to me and it makes me quake with fear to think I live with a man who could do such a thing.

My home is become like a prison to me, for he does control my comings and goings so effortlessly. He has no need of physical restraint for he is able to do so with misinformation or by withholding information. Morgan's harvest too, has come and gone, and Eli did not tell me until he knew it would be too late for me to offer Beulah my help. What must she think of me?

Chapter Fourteen

Morgan does a-wooing go.

"I'll go and have a word with her, if you like," I say to Beulah.

She wraps her shawl tighter around her shoulders and folds her arms. We're down in the hay field where I'm turning the hay with my pitch-fork, so it can ripen in the sun.

"No, indeed, we'll not go begging for her help. Megan knew full well that yesterday was your harvest day, for Eli will have told her long before. She had time-a-plenty to offer her help, and she didn't come near. She's made her feelings perfectly clear, if you ask me. She doesn't want anything more to do with me."

I lift a fork full of hay and toss it up as I turn it, so the air gets right through it. Though she has not said as much, I know Beulah is deeply hurt by Megan's rejection. Beulah is a proud woman, and I am sorely disappointed in my sister. I do not know quite what has happened but she seems to have taken against Beulah. I understand if she bears a grudge against me, but Beulah has been the best of friends to her.

"What are we to do, then? You say you will not accept a lift with Eli again. Megan will not take you."

Beulah shrugs and pulls down the corners of her mouth and sniffs.

"I suppose you'll have to teach me how to drive that pony and cart."

I know it's the last thing in the world she wants to do. I know she's a-feared to go anywhere near the pony, let alone trust it to take her to town and back.

"It's not as bad as you fear, I swear. And I won't let you go alone until I'm sure you've mastered it."

She shrugs again with a sulky look on her face, as if what I say makes no difference at all. I pause in my work, and lay down the pitchfork. I reach out and take her hand in both of mine.

"I wouldn't let any harm come to you. You must learn to trust me. You mean more to me than…"

"We got a visitor!" Fortune comes running down the path, shouting, and spoiling the moment. Other than one kiss, this fumbled gesture and bungled attempt is the nearest I've come to openly declaring my feelings for Beulah. Dafydd appears behind Fortune, and I let go of Beulah's hand as quickly as if it had been a wasp.

"Hay's coming on, then. It'll be ready to stack in a day or two," Dafydd says as he walks towards us.

"Aye! Just so long as this weather holds."

"It'll hold a while longer yet. The flagstones in the house are still sweating nicely, always a good sign."

186

Beulah makes her excuses to get back to her chores but Dafydd tells us he wants a word with the both of us, and we look at each other, wondering what ever it can be, for he is not his usual, jovial self.

"Go on up to the house, Fortune, and gather some vegetables from the garden for our supper," Beulah tells her, thinking the same as me, that Fortune has eyes and ears that do not miss a thing.

Fortune goes reluctantly and Dafydd remarks upon Megan's absence at yesterday's harvest. I tell him we have not seen or heard from her in weeks. Dafydd tells us he is worried about her, says he was down there not so long ago, and found Megan in some distress.

"What ails her now?" I say with some impatience, for there always seems to be something with our Megan.

Dafydd looks sharply at me as if I have said something to offend him.

"Have you given any thought to how awkward things are for her, knowing her daughter is up here, while having to pretend she is not? And I don't think Eli is too impressed with the situation, either."

That shakes me. How in hell did he come to find out that Megan is Fortune's mother? It is Beulah, though, who asks the question.

"Did Megan tell you that?"

Dafydd kicks at the hay beneath his feet.

"She had no need to tell it. I've known for years she'd had a babe, just didn't know what had happened to it," he says to Beulah, and then turns to me, "thought your mother might have done away with it, if truth be told."

I cannot look him in the eye. He always was a clever old devil. I never imagined he knew all along about Megan's secret, though.

"Why in hell steal the babe from her only to bring her back? And after Megan married, and all?"

His anger is up, and, stammering, I explain how I had no choice due to the circumstances in which I found Fortune was living.

"Who else knows?" I ask him, fearing he, or more likely that wife of his, will have told the whole parish by now.

"I've told no one, and will not either. But Mary suspects the truth, and you know how she is, she won't rest until she's uncovered it."

Beulah speaks up, her voice full of indignation. "Your wife should learn to mind her own business! Busybody that she is!"

Beulah follows with a quick apology for having said such about Dafydd's wife, though Dafydd seems not the least perturbed by Beulah's outburst.

"I only came to tell you to watch out for Megan, that is all. I need not tell you, Morgan, she is not as strong as she appears on the outside. She takes things hard, always has. I wouldn't want to see anything bad happen to her."

His words take me back to that day by the Wildwater when I thought Megan had thrown herself in. Surely to God, she is Eli's responsibility now. I cannot forever be chasing after my sister for fear she will harm herself.

"Well, it is she that is avoiding us, not the other way round!" Beulah tells him. "It seems I am not good enough for the likes of Megan now she is married!"

"Tosh! Megan's never been that sort," Dafydd tells her.

"It is actions that speak," Beulah says, a picture of hurt indignation, folding her arms across herself and turning to go.

"I'll go and see Megan, try to smooth things over," I say to Dafydd as we watch Beulah go out through the field gate.

"See that you do, Morgan. I wouldn't have said anything, but Megan's appearance when I last saw her, well, it left me concerned for her."

I hope she isn't thinking of throwing herself in the river again. Dafydd knows nothing of that and I shall not tell him. Megan has brought enough trouble on us all without adding that particular shame into the bargain. Dafydd has always had a soft spot for Megan but then he's only seen the one side. He isn't the one that has to live with the consequences of her reckless and selfish frolics.

Dafydd shoves his hands in his pockets and starts to walk away. He turns his head and speaks over his shoulder;

"You might have a word with Eli. Tell him to go easy with her."

I know not what he means by that, and it is not as though Eli would ever listen to anything I ever said to him. He didn't much like me before I brought Fortune home. I don't suppose my doing so has endeared me to him. I've not seen him since, but I don't doubt he bears me a grudge. I pick up my pitchfork with a sigh, and go back to tossing the hay. I thought it was Dafydd's wife who was the meddler in that marriage but it seems Dafydd, too, cannot mind his own business. I suppose I will have to make a trip down there, if only to scold Megan for the way she is with Beulah.

When I've finished turning the hay, I go up to the house to tell Beulah I'm going down to see Megan. I have gone no further than Eli's wood when I see him, instructing some of his men who are coppicing there. When I go up to him and say good day, he does no more than give me a curt nod of his head. I feel like turning round and going back home but don't know when I will get the chance again awhile, what with all that hay almost ready for stacking. I explain that I'm on my way down to see Megan, but he tells me she is not there.

"Not there? Where is she gone?" I ask him.

He shrugs his shoulders. "Who knows where your sister goes off to for hours on end? I have quite given up trying to guess."

There is something in his tone I do not like. I feel he is only telling so much, and in between the lines is some kind of slight on Megan.

"She'll be off walking and picking flowers, I expect. She always did do that, any chance she got. Away with the fairies half the time is our Megan!"

I say this with a laugh, meaning no harm by it, but what he says next surprises me. He takes me by the elbow and steers me out of the earshot of his men.

"It is no laughing matter, Jones," he growls at me. "No doubt you're laughing behind my back at my taking her off your hands. You rub my nose in it by bringing that bastard of hers back here, but I'll have the last laugh on you, I promise you that."

"It wasn't my intention to rub your nose in it, as you say. I could not leave the child where she was, Megan must have explained to you why."

My words do not placate him as I'd hoped but only serve to increase his fury.

"And neither of you thought fit to tell me about that bastard, did you? Oh, well done, Jones, no doubt you're pleased with playing your tricks on me, but I will have my day."

He is clenching and flexing his fists in readiness for a fight. I don't doubt that I would win, he is not built as I am for he hasn't had to do a day's hard work in his life, but I'm in no mood to start a fisticuffs with my sister's husband.

"Now, look here! If I had known Megan hadn't told you about that, I'd never have let her marry you. So, don't go blaming me. I thought you knew!"

"Thought I knew? What do you take me for?"

"Well, if I'm honest, I took you for a madman."

That takes the wind from his bellows. He stares at me for a few long moments, then twists his mouth into something like a smile.

"It is not I who is mad. It is that sister of yours."

"What do you mean by that?"

"You know very well, Jones. You said yourself; she is away with the fairies half the time."

There is something about the way he keeps calling me Jones that irks me; as though he is speaking to one of his work men. But what irks me most is his calling Megan mad, and twisting my words to make it seem like I agree with him. That's no way for a man to talk about his own wife and I tell him so.

"I only speak the truth. And she is, as you say, unfortunately for me, my wife and I can say and do with her what I like."

It is one of the ironies of my life that my own words and jests do find a way of coming back to me in the ugliest of ways. Only recently, Beulah admonished me for making light of a man selling his wife in the market place. To hear Eli speaking of doing with Megan whatever he likes, it is no longer amusing, and I am as outraged as Beulah was. My voice shakes as I speak.

"I urge you no longer speak of my sister in such terms. You will not do as you like with her, as you say, so long as I live and breathe."

It is I, now, who is ready for a fight. I am ready to knock his simpering head from his shoulders.

"I think you will find, Jones, you have no rights in the matter. From the day you and your sister tricked me into marrying her, all the wrong is yours and the right is on my side."

There is only one remedy for a man who refuses to listen. I throw a punch that lifts him off his feet and he lands upon his back. He puts his hand to his bleeding nose and attempts to get to his feet, but he gets only as far as his knees before rolling over onto his side, groaning. His men, working down in the wood, have dropped their axes and are contemplating whether they should come to their boss's aid. I do not wait to find the outcome of their decision. I head for home, climbing back up the hill, though wobbling at the knees, and the fist that hit him aching like hell.

Beulah kneels at my feet, and gently bathes my swollen fist with salt water. "You never did!" Beulah exclaims when I finish telling her the story, along with a few embellishments to impress her.

"He had it coming."

"Well, Morgan! To think of you standing there telling his workmen you'd take them on and all! That was very brave of you!"

"Aye, well, need drives the devil!"

"Didn't dare though, did they, after they seen what you did to Eli! Oh, I'd have loved to have been there to see it!"

I bask in the glow of Beulah's pride in me. I look down at the raven-haired head, bent over my hand, and think this is the perfect moment.

"Gone up in your esteem, have I Beulah?"

"Well, yes, I suppose so. But I didn't think *so* bad of you, anyway."

I'm not quite sure what she means by that but plough on.

"I've been thinking a lot lately…"

"Oh, now, I wouldn't do too much of that!" she says with her usual humour, but I don't laugh.

"For hell's sake, Beulah! Do you think you might consider marriage?" I blurt it out, and then lose my courage. "Some day! One day?"

I have shocked her. She doesn't know what to say. She sits back on her heels and places her hands in her lap.

"Well I might. But someone would have to ask me first."

She picks up my fist again and returns to bathing it. I never imagined it would be this difficult to ask a woman to marry me. My exasperation with myself makes me shout.

"I am asking you, you stupid woman!"

Beulah stares at me, then drops my hand and gets to her feet.

"And why in hell would I want to marry a man who calls me stupid?" she asks me.

She throws the cloth down on the table and I watch in silence and despair as she makes for the stairs. I hear the scuttling of little feet across the landing. Even when we think she is fast asleep, Fortune is listening. You bungled it now, I say to myself.

Chapter Fifteen

In the deep, dark corners, shadows lurk.

When my husband comes in for his supper, I am so alarmed at the sight of him that I cry out.

"Why, Eli!" I shriek, and say no more for he does silence me with such a chilling glare that I dare not say another word.

Even Branwen is silent during the meal. Eli's nose is so swollen and bloody he cannot breathe through it, so does chew his food with his mouth wide open. It is a most off-putting sight and my appetite is quite ruined. The same cannot be said for Branwen, I fear, for she gobbles her food with her usual ravenous appetite.

The more I think on it, I believe that her parents, whoever they were, were quite inspired in naming her after a raven. Perhaps they knew, from the moment she was born, that she was going to be trouble. Perhaps, she did suck her mother dry from the first feed and that is why they so named her. Now my train of thought has led me to think on her parentage, I feel curious, for I realise I know nothing about her life before she came here. My curiosity emboldens me to query.

"Branwen!" I say to gain her attention, and she pauses, her mouth wide open to receive the food that was travelling so swiftly towards her mouth. She stares at me for a moment; her surprise at my having spoken directly to her is quite comical and a titter escapes me.

"Where is it you come from?"

She scowls at me. "What business is that of yourn?"

"You are living in my house. Therefore, it is my business to know something about you, surely."

To my surprise she does not answer with more insolence but shrugs and says she was raised in Cardigan town.

"And what did your father do, pray tell me?"

She looks to Eli, as if waiting for his permission to speak further, but he is too engrossed in removing a piece of gristle from between his teeth to notice. I raise my eyebrows and smile in expectation of an answer.

"He were a weaver; spent his days bent over a loom."

"A weaver, indeed! And were you an only child or were there more of you?"

Her eyes dart to Eli again before she speaks. "I were one of six; four sisters and two brothers."

"And where are they then, your siblings?"

"Two of my sisters married and left for pastures new, two of my sisters died of the cholera. One brother went to sea, one stayed to weave alongside our Da."

"And your Mam, do you take after her? You must miss her sometimes."

"Not really. I never knew her. She died giving birth to me."

I did not expect this at all, of course, and I am quite taken aback. I feel a rush of sympathy which I do not want to feel.

"I am sorry to hear that. It must have been difficult growing up without a Mam."

She shrugs off my sympathy, her face sullen again.

"But your Da is still alive?"

"Aye. What of it?"

"Do you never go to visit him?"

She curls her lip with derision and looks over at Eli, not me, when she replies.

"I've not any plans for leaving, if that's what you're angling for!"

Eli seems not to have noticed our conversation at all. He has finished his meal and shoved his plate away, and is now staring into space, his eyes black and the tic pulsing at his temple. He is enraged about something but I know not what, unless it is the pain he must be feeling in his nose.

"I never hoped or imagined that, Branwen!" I say, wishing I had not made any attempt at conversing with her. She was a sullen, bitter thing, full of suspicion and malice.

I rise from the table and gather up our plates. Branwen looks at Eli with caution, as if she is about to speak to him but is unsure if it is wise. She is not graced with much intelligence or patience, I think, for she does not know when it is wiser to let things be, and cannot contain her curiosity any longer.

"So what in hell happened to you, Eli?" she says. "Did you have a run-in with the bull?"

He throws an angry glance at her.

"What business is it of yours?" he snaps, getting up from his seat.

He goes out without another word, and I see she is chastened by his lack of friendliness towards her, and I am glad of it. A mottled flush has covered her milky throat and she cannot look at me. Let her have a taste of what it is like to be on the wrong side of his temper, I think, watching her waddle out the door, her back all stiff and proud. It heartens me to know that being my husband's bed mate does not absolve her from feeling the lash of his tongue.

I do not hear him come back to the house, and so when he enters the parlour I am startled, and quickly hide the thing I am stitching behind the cushion of my chair. I fold my hands in my lap and sit up straight. I compose my face into an innocent expression, to cover my guilt and embarrassment. I fear he has seen, and is going to interrogate me as to what it is I am sewing. So it is a mixture of relief and consternation I feel when he speaks, with a nasal twang on account of his swollen nose.

"Your brother and Beulah are most upset that you did not go and help on their harvest day."

He is stood near the fireplace with one hand resting on the mantle. I cannot bear the look in his eyes these days, so cold and full of condemnation they are.

"But I did not know!" I tell him. "How am I to help if I am not told?"

He has done it again, sought to control my comings and goings by withholding information. I am upset, distressed and angry. I get up from my chair and my voice rises with indignation. "When was his harvest? You knew didn't you, and did not tell me. You are too bad, too bad."

"So I am to be blamed for this, and all, am I?" He says, shaking his head with disbelief, and then closes his eyes and clasps his forehead as if he is a man overburdened with worry. "I told you days ago, Megan, so do not attempt to blame this on me."

His words throw me into a flurry of confusion and doubt, for I cannot recall him telling me at all.

"When did you tell me?"

He looks up at the ceiling, and narrows his eyes, as if trying to remember.

"Let me see, oh, yes, I remember, it was when you were down in the orchard picking blackcurrants. I came down immediately, the moment I heard, to tell you.

The Lord God knows, I did not want another scene, should I forget. But it seems that even when I do the right thing, I am to be berated."

I remember being in the orchard. I remember picking the blackcurrants. For the life of me, I do not recall his coming down there to speak to me.

"I do not recall your having told me. I would not have forgotten such a thing."

"Well, clearly you have forgotten, Megan. Or perhaps it is that you simply did not listen, for you spend so much of your time in the world of your own wild imaginings."

He has turned on his heel and gone out through the door before I have properly heeded his words. Either my husband is a convincing liar or I am truly losing my mind. I am sorely afraid. I sit back down in my chair, and rub my forehead in an attempt to clear my confusion. I do not think Beulah will ever forgive me for not helping her, yet again. There is no excusing it, for I cannot say with certainty that Eli did not tell me. I am no longer certain of anything at all.

What am I to do? Go to Beulah and say I am sorry but I forgot? Ha! I can imagine too well her response to that! Or am I to go to her and contradict what my husband will have told her on their weekly jaunts to market; that he told me of the harvest. She will think me a liar. Oh, what a rat in a trap, I am. There is nothing I can say in my own defence to regain the lost friendship and esteem of the only friend I have in this world.

Dark thoughts do begin to enter my mind as the daylight begins to fade. The window panes blacken, the room falls into gloom, but I do not rise to light lamp or candle. There is only the red glow of the dancing fire, and Eli's parents standing stiffly in their portrait, to keep me company. I stare into the flames and do begin to think there is something very wrong with me. The fault must lay with me, for surely every person I know or have known cannot all be wrong.

All these years, I have tried to convince myself that I have done no wrong; that I do not deserve the blame attached to me by mother, brother, husband, friend. While the shadows in the corners of this room do darken, and by the flickering light of the fire, I come face to face with the self I would deny. *You brought it all on yourself,* Mam used to say to me. And for the first time, I wholly know it to be true. I am a wretched, unworthy person.

Oh! It is an ugly sight to see oneself through the critical eyes of others. To judge myself as they do judge, with all my sins laid bare. Through discontent and wanting more than life allotted me; I did grasp at a man who promised more than he was ever prepared to give, and I gave him more than any man has a right to ask. I gave him the body, the body that ached, and should have been Eli's first to know. Through discontent and wanting more than life allotted me; I did deceive and marry a man that I had no right to marry.

I shiver in the deepening gloom. My husband does despise me as my mother did before him. My brother would gladly disown me. My only friend must think I am no friend worth having at all. I wonder what Myfanwy would think of me, now. Would she condemn me like the rest?

I hear bedsprings creak as Eli turns in his bed. He is not gone for comfort to his dairy-maid this night. If that is what he ever did, if that is not the product of my wild imaginings. Is it possible for a mind to conjure such things out of air? Is it possible I forgot a thing which was so important to me to remember?

I think back to the night when I heard them upstairs, the night of the lightning storm. If I imagined that then surely I must have imagined the rest too, for I do not only recall what I heard upstairs but the whole of the happenings of that night; the dog too hurt and too pained to lift its head; the sycamore rent in two by lightning.

So afraid am I that I am losing my mind, I take a spill from the fire and light the lamp and go out into the night. Beyond the pool of lamplight, the night is as black as a raven's breast. My only guide the pool of light, I go around to the back of the barn with trepidation, for I fear that when I get there I will find the sycamore standing there as it has done for a hundred years or more. If it is still standing, then I am quite mad.

I hold the lamp high, and though its light is dim, there is no doubt what I see illuminated there. The tree lies, split in two, its roots reaching up like crooked fingers to the sky. Relief floods through me, and I have to lower the lamp for my limbs feel suddenly weak.

I go into the barn where the dog sleeps. I hear it whimper on my approach. I place the lamp upon the cobbles by its side. Eli has hobbled the poor thing; tied its paw to its neck with a rope; so tight the dog can hardly breathe. From this rope around its neck is another tied to a post. This length of rope is so short, the dog cannot lie down to rest. It is being slowly strangled. I get down on my knees and free the dog from its shackles.

My husband is a cruel man. My husband is not the man I thought he was. My husband is not a man but beast, to inflict such cruelty upon a helpless animal. The dog rolls on its back, wagging its tail wildly, in an act of grateful submission. I ask myself, what kind of man would do this to an animal that has shown him nought but loyalty? The dog does not deserve to be so cruelly treated!

I get to my feet with the lamp. Never have I been so a-feared as I am at this moment. My mind reels with confusion, there in the great, looming space of that barn.

Would he have me thrown into one of those places, even while knowing I am not mad, and that he has done these things of which I have accused him? A man that would do this to his dog is capable of such, I think. Oh, dear God, help me in my hour of need!

I see it all now, as I beseech my maker. I see why I have believed I am not deserving of the punishments meted out on me. It is because I never once did intend one soul to harm. Yet my husband and his dairy maid, would do me the greatest harm of all, and seemingly without conscience. If God is just, then it is on my side he should be.

I never once felt close to God within the hallowed walls of our chapel. There, I have only felt close to terror. Why would any preacher think it possible to love something so feared? To obey, as I must obey my husband, out of fear, and because it is that which is expected of me; this is not done out of love but fear of what will happen if I do not.

Surely, as God has made man, and thereby woman, in his own image, then he would want what we do crave; a love that is not conditional on what others would have us be. All I ever sought in this life was to be loved for myself, whatever my flaws and shortcomings. Is that not what God would want; not that we should live in fear and trepidation of his presence, but to adore him with all our hearts? Why then, does the preacher preach fear and condemnation? Why does he seek to force us into fearful submission, as if we are poor, lowly dogs?

I have taken to closely observing our preacher of late. I have seen him, the preacher, his eyes agleam with excitement, as one or another drops to their knees in the aisle, overcome and quaking with terror when he promises them the fires of hell; sinners that we all are. I have seen him, the preacher, in an ecstasy, when he has those same people jumping up from their seats with glee when he offers them salvation. I have seen the heart of that preacher, when he points his finger of condemnation into the congregation. He is a man who gains great pleasure, wielding power and punishment, in the name of his fearsome God.

I never saw God in the chapel, but I felt his presence once; up there by the crashing source of the great Wildwater, where the sun shines through the spume and spray, creating heavenly rainbows. I felt his presence in every single thing; in the sheep, the trees, the sunlight and the shadows; in the flowers, the rocks, the beautiful and the ugly, the living and the dead. And he offered me hope when I thought all hope was gone.

After breakfast, my husband admonishes me for having freed his dog. When I enquire why the poor animal must be shackled thus, my husband says;

"Because he must learn who is his master."

"You will only ever be his master if he respects you. Obedience out of fear is as nothing against obedience from desire. No body loved or respected a person out of fear, Eli."

I am aware when I say this that I do not only speak for the dog. I want to impress on him that he is destroying my love for him by treating me as he does. I want him to understand this before it is too late.

"And what would you know about respect, Megan? Do you imagine yourself respected and loved by anyone who really knows what you are?"

His contempt for me all but drips from his mouth as he speaks. The nasal twang created by his swollen nose only makes him sound all the more superior. I will politely speak no longer.

"Only a lowly coward would take out his anger and malice on a defenceless animal!"

"I do nothing of the sort. I am merely teaching him a lesson."

"You've taught a lesson, alright, Eli. Both he and I have learned all we need to know about you. I am only sorry I did not know you fully, before I agreed to marry you."

I have dared to say too much. I stumble backwards as I see him raise his fist.

"You are not the man I married," I say, my eyes welling up with tears.

"And whose fault is that?" He says, letting his fist drop to his side.

I do not shout after him as he goes, for fear he will return and strike me a blow. But in my mind I am shouting, screaming, tearing out my hair; I am going quite mad.

Chapter Sixteen

Oh, to ride a white cloud and go wherever the wind blows.

The weather is on the turn, again. On the western horizon, layer upon layer of rain clouds gather. Eli's men are in the boggy meadow which lies on the other side of the river. They are cutting the waist high rushes which grow in abundance there. They are in a hurry to gather them in and get the haystack thatched before the rain comes in. Swish, swish, their blades do go, and the rushes fall with a whisper to the ground. The young boys run up behind, gathering the rushes into sheaves and stacking them onto the gambo.

There is a wind picking up, soaring through the tree tops and blowing them about, making a loud hushing sound as it catches the leaves. I have a shawl wrapped about me for the wind is cool but when the sun breaks through the scudding white clouds, sweat breaks out on my brow, for the heat of the sun is hot.

Now I am resolved as to what I must do, and the time left to me being limited, I climb the hill to Carregwyn. I go in hope of catching a glimpse or two of Fortune. I want to commit her dear little face to memory, so that I may carry its image with me when I leave this frightful place. Eli places all blame upon my shoulders even while it is he, and only he, who has the power to make choices. I have only one choice left to me for he has removed all others.

I make a little posy on my way up. On the mountain slopes, scattered gatherings of delicate blue harebells dance and shiver in time with the wind. White clustered flowers of yarrow, on their sturdy thick stems, bend and sway. On the short, sun-burned turf of the hill top, the lichens are crisp underfoot. The ladies-bedstraw creates large splashes of shimmering yellow, the flowers as tiny as the mites they are meant to deter. Yet, despite their seeming fragility, they withstand and continue to bloom in all weathers.

I do not stop at my usual hiding place for it is too far away to properly see her. I go down to the little coppice behind the house and hide myself behind a tree. What a stirring noise the wind does make through the trees above. It makes me think of freedom, of soaring like a bird unfettered by man or duty. I lean my back against the trunk and tip my head back to look up through the shivering canopy of leaves. To ride upon a white cloud and go wherever the wind would take me! My heart yearns to be so free.

So loud is the wind through the canopy, that I do not hear her until she is quite close. I shrink against the tree trunk, and sneak a peek around it. My face crumples at the sight of her and my vision blurs with tears. I flick them away with my fingers and watch. She is no more than five yards from me. She is kneeling at the base of the hollow tree where I used to leave gifts for the fairies when I was a child. In her lap she has a corn-dolly and she is chattering away to this with an earnest expression on her face.

"And then Da did punch him on his nose, and did box his ears 'til he cried like a babby. But it is a secret 'cos I isn't supposed to know. I did hear Da telling Beulah when they thought I was sleeping."

So it was Morgan who punched Eli! Whatever did they fight about? Fortune walks the corn-dolly across her lap.

"And Da says he'll not set foot on Wildwater ever again, sister or no sister. He doesn't care if he sees either of them ever again." She pauses, "Megan's been nuffin but trouble since the day she was born."

Fortune reaches into her pocket and pulls out a handful of redcurrants. She shifts from her knees and sits down, brushing bits of dirt from her dress. She places the corn-dolly in the crook of her arm, as if it was a baby, and pretends to feed it the fruit.

"Dat's what Nesta used to say about me; 'you are nuffin but trouble'!"

She sighs to herself. "I did like Aunty Megan. I don't know why people always must fight and fall out."

The sound of Beulah's voice calling startles her for a moment. She gets to her feet and shouts in answer,

213

"I's coming!" and then she is gone, skipping down to the house, and I shall probably never see her again.

I go to the hollow tree. Deep inside the hollow, where it is always dry, I place the posy of flowers and the little gift I have been sewing for her these past weeks. It is all she will ever have of the mother she believes is already dead.

Chapter Seventeen

When Does a lie cease to be so and become the dreadful truth?

I am down in the hay fields, tying in the last of the thatch on the haystack. It is already spotting with rain and I've got the job done by the skin of my teeth. The tops of the clouds are blindingly bright in the sunlight, but their black underbellies are swollen and pregnant with rain, and the blue gaps between the clouds are getting fewer and farther between. I've done the job near one-handed, on account of my still swollen fist. Beulah says it is broken and I should put it in a splint or it may set crooked. I will do it now this job is done when it will not be more of an encumbrance than a help.

As I step on the ladder to climb down from the rick, the last person I expect to see comes riding up the track. I didn't think I'd be seeing Eli Jenkins anywhere outside of chapel from now on, so a worm of worry crawls into my stomach as I think he can only be coming to bring bad news. My immediate thought is of Megan, for there is always some bad news or other mixed up with her.

It is with slow caution that I walk back up to the yard where he is dismounting his horse by the block on the side of the barn. I cast a wary look in his direction as he jumps down onto his feet. I hope he hasn't come to resume his fight, for I'd not be able to punch him with my hand in its present state. I try hard not to look pleased with myself when I see his nose is even more swollen than my hand, and I hope Beulah gets to see it.

I wait for him to make his reasons for this visit clear. I shall not be the first to speak. But I can only watch aghast as he brushes past me, with his long riding coat billowing out behind him, and strides across the cobbles to the house. Who in hell does he think he is? I follow after him to ask him so. He is now beating hard upon the door with his fist, and shouting.

"Megan! Come out of there! I know you're in there!"

"You'll knock my door off its hinges if you're not careful. Megan's not here. Why would you think she was, man?"

The kitchen window opens and Beulah's head appears.

"I'll answer no door to you unless you stop that banging," she yells at Eli. "How am I to answer the door without the risk of you knocking me senseless?"

He lets his hand fall to his side then, and stands staring at the door, waiting for it to open. The moment it does, he is inside, almost knocking Beulah off her feet with the force of his entry.

"Where's Megan? Where is she hiding?"

He stands there with his head skimming the beams of the ceiling. His face is like thunder, his eyes darting from the scullery door to the stairs, thinking Megan will have gone one way or the other.

I may not be able to punch him, but Beulah has picked up the skillet and is holding the handle with both hands. One thwack across the head with that would knock the bugger out cold. This knowledge emboldens me to speak up.

"She isn't here, you fool. What makes you think you would find her here?" I say to him, raising my voice in anger.

He narrows his eyes at me, "And why would I believe anything you have to say, Jones? Where is my wife? Eh? I'll have the law onto the both of you before the day is out."

"You'd better hurry then," Beulah quips, "for it's a long ride to town and it will be dark soon."

I have to hand it to her; she seems not the least afraid of him. I'd have thought twice about making light under the circumstances.

"I know not what you are talking about. Why would we lie to you?" I say to him.

"I'll wager you are behind her disappearance, you spiteful bugger. You always were jealous of me because I had more than you!"

"What do you mean? Megan has disappeared?" I say, a cold shiver working its way up the back of my neck, making my hair rise. The memory is still fresh in my mind of the day she was about to throw herself in the Wildwater.

"I do not think it coincidence that a great deal of money has disappeared along with her. You'll swing along with her for your part in it."

I swallow hard. "You want to be careful what you say. My sister is no thief and neither am I."

As I am saying this, I am thrown back to that time when Mam said Megan had been pilfering the profits from her sales at market. Megan denied it with all her might but I was never sure of the truth. Leastways, if Megan has stolen from Eli, she is a bigger fool than I imagined. But he will never hear that from me.

Beulah tells Eli to calm himself and sit down.

"I'll not sit at the table of a thief and a scoundrel," says he.

"You're talking daft, man," Beulah says to him, "Morgan is no thief, and neither is Megan. Shame on you, for accusing your own wife of such a thing! Where was this money kept? In the house? Your door is always open. That day I came to visit, I could have walked right in and taken what I pleased. Anyone wandering vagabond could have stolen your money, but no, you come here first with your accusations!"

There is no stopping Beulah when she gets going. "In all my life, I never heard the like! And where is

Megan? Gone for one of her rambles no doubt! I think you owe us an apology."

Beulah folds her arms across her chest as though she is prepared to wait forever if need be. Her mouth is a tightly-closed line of defiance. Eli knows not what to say; he looks about the room as if he will find his money, or Megan, there. He stares hard at Beulah, then at me, a tic pulsing in his jaw as though he is grinding his teeth. When he speaks, his voice is no longer raised and he is as near as he will ever get to looking like he has made an ass of himself. The satisfaction in this lasts only until he speaks.

"Megan is not gone for one of her 'rambles'. She has been gone since yesterday morning. If she is not here, then where do you suppose she might be?"

In the river; that is the first thought that leaps into my mind. She has done it and I not there to prevent her. I look at Beulah and her face mirrors my own shock and anguish. It is like a punch in my gut, the shock of it, and I am reeling. Eli looks from me to Beulah with puzzlement. He has not thought of it for himself, has not imagined the most possible of all explanations for Megan's disappearance.

"I will go and tell Dafydd to gather the men to search the river," I say, like a man speaking within a dream.

I look to where my coat hangs on the peg. I look at the window where the rain is already splattering the panes. I know what I have to do but I am rooted to the ground beneath my feet. I cannot do it, cannot find my sister as I once found Sian; her hair matted with river weed, her lungs filled with filthy water. I cannot bear it.

"Why? Why now?" I say, with bewilderment, to myself more than him.

When I do finally look at him, I see he understands now. His mouth hangs open just as it did, the other day, when I hit him. Bloody fool that he is, coming here with his wild accusations when all this time my sister was in the water. I do not realise I have said this aloud until he answers back.

"I never thought... it did not enter my head..."

Beulah interrupts, "We do not know that is what she has done. I will not believe it until I know it for sure."

She finishes with a sob and her hand flies up to cover her mouth, tears welling up in her eyes. "If only she had come for the hay harvest! I would have known, I'm sure of it, if I had only seen her."

"Dafydd told us. Dafydd said he was worried about her. I was on my way to see her when ..when I bloody well ran into you," I say to Eli.

He has turned the greyish colour of Beulah's not-so-white apron.

"What would Dafydd know!" He says, and I don't like the way he says it, as if he is nervous of the answer.

"He saw Megan, said she didn't seem herself. Said I should have a word with you..."

"When did he see her? She said nothing..."

"Will one of you please go and see Dafydd!" Beulah shouts at us.

"I will go. It is on my way home, anyway," Eli says, making for the door like the hounds of hell are at his heels.

I am trying to put all the pieces together. They are all of a jumble and I don't like the way they are falling. If my sister is in the river because Eli has not been treating her right, he will wish he had never returned.

It seems that only moments have passed since Eli went out the door when Fortune rushes in, breathless with excitement.

"Look what I found in the hollow tree!"

She holds up a rag doll to show us. Beulah gasps. It bears an uncanny resemblance to Fortune, and therefore, Megan. At the sight of it, I am overwhelmed by a grief I fear will fell me, like a tree, to the ground.

"Look!" Fortune says, unaware of the effect on Beulah and I, "She has an M embroidered on her skirt!"

Fortune's face is full of eager excitement while I can only gawp.

"Do you think it might have been my Mam that left it?"

Without thinking at all, so practised am I at living this lie, I say;

"Don't be daft, Fortune, your mother is dead…"

God in heaven, have mercy on my soul, I'm sorry Megan, I fear I have made the lie come true. Fortune's face crumples. Beulah stares at me. She reaches out a hand to me. I turn away and stumble past Fortune, out of the door. I run for the hills where no one can hear me roar my sister's name. Megan! Megan! I shout into the dusk and the echo of her name is the only answer I receive.

Chapter Eighteen

Oh, the fiddler he played to make us all dance to his chosen tune.

If Megan is in the river, there is no saving her now. She has been missing a day or more. Morgan is bereft, has not slept the whole night but stayed down here by the fire. How will I ever sleep? he said, in answer to my advice that he go to his bed to rest. He thinks he tempted God or fate when he declared Fortune's mother dead. There is no persuading him otherwise. God has done this to punish me for telling lies, he says. God has said 'if you say so, Morgan, then so shall it be'.

There he is still, brooding by the fire, when I come down. I have not slept, either, but was damned if I wasn't going to lie down and rest my body, at least. Whatever happens this day, whatever they do or do not find in the river, the chores still have to be done. I open the shutters and my eyes protest at having to face a day without having had sleep; I feel a pain, like sharp, hot needles it is, shooting through my eyes. I feel so weary of it all; how will we ever get through to the other end of this?

"I'll murder the bastard," Morgan says, and I turn to him in surprise.

"Eli," he says when he sees my questioning look, "if he is the reason, I will kill him with my bare hands."

I say nothing but go out to the scullery and bring back bread and cheese.

Morgan carries on as if I have not left the room. "I should have heeded what Dafydd said. Should have warned Eli to treat my sister right."

"There is no point in tormenting yourself like this, Morgan. You don't know for sure what has happened."

"My sister is missing. What else do I need to know?"

I tell him there is no need to raise his voice; he will wake the little one.

"And that's the other thing. Why else would she leave that doll for Fortune, like she did? It made my blood run cold when I saw it."

Let us wait and see, I tell him, what the men do or do not find in the river. But he is not listening, is wandering along a path in his mind which it would be better not to follow.

"And him coming here, accusing her and me of stealing his money; that's all he cared about, didn't give a damn what might have happened to Megan."

He does not move out of the way and I have to reach round him to hang the kettle over the fire. I do not think he even noticed me there, his gaze turned inwards as it was.

"What's he been saying to her, eh? What's he been doing to make her want to throw herself in the river?"

I leave him sitting there while I take up the pails and go down to the gorge. As I dip the pails into the cool, crisp pool of water, I think about what Morgan has said. Though I tell him not to so torture himself, I cannot argue with what he says, for there is a horrible ring of truth chiming through his words, like the bells of the village church being rung to alert people to an outbreak of fire. And while I do not want to leap to conclusions before we know for sure what has happened to Megan, there is a dread inside me, forcing its self upon me until I cannot ignore it any longer.

The dread is this; that I ignored all the signs of Megan's deep unhappiness because I was too hurt to think upon it, after discovering Megan was no friend of mine. Morgan is right. We should have heeded Dafydd's words. What had he said? That Megan was not the sort to think herself too good for the likes of me or anyone else.

I sit for a moment, beside the falling water of the gorge, and ask myself why I was so ready to believe that Megan thought I was no longer good enough for her. If the cap fits, my aunt Suzannah used to say. How quick I was to don the cap of unworthy, village peasant. And who was it told me that Megan saw me this way? Eli. Not Megan.

With a shock that makes me swallow hard on my own spit, I think he has played me like a fiddle. I have allowed him to blur my vision and dismiss what my own senses told me, on that day I went down to Wildwater and got a whiff of the foul wind that was blowing through that place. If the cock has killed our little hen, I will be elbowing Morgan out of the way to be the first to wring his scrawny neck; for if she has thrown herself in the river, it is he who will have killed her, as surely as if he had thrown her in there himself.

So enraged I am by my own thoughts, I hardly notice the weight of the yoke upon my shoulders as I climb the hill back up to the house. Far heavier upon me is the weight of my own rage, guilt and grief at my own folly, and what we may have lost on account of it. I will never forgive my own hot-headed pride and stupidity if Megan is gone from us forever. Now this vision of Eli as duplicitous scoundrel has entered my head, the more convinced I become with each fleeting memory of the things he has said.

I think back on that day I went to town with him and Branwen. As thick as thieves, the two of them; and Megan at home with things she much preferred to do than help a friend in need, was what he led me to believe. And them turning up on the last night the wool-pickers were here, and Morgan's disbelief that Megan hadn't wanted to come. She wouldn't have missed it for the world, he'd said, couldn't understand what had got into her. And then to top it all, her not coming to help with the hay harvest, leaving me alone to cook for all those sour-mouthed women.

By the time I have reached the house and hoisted the yoke from my shoulders, this is what I am thinking; he was my only source of information as to the reasons for Megan's supposed rejection. Likewise, he was her only source. What if he never told her? In not telling her when I needed her help, he would have known I'd think even worse of her than I already did.

But why would he do such a thing? Why would he want me, and Morgan too, to think badly of Megan? What did he seek to gain by that? It ensured we kept our distance. Only the other day, Morgan was saying he would never go to Wildwater again. And I've said much the same over the past months. God help us, we have both said we wouldn't care if we never saw Megan again. What fools we have been, and like all fools we realise our own folly when it is too late. He could treat Megan however it pleased him, couldn't he, if there was no one who cared to witness it? This thought is like a physical pain to me.

"Is you alright, Beulah? Did you hurt yourself?"

Fortune is stood in the door with that doll clutched to her chest. She has not put it down since finding it yesterday. Oh, Megan, I think and fresh tears spring to my eyes.

"Yes! Yes, I think I pulled my shoulder carrying the water," I say to Fortune, rubbing at it in the hope of convincing her.

"Why was Da crying in the night? It woke me up."

Her pinched little face is so serious, and her eyes are filled with sadness. We are all so broken, so very broken, how will we ever be mended? I cannot lie to this child any longer. I remember, as a child, what I imagined to be wrong was far more frightening than the worst possible news.

"His sister, Megan, is missing and we don't know where she is. The men are going to look for her today. We need you to be a good girl and not bother us too much because it is a big worry. Will you do that?"

She nods her head and pulls the doll into her arms and rocks it as though it is baby.

"Is she lost on the mountain? I hopes they does find her. We love her, we do, don't we dolly?"

"Perhaps you could think of a name for your doll?" I say, carrying the pails of water into the house.

"It's a secret!" she shouts.

I take a closer look at her. She is looking peaky this morning. Her face is all pinched up somehow, and there is a puffiness around her eyes. Morgan and I were not the only ones who lost our sleep last night, I think. Goodness only knows what goes through Fortune's mind. She gave us both such a turn, coming in with that doll that looks the spit of Megan. And her saying perhaps her Mam had left it there, well, she must have been hoping her Mam was not really dead as Morgan had told her. Perhaps she was more upset by Morgan's outburst than she let on. Poor little thing. Poor Megan.

I have often thought of late that we should tell Fortune the truth about who her mother is, and trust her to keep Megan's secret safe. If Megan is in the river, then, that will never happen now. Morgan will be able to tell Fortune her mother really is dead and it will be the truth. Please, Megan, please God, don't let that have happened.

Fortune has run off before I have a chance to offer some words of …of what? Comfort? What can I tell her that would be of any comfort? I lug the pails into the scullery with the water splashing against my skirts. I've yet to get the hang of carrying them without wasting any. I need to get the hang of it, else I'll be forever going up and down from that gorge.

To think I felt sorry for that bugger, Eli. Poor Eli, I thought, Megan doesn't know how lucky she is. I only thought like that because my anger at her blinded me to the truth. And it was he that stirred that fire into life and kept it stoked. Oh, I hate him now, I do.

Morgan is still sat where I left him, staring at goodness knows what inside his head.

"Go and do your work, Morgan. You need to keep yourself busy," I say with a harshness born of fear. I need him to be strong; I can't be strong for all of us.

He looks up at me, his eyes glazed, still there in that place inside his head. Then he properly sees me and takes in what I've said.

"Perhaps I should go down there, go help them search." His face is that of a man who is haunted.

"No, Morgan. They won't expect it. You are too close of kin."

"But they may not do it properly. How will I know if I am not there?"

"Dafydd is in charge, Morgan. You know he loves Megan like a daughter. If there is anything to find, he will find it."

Morgan nods his head. He is like a man who has been in a fight, dazed and bewildered by the punches life has thrown at him. My heart goes out to him. I go and stand beside his chair, cup his head in my hands and hold it to my breast. Poor, poor, man. There, there, I tell him with the tears pouring down my face. There, there, I say as much to myself as him.

He throws his arms around my waist and clings to me as if I have the strength to keep him from drowning in his grief. Oh, Beulah, he says, where would I be without you? He pulls away and gazes up into my eyes, his face full of anguish. Marry me, Beulah, he says, marry me, please. Not now, I think, do not ask me now, not now when you are only asking me because I am a rope to cling to and bring you back to shore. I will bring you back, for the love of you; you don't need to marry me for me to do that for you.

I don't say this, of course, instead I tell him to hush now, this is not the time to be asking such things. I tell him to go now, go and do the jobs that have to be done, come what may. They will bring word, if and when there is something to be told. Go on, go, I tell him, and he does. He goes like a child who has been told what to do. He goes, because, what else can he do?

I fear I have lost all faith in the sanctity and security of marriage. Better to be a housekeeper, I think, than to hand a man all the power over my destiny. I could walk away, tomorrow, even though it would break my heart. I would have that choice though, a choice I would not have if I married him. I would be his chattel then, for better or for worse. God help me, I never wished to fall in love with this man but it has happened despite me.

Dafydd comes to us near dusk, tethering his pony to the gate and loping across to the house. I am at the window so am the first to see him arrive. I try to read his expression as he comes nearer to the house. His head his bowed, his shoulders bent and when he comes to the door, he looks up and I see that he is grey in the face with deep shadows beneath his eyes.

Morgan is over in his far flung fields, weeding the turnip patch. I sent him back out there after he'd come in for his meal. The waiting was driving him to distraction and I thought it best that Fortune did not see it. Even though I am expecting it, I flinch at the bang on the door. I straighten my pinafore, smooth back my hair, and take a deep gulp of air.

"Go up to your room, Fortune, and do not come down until I say so."

Something in my tone or face must tell her this is no time for argument. She leaps down from her chair and goes straight up the stairs, carrying that doll in her arms. I am silently praying to God and all his angels when I go to the door. I pull back my shoulders and compose my face but my hands are trembling like the leaves of an aspen tree in a breeze.

"Come in, Dafydd," I say, as if this is a normal social call.

"Beulah," he says, with a curt nod of his head, "is Morgan inside?"

"No, he is over in the turnip field. He needed to be doing something; the waiting was driving him out of his mind."

"I'll go up there, then," he says, and turns to go.

I cannot possibly wait on his news until he has told Morgan.

"Wait! Did you find her? Was she in the river?"

"We found nothing. We've been up and down, I don't know how many times, but found no sign."

He drags his hand across his forehead and through his hair. He looks done in. He opens his mouth to speak but is too overcome, blinking rapidly against the tears that have sprung to his eyes.

"But that is good news, isn't it?" I say.

It is some moments before he has composed himself enough to reply.

"Is it? That we haven't found her doesn't mean she isn't there. Where else would she be? We've searched every empty barn and hut for miles around. If she's not in the river, where is she?"

I have no answer to give him.

"I shall never forgive myself," he says, "if she has come to a sorry end. I should have said something to Eli but instead I told Morgan to do it. I thought it would be better coming from him, him being her brother and all."

"We will all be wishing we had done things differently, Dafydd. No more so than Morgan and I. How is Eli taking it?"

"Eli? Shaking like a leaf he was when I asked him what could have driven Megan to do such a thing. I'll have my day with him, I promise you that."

"You'll have to get in line behind me and Morgan, then."

I tell him how I feel that Eli has played me like a fiddle; how I would never have fallen out with Megan if he hadn't been talking behind her back, telling me things she was supposed to have said, telling me Megan no longer thought I was good enough for her.

"He's a canny bugger; kept you away so she wouldn't be able to tell you if he wasn't treating her right. And Megan said nothing to Morgan? Left no word to explain?"

"No. But she left a gift for Fortune in the hollow oak tree, a doll; it gave Morgan and I such a turn when we saw it."

Dafydd stares at me. "It doesn't look good, Beulah, I have to say."

I nod, fighting back a wave a grief.

"I'll go and have a word with Morgan. In the turnip field, you say?"

I can do no more than nod in answer, and I quietly sob into my apron the moment I've closed the door behind him. Fortune comes to the top of the stairs and asks if she can come down now. Drying my eyes, I tell her of course she can, come and sit here at the table. She climbs up onto her chair and I am only half listening when she tells me, 'look, Beulah, her clothes come off, can you make me a nightgown for her, for when she comes to bed with me?'

I have gone to the window, and am watching Dafydd go up to the turnip field. I half turn to Fortune, saying yes, I could probably manage to do that. She has undressed the doll, and folded its dress and pantaloons in a neat pile beside her.

"She will be cold without a nightgown," Fortune says.

"What's that you have there?" I ask, seeing her neatly folding a piece of paper.

"It was inside the dolly's pantaloons," she says with a blush and snigger.

I stare at it for a moment, my heart racing, before I go to her and ask her to let me see it. I all but snatch it from her hand. When I have unfolded the piece of paper and seen there are words written there, words I cannot read, I am running across the cobbles and out of the gate, startling Dafydd's pony so that it rears up onto its hind legs. I keep on running, stumbling in my haste to give Morgan the note his sister has left him.

Part Two

Chapter Nineteen

Run, little fox, run for your life, for the breath of
the hounds is hot upon your heels.

I bring her a bowl of water and a cloth to wash the blood
and dirt from her face. When she is clean again, she
takes a comb from her bundle.

"I prayed to God I would find you still here. I
have walked the whole day long to be with you," she
says, wincing as the comb snags on a tangle of hair. "Is
the cut on my face very bad?"

She turns her cheek to me for my inspection.

"It's a deep scratch but I don't think it will scar."

The dog lies fast asleep beside her chair. She has
fed him some of the ham and bread and given him water
to drink.

"I heard a trap coming along the lane and feared
it was Eli coming for me. I jumped the stone wall and
fell upon a pile of loose stones on the other side."

"You must be worn out," I say, looking to the
window and the black of the night outside. My

neighbours have long been in their beds but I fear I shall not sleep this night.

I get up and close the shutters. Who knows who might be looking in, searching for her already? How to tell her there is not a thing I can do to help her? If she stays here with me they will catch up with her in no time at all. That friend of hers, Beulah she called herself; she knows of our past friendship. My humble dwelling will be one of the first places they'll come to look for her. Dear God, it is a fine mess she has got herself into, now.

"Just think, Myfanwy," she says, "you will not want for anything again."

"Dear Lord, how much did you take?"

"I did not take it all!" she says, as if that makes it alright. "I have not counted it but I heard them discussing it, when that whore of his was telling him he could afford to put me away forever. It came from the sale of his Uncle's farm."

I do not say she will be locked away now for certain, and not one will be able to speak up for her and say it was without good reason.

"Don't look like that, Myfanwy! What else was I to do? How far would I have got without a farthing? I was a rat in a trap with those two."

She tucks the comb back into her bundle and begins to untie her boots. The flame of the candle begins to gutter and I use it to light another. We have burnt more candles this night than I would use in a week.

"It's just that I am worried for you, cariad. I don't think you realise…how much trouble you are in."

"What difference does it make? It was run or have them put me away as a mad woman."

She grunts as she tries to tug the boot from her foot and I kneel down at her feet, take hold of the boot and pull it off.

"You do not know that for certain, you said so yourself, they did not say that exactly."

"You don't believe me. You think I have imagined it!" She stares at me with a wild look of fear in her eyes, her voice shrill. "I thought I could rely on you. You, who know how these things happen."

I unlace the other boot thinking it is hardly worth her taking them off for she will have to put them back on very soon.

"But what if you were wrong in your suspicions, Meg?"

"It makes no difference. My husband despises me, seeks only to punish me for the rest of my days. If I had stayed there any longer I surely would have become the lunatic they purported me to be."

I understand then. It makes no difference what their intentions were, for little Meg the outcome would have been the same. I pull the other boot from her foot. Let them come, I think, let them dare to come here for her and I shall give them a piece of my mind. Silly that I am; as if a piece of my mind will save my poor friend.

"You must get some rest, Meg. Sleep now, on the cot there in the corner. I shall wake you as soon as it's light."

"You will help me, then?" she says, tears welling up in her eyes.

"I will help in the best way I can," I say, not wanting to say more for fear of upsetting her. She will need what little time is left to her to sleep this night.

She lies down on the cot and closes her eyes. "I'm so tired, Myfanwy, so tired of it all," she mumbles.

I pull the blanket over her. "Aye, I know, cariad."

I take my shawl and wrap it around myself. I sit myself down on the chair beside the cot and stroke the hair back from her face. I take up my knitting and begin to knit. It just goes to show, you never can tell what God has in mind for a person; never can tell what lurks ahead upon life's path. I always thought Meg would do well for herself; that she'd be snapped up by some wealthy farmer or such and have an easier life than me. And so she was, it's only a shame he didn't snap her up before that ne'er-do-well came along.

Now I come to think on it, knowing what I know now, I should have seen that Megan's head would be easily turned. If only I'd seen it then, if only I'd known how little she knew of the ways of men; I could have warned her, told her how to handle them, like I told my girls. But then, she was in love and when did anyone in love listen to common sense?

Men it is who own the chains that bind us; men it is who dictate the rules we must abide by. While we are married to them, they are our only shelter and our sustenance; we cannot survive without their will for they own all there is, even our own selves. Megan does not realise this, yet, I fear; that she is as much her husband's possession as the stolen money in her purse and the dog that lies at her feet. He can do as he pleases with the both of them for they belong to him.

I shift in my seat. I am too old for sitting up all night, as I did with my girls when they were young and ill with one thing or another. My shoulders ache and my hips are bad. The air becomes chill as I sit and wait for the first glimmerings of dawn. Megan sleeps the sleep of an angel. The dog has crawled beneath the cot but is not properly asleep. He opens his anxious eyes every now and then, as if he too senses the need to protect his mistress from impending danger.

The first sounds of morning begin to stir outside. Ravens begin their chatter and squawk, on the roof of the house across the road. The clatter of a barrow's wheels upon the cobbles tells me the gingerbread man is up and on his way down to the marketplace. He is always the first to rise. Soon after, I hear the wheels of another barrow; the creak of the unoiled wheels and the hacking cough that accompanies it, tells me it is old Rhys, the cobbler. His days are numbered, I fear. He has grown so thin these past months, and the cough that plagues him will surely take him when the next winter comes.

I rise from my chair, stiff as a bed-post, and shuffle across the room to open up the shutters. I too am grown old. I am well into my forties now. There are plenty who have died before my age, from one ailment or another. Who knows how much time I have left? I look out of the window; a pall of smoke hangs over this narrow, little street, giving a yellow-grey tinge to the dawn. Soon, neighbours will be throwing their slops from their chamber pots out of the windows and going about their business. I will have to do what I must before people begin milling about.

Through the wall behind the cot, I hear the clatter of old man Seth, already at his loom. Megan stirs and half opens her eyes. I bid her good morning, though there is no good in this morn, none at all. She sits up and stretches her arms above her head and smiles at me with such sweetness it makes my heart turn over. She thinks she is safe now, that all her troubles are over now she is here with me. I wait until she has broken her fast before I tell her what I must.

"Will you willingly go and hand yourself over to the law?" I ask her.

She looks at me with confusion and fear in her eyes. "You know I will not. Why do you ask me this?"

"They will be looking for you, Meg. You wish to be free, but what kind of freedom is it to be hounded like a fox until you are run down?"

"Hush, Myfanwy! You are making me feel ill!" she says, her eyes pleading.

"You could return to your husband, now, today, apologize and plead you will not do the like again."

"Have you not heard anything I have said..."

"Yes, I hear you, but you have made your situation worse than it ever was before."

"How could it be worse?!" she says with a snort.

I stare at her with disbelief. It is time for plain speaking.

"You have not only stolen away yourself from your husband but stolen a large sum of his money, too?"

She shrugs and averts her gaze, a sulky pout to her mouth.

"And what of your brother and daughter? They will be worried sick about you."

"I have told you, my daughter does not know she has a mother alive. She cannot feel the loss of a mother she does not know she has."

"Your brother, then? He will think you have gone through with that from which he saved you once already."

She smiles at me. "No. He will not. I left a note, you see, tucked inside the bloomers of the doll I made for Fortune; a note to let him know I am safe and well and staying with a friend."

"You cannot stay here, Megan." I speak more harshly than I intended.

She swallows hard. "Then you are not the friend I believed you to be."

"I am telling you this because I *am* your friend. If you are determined not to go back then you must go on. If you stay here, they will track you down and they will lock you up for a thief or a madwoman. You will have risked all for nothing."

"But where will I go?"

"Is there nowhere else? Not one other you know who would help you?"

"No. Not one!"

"You spoke of the wool pickers with such fondness. Would they not give you refuge?"

"But they are such a long way away!" she says with much dismay.

"The further the better, for you, my friend."

"But I do not know the way."

"God will show you the way. You must not tarry any longer. They could come here looking for you at any moment."

"I don't want to go," she cries, like a child who is afraid of the dark.

"You have no choice now, Megan. I will take you down the road and show you the way the drovers take, over the Elenydd. You cannot take the stagecoach, and you must not go near any toll gates, for they will leave word in these places, and with these people, to look out for you."

"Who will do this?"

"The law men, Megan. You have committed a crime, now. Oh, come here, cariad, give Myfanwy a hug. Don't take on so, there, do not weep. If there is any justice in this world, God will keep you safe."

She weeps upon my shoulder and clings to me, her arms about my neck, as a child does cling to its mother when afraid. I unclasp her hands from about my neck and push her away. Sometimes, we do not know how strong we can be until we are put to the test.

"Do you really think so, Myfanwy? Do you really think God will keep me safe?"

Of course, I do not. I have seen enough injustice in this life to make me think if there is a God, he has not the power, or the will, to help those in real need. But I tell her I believe, in the hope it will assuage her fear and give her the courage she needs. She sniffs back her tears, and gives me a smile that quivers at the edges.

"Yes, I think you are right. God will keep me safe, for God knows how cruelly and unjustly I have suffered."

"Come, then. I will show you the way you must go."

She gathers her bundles together and is going to leave all the food she has brought for me. I tell her she will need all she can carry for the journey she must make. Take this money, then, she says, I do not need it all.

"I cannot take it, Meg. If I were to start spending sovereigns about the place, people would know I could not have come by such money honestly. They will think me a thief, or worse, they will know that you have been here."

I hurry her down the cobbled street. The dog runs along by her side. She will have to share what food she has with the animal but it will be worth it for the protection it may afford her. You never know who is walking the roads these days. I wonder if I should warn her, but then, what would that do but make her more a-feared?

"Keep your money well hidden, let no one see how much you have or they will rob you."

Her mouth drops open. "Surely not!"

I tell her to trust what I tell her and to keep her wits about her. My neighbours are milling about, sweeping their steps or throwing out slops. I tell Megan to keep to the middle of the street else she will step into something she'd rather not, or find it tipped upon her head. Oh, she says, and quickly veers away from the filthy gutters. Too good for this she is. I am ashamed for her to see the ways in which we poor town people live.

Not that she'd ever let me see the disgust she must surely feel.

"And tell no one, not a soul, from whence you came. Mind now, not a soul, until you reach your destination."

She nods her agreement, her face full of anxiety and dread.

"The wool picking women, you're sure you can trust them?"

We have reached the end of my street and have to cross another and pause for the ponies and carts trundling up and down.

"Yes, I'm sure if I were to tell them what has happened, they would be sympathetic. They are good women who have suffered much."

I take her by the elbow and lead her across the thoroughfare, then down the next street which leads to the road due west.

"Now, you follow this road only as far as the milestone. When you see that, you will find a green road leading off to the right. That is the route you must follow. It is the ancient drover's road that leads over the Elenydd. Keep to the trodden path, do not wander from it. If you see a drover heading your way, which you surely will, find a hiding place until he has passed by."

"But what if I don't see him coming?"

"You'll hear them long before they come into sight. There is such a racket, what with the bells on the cows, and the barking dogs, and the drover shouting."

She turns her gaze from me and looks to the road she must follow, her eyes wide with fear. I reach out to hug her once last time.

"You will be alright, cariad. Do not be afraid, lest your fear take hold and addle your senses. There is nothing to fear but fear itself. Go on now."

I nudge her gently in her back and it is enough to start her walking. She walks a little way down the road before turning to raise her hand in farewell.

"Fare thee well, dear friend!" I call, raising my hand to wave.

I watch as she pauses before turning back to the road. I close my eyes, holding in my mind the vision of her cloaked figure carrying her bundles, and the dog trotting along beside her. I want to remember it well, for it is probable it will be the last time I ever see her.

Chapter Twenty

When running from the hounds, beware of the wolf up ahead.

They are standing side by side when I get to the turnip field. They turn their heads as one on hearing my shout as I reach the gate.

"She has left a note!" I tell them, panting from the run up here, and hand the note to Morgan.

It is as well that Morgan is leaning upon his hoe for his legs almost buckle beneath him. He grabs the note from me like a hungry man being passed a hunk of bread. He pours over the words on the page before throwing the note on the ground. I exchange a look with Dafydd, and bend down to pick the crumpled paper from the dirt. I hand it to Dafydd so he may know the source of Morgan's anger.

"I'll be damned! So Eli was right in his suspicion that Megan had stolen from him," he shakes his head, a flicker of a smile playing at the corners of his mouth.

"I don't know what you're so amused about!" Morgan admonishes him. "She'll have the law after her now. Trouble, that's all she's ever been and ever shall be."

"Don't talk daft, man," Dafydd says to him, "Eli doesn't know for sure it was her."

"He knows well enough, and he'll want his revenge. You don't know him like I do, he's a vengeful sod."

Morgan spits on the ground as if there is a bad taste in his mouth.

"Well, I take my hat off to her. What else was she to do, eh? She wouldn't get far without money. And if he had been treating her right she would not have been forced to go."

Morgan goes quiet then and his voice quavers when he begins to speak.

"Who is this friend she is meant to have gone to? I'll wager she's taken up with that rogue, again, that's what she's done."

"She would never have done that!" I say, "Megan hated the ground he walked on for having told Eli the things that he did."

Dafydd turns on Morgan then, his face a picture of frustration.

"Beulah's right! Morgan, bach, will you never learn? Moments ago your heart was breaking at the thought of your sister in the river. Now you discover she is alive and you're back to your old ways, with not a good word to say for her. You want to ask yourself this! Why it is that she didn't feel she could come to you for help? Why did she feel she had to run rather than do that? You know where to find me when you are prepared to answer that!"

With that, Dafydd strides off out of the turnip field without so much as a backward glance. I cast a wary glance at Morgan who is red-faced and cannot look at me. He turns back to the hoeing of the weeds.

"Isn't it time you finished here, today? It will be dark soon."

He says nothing. I stand for a few moments longer, watching him wield the hoe, slicing through the weeds. And then I leave him be, to lick the wound which Dafydd has opened up. It is not easy to see ourselves as others do when the sight is not to our liking, and it is always the truth which strikes the hardest blow.

I smooth the creases from Megan's note, fold it neatly and place it in my pocket. I pause at the gate to gaze upon the blazing sky the sun has left in its wake. There's a soft breeze blowing up from the valley and it plays with the tendrils of my hair. A raven flies past, hurrying, and then another, wings beating rapidly through the air, heading for home. Oh, to be free as Megan is now, free of the toil that is our women's burden to carry.

Wherever she is, I wish her luck and do not blame her one bit for stealing some of Eli's money. He owed her something, surely, for robbing her of the future she should have had if only he'd had it in his heart to forgive her one mistake. Poor Meg, things must have taken a bad turn at Wildwater for her to up and leave. I listen to the sound of the wind rustling through the leaves of the sycamore. Megan loved all of this, it must have been hard for her to go.

And then it strikes me, and I catch my breath with surprise. Of course, she would not have asked Morgan's help for she would not have come here and brought shame on him. Oh, Meg, I've been such a fool, I'm so sorry, I whisper into the twilight. If only I had not listened to Eli and my own stubborn pride, she would have confided in me, I'm certain of that. When I think of what she must have endured to make her run away, and endured alone, I am filled with sadness and guilt.

"Where in hell would she have gone? Who is this friend she says she's gone to stay with?" Morgan comes to ask me the next morning while I am up to my elbows in bread dough.

I blow flour from the end of my nose and then I remember the woman I met in the market place. What was her name? Myfanwy, that was it!

"I know! I met a woman when I was at market. She enquired after Megan after she discovered where I'd come from. They were big friends when Megan used to go there. I'll wager that's where she's gone."

"Then I'll go and fetch her back. It isn't right her staying elsewhere when she should be with family."

I tell him then, why I think Megan never turned to him for help. And as I say it, another thought comes to me. It wasn't just that. I remember the stricken look on her face when Fortune told me she loved me.

"She won't come back here, Morgan," I tell him, giving the dough one last good punch before setting it in a bowl by the fire to rise.

"Why not?" he asks.

I brush the flour from my arms and do not answer him until I have been to the window and looked out to make sure Fortune is not headed back to the house. She is up in the dairy, teaching that doll of hers how to churn butter. She loves the task and I am grateful that she does for it is one less chore for me to worry my head about. I lean my elbows on the windowsill and tell him how Megan can't bear to come here and have to pretend she's not Fortune's mother; and of the pain I saw in her face when she saw Fortune hugging me.

"It was a cruelty to take her child away, and it added insult to injury to expect Megan not to be hurt by seeing others raise her child in her place. It was my idea, Morgan, so don't stand there looking like you want to put a noose to your neck."

He stares at the floor but I can see by his face it is not the floor he is seeing.

"It will never end, will it? For the rest of my days I am to be haunted by the hounds of hell for what me and Mam did. It is a wrong that can never be put right."

253

I fear that he is right, and have no words of comfort to give him.

"The best we can do is care for Fortune the way Meg would want us to."

He nods his head in agreement.

"Let's go to the town today, Morgan, as soon as I've baked the bread. I know that, like me, you will not rest until you know Megan is in a safe place."

He is cheered by this idea and goes off to do his work before preparing the pony and cart for our journey.

The sky is warm and overcast with no breath of air and so the breeze created by the motion of the cart is a welcome relief. Fortune is sat between us with her doll on her lap, overly excited by her first trip to market. As we trundle along the narrow lanes, I rehearse in my mind the apology I have to give Megan. Morgan hopes to persuade her to come home with us. I hope he is successful. While Fortune changed into her best chapel dress upstairs (a cast off from one of Mary's daughters, unfortunately), we spoke out in the barn of how we might make things right for Megan.

We are both agreed that the best thing of all would be to tell Fortune the truth, so that at least if Megan would come and live with us she would no longer have to pretend. But of course, we can only do this with Megan's agreement. From now on, what is right for Megan must come before all else. We owe her that much, at least. And as for Eli, well, she need not see him again outside of the chapel. He can say what he likes about his rights as her husband but Morgan will never let him go near Megan again. Morgan says he will kill Eli first.

"The first fing I is going to buy me is a good pair of boots!" Fortune says to her doll.

Morgan and I exchange amused looks over the top of her head.

"Oh, aye, so you are rich now are you?" Morgan says to her.

"Yes, I am! For I have these coins in my pocket!" Fortune tells him.

She fumbles in her pocket and pulls out two gold sovereigns.

"Where in God's name…?" Morgan splutters.

"The fairies did leave them in the tree with dolly!" Fortune tells him, as though it was nothing unusual. "Will it be enough for a new pair of boots?"

"A dozen pairs, I should think!" Morgan tells her. "That's a lot of money you have there, Fortune. Give those coins to Beulah, now, lest you should drop and lose them."

"There's plenty more where they did come from!" Fortune says with a laugh.

I can see by Morgan's face that he is livid but does not want Fortune to see his anger.

"The fairies should be more careful where they go leaving that sort of money," Morgan says to her but it is me he looks at with a shake of head.

"How many more of those coins did you find, Fortune?" I ask her.

"Oh, I didn't count them all but the purse was full."

"A full purse of gold coins?"

"Yes, it was too heavy for dolly to carry so I had to carry it for her."

Dear God. Megan was certainly making sure that Fortune would want for nothing. Eli would commit murder if he ever found out that some of his money was going to provide for Megan's 'bastard'. We should hand it over to him, but I don't know how we can do that without him then knowing for sure that it was Megan who stole from him. Perhaps if we can persuade Megan to come home with us, she will own up and hand the money back. Especially as she would only have took it out of desperation, thinking she would need every penny. She will want for nothing when she comes home. She and I will go to market together, just as Morgan wanted. We will be better off then and in no need of stolen money.

I think all this as we hurtle along the bumpy lane, splashing through fords and scattering geese in the farmyards we pass through. For the first time in months, I feel a restless excitement swelling inside me at the thought of having Megan back with us. We had some fun, her and me. And the load will be so much lessened when we can share it. Oh, yes, things will come right now, I'm certain of it.

The marketplace is teeming with people. I hold tight to Fortune's hand for fear of losing her in the crowds. She is insistent we go to the cobbler first, so that he can measure her feet for new boots, but he is not there in his usual place and someone nearby tells us he is not well.

"There is a shoemaker down Church Street, you can try him instead," we are told.

The shoemaker measures Fortune's feet. She is most disappointed that she will have to wait another two weeks before the boots will be ready, until I explain that it will mean another trip to market with the pony and cart. At last, we are free to go in search of Myfanwy and I find her quickly enough. I know, the minute I see her face, that she knows we have come about Megan. Shocked to see me she is, but not surprised. She casts wary eyes from me to Morgan and looks almost afraid. She crams her knitting inside her pinafore pocket and folds her arms across her chest.

"I thought perhaps you'd arrive one of these days," she says.

"We've come to tell her to come home, Myfanwy, to us, her family."

"Bit late in the day for that."

"We didn't know how Eli was treating her," I say, thinking she is admonishing us for not having looked after Megan before.

"Well, I do, and I'll not be telling him where she's gone. Law or no law, I'll cut out my tongue before I'll hand her over to their kind of justice."

"So she told you about the money?"

"Aye, and the rest."

"He won't be setting the law after her. He doesn't know for sure it was she that took it. And Morgan here won't allow any more harm to come to Megan, even if Eli was of a mind to do that."

All the rosy colour fades from Myfanwy's cheeks.

"But I thought they'd be after her, else I'd never have sent her away."

Morgan and I stare at each other. "Sent her away where?" Morgan asks her.

"She's headed for the coast, along the old drover's road, over the Elenydd. I thought it was her best..."

It is Morgan now who has changed colour, his face a pale shade of grey. When he speaks, his voice is a growl.

"Have you ever been along that road yourself, you stupid ruddy woman?"

"Well, no, but..."

"You've sent a woman, my sister, alone across the Elenydd!"

People are looking our way, wondering what the argument is about.

"Hush, Morgan, stop that shouting. Myfanwy was only doing her best to help."

"Help? She has probably sent my sister to her death and you tell me not to shout?"

"Where is this Elenydd? It can't be so bad, surely?" I say to him while placing an arm about Myfanwy's shoulder as she has now began to weep inconsolably.

"It is no place for a woman alone," says he.

"She's not alone! She has a dog with her!" Myfanwy says through her sobs.

"A dog is no match for a wolf," Morgan says, making Myfanwy startle and her weeping takes on a hysterical edge.

"Whatever are you going on about, Morgan?" I admonish him.

"Wolves roam wild on the Elenydd, and not just the kind you read about in fairy tales. Vagabonds, beggars and cattle thieves roam there too, waiting to pounce on some unsuspecting drover. Well, they shall have easy pickings with my sister, shan't they?"

As we too often seem to do, we have forgotten that Fortune is listening to all until she flings herself around my legs, wailing loudly.

"Now see what you have done!" I say to Morgan.

"What I have done? This woman here is the one you should admonish, not me!"

"I didn't know. She said she had friends, some wool-pickers at the coast. I knew the drover's road went that way. How was I to know?"

"You weren't to know, Myfanwy, dear," I say to her while Morgan continues to glower.

"I shall never forgive myself if any harm comes to her...."

"And neither will I forgive you," Morgan growls at her.

"Is the nasty wolves going to eats Aunty Megan?" Fortune asks me through her tears.

"No, of course not, Uncle Morgan is just being silly, don't listen to him," I tell her.

She dries her tears and begins to tell her doll the fairy tale of the wolf and Red Riding Hood. "But you mustn't be frightened 'cos it is only a story," she tells the doll.

How much better it is to be a child whose fears can be quickly dispelled. I have hardly begun to think on the meaning of Morgan's words and am already feeling the chill of fear tingling in my spine.

"I'll have to get together some of the men to help me go in search of her. She has hopefully not gone too far." Morgan turns to Myfanwy. "How long ago did she leave? Was it this morning?" Morgan asks her.

She looks from him to me, her eyes filled with fear.

"She's been gone days since. I sent her off the very next morning after she came to me."

Chapter Twenty-One

The Dairy Maid's Lament.

She is gone and my path is clear! Surely it is better this way, I say to Eli. Better? He shouts at me and asks me to explain how it is better. He has no idea where she is and half the community, including her mad brother, are against Eli because they think he has driven her away with his cruelty. I do not think it a good time to remind him that what they think is right. Instead, I go to him where he is sitting in his chair by the fire and I curl my arms around his neck, and rub my groin against him.

"Get away from me!" He says and pulls my arms away with a look of such disgust and horror you would think I was a serpent he was uncoiling from around his neck.

I feel a hot flush of shame and humiliation, as though he has slapped my face.

"Why do you treat me so? It is what you wanted, her gone so we could be together!"

"It is what YOU wanted," he says.

I stand and stare at him. He wanted it, too. He said he would get her locked away in one of those places for mad women I'd told him about. I remind him of this and he tells me to keep my mouth shut or he will shut it for me.

"I am only saying the truth!"

He is changed since the day Megan disappeared and the men dragged the river, looking for her corpse. How I curse her! If she had not gone, his feelings for me would not have altered.

"Why does it make such a difference whether she went of her own accord or you had her put away? Surely, all that matters is she is gone?" This I asked him yesterday, when he stood as still and cold as an oak tree when I passed him down in the meadow. He stood with his arms at his sides and his face closed to me when I reached up on tip-toes to kiss him. I pulled away as if stung and carried on my way to the cow with hot tears stinging my eyes. I was so upset that the cow kicked over the bucket the moment it was full. Cows are the most spiteful of creatures at times; they have no sympathy for the pains of a dairy-maid and seek only to punish us if we go carrying our sorrows to them.

I fear a dairy-maid I shall forever be, now. Last night, by the light of the moon, I clambered out of my bed above the kitchen. I had been waiting all these nights, since Megan went, for him to come to my chamber and had grown impatient. I crept along the landing and past her door as if I feared she was still here and would come out and find me. When I turned the handle on his door it was to find it locked.

Oh, the fickleness of men! When he had no right to have me, he wanted me all the time. Now he can have me whenever he wants, he no longer desires me. He did not want his wife when she was here but now she is gone he is enraged. He can pretend what he likes to get himself off the hook, but I know; he loathed the sight of her for she had lain with another and pretended to be pure. Did she not tell me as much herself, when she came to me in the dairy to warn me he would never marry me because I would always be a whore in his eyes?

I leave Eli to fester in front of the fire and I take a candle up to my bed. I fear this is God's way of punishing me, for in the back of my mind is the niggling feeling that I am being shown what it was to be Megan; to love a man who does not love her and treats her cruelly. In my chamber I kneel upon the cold, hard boards and whisper a prayer to God to forgive me and have mercy. I ask him to show me why is it wrong to take another woman's husband if that husband does not want her?

I get up from my knees and rub them for they are cold and sore. I climb into my bed and wonder where Megan has gone. I am sure she has done this to spite me, to show me she was right; that Eli will never marry the likes of me. A worm of suspicion enters my mind; that he has used me as a way of punishing her. If he'd had nothing to punish her for, would he have taken up with me again? That day I was at the hiring fair, the day he ran into the man who left Megan with child; would he have hired me that day if he had not wanted revenge on Megan? And who better to rely upon than one such as I who had been so loose with her favours with him in the past?

He could be sure I'd take up with him again for I never could resist him. When we were on his Uncle's farm together, I fancied he would marry me. Always wanting a tumble in the hay with me, he was. No matter what time of day or night, he'd come looking for me like a bull for the cow. But he took off back here the minute his Uncle died and not a word of farewell to me.

I have been a fool to imagine he would marry me. There is one rule for the men of this world and another for us women. Eli punished Megan for laying with another before him, yet he had done the same himself and not thought bad of himself for it. All the men I've ever known have been thus, taking what they want without conscience.

When I was hardly grown from a child, my own Uncle Isaac saw me as his property, to do with what he wanted when father and brother were busy at their looms. He'd take me out into the shed, at the back of the house, and I never thought I could tell him no. I thought I had to do as I was told for that is how I was raised. I never dared but obey anyone doing the telling for fear of the slap I would get if I did not. And so I let Uncle Isaac do what he wanted even though I sensed that what he was doing was forbidden. It wasn't for me to tell him, and with Mam dying when I was so young there was no woman to tell me the right and wrong of such things.

A pitiful tear has slid down my cheek and dripped upon my pillow. I have been taken for the fool that I am. Eli never loved me as he told me he did; if he had he would love me still. Now Megan has gone, he no longer has use of me to punish her, and he is casting me aside. I face a winter without work unless I take field work wherever I can find it. Better to stay on here as dairy-maid until the spring hiring fair. Eli will not want to be without a dairy-maid all winter, and now Megan is gone, he needs my help in the house, too, so surely he will not throw me out.

I cannot go back to father for he threw me out long ago, when I was heavy with Uncle Isaac's child. I was but fifteen year old and the birth almost did for me as it did for the babe. She came into the world on a starry summer night, in a derelict barn where I'd taken shelter. She took not one breath and I think it was because she knew I didn't want her, couldn't want her, couldn't care for her in this world where no one wants to know a mother with a bastard child.

They would have hung me by my neck if anyone had found me with a dead babe in my arms. That happened to a woman in Cardigan, but a year or two before I was with child. They said she had killed it because it had no father. But how could they know she had done it? They said she had smothered it at birth. If her child had died at birth and she had been married, they would not have accused her so. But because there was no midwife present to say otherwise, they said she killed it because she was not married.

I swear I never did that, but neither did I do anything to help her breathe. Dear God, I am a vile and wicked person, I know. When she had grown cold in my arms, I wrapped her little body in my shawl. I looked at her face one last time, and oh, she was the prettiest babe you ever saw! She looked as though she was sleeping and for a fleeting moment I wanted her to wake and look at me, so that she would know what her mother looked like. For she would never see me again, do you see?

There was a length of old rope hanging from a peg in the crumbling stone of the barn wall. I went outside and found a rock and tied the rope around it. The other end of the rope, I tied around the little bundle. I'd passed a river on the way to the barn, it was only a short distance away. They mustn't ever find her, you see, or they would think I had smothered her.

Standing on the riverbank, I kissed her dear little mouth then wrapped the shawl over her face so she wouldn't see what I was about to do. I don't know why I did that, because she couldn't see, could she? But I felt she knew, anyway, even though she was already gone from me. And then I waded out into the water, though I didn't know how deep it was, and didn't care, for it seemed it would be a blessing if it would take me, too. With my arms outstretched I laid her on the water, as if laying her down to sleep in a cot. And then I let her go.

It was nothing short of a miracle that I lived to tell the tale, for I was struck low with such pain and fever afterwards, I thought I would surely die. I don't know how long I lay in that barn following my return there, but I was almost too weak to walk when I emerged, and the stench of my own body repulsed me. I do not know of any good reason why God allowed me to live for I am a barren woman since. All the tumblings in all the haystacks in the world have come to nothing over the past fifteen years.

I have not told a soul before, not even Eli, and shall never tell him now. And who will have me if not him? Who would want me once they knew I am as barren as a long-toothed ewe? It is my secret to keep, for the telling will never help me.

I wake to unfamiliar sounds coming from outside. I know by the light coming through the shutters that I am long overslept. I had lain awake until the moon was sailing high in the sky, thinking on what my future holds. I leap from my bed and open the shutters, shielding my puffy eyes from the sunlight pouring in. They are cutting up the sycamore tree which fell behind the barn on that night of the storm when Eli and I heard not a thing above the sounds of our amorous rutting. I listen to the swish-swoosh of the two men pulling and pushing the saw between them, carving up the trunk of the tree; and the crack and clap of the turner splicing the logs and throwing the slices into a pile beside him. He will carve them into spoons and platters; sycamore has a close grain which does not easily take up moisture, and so is the best wood for such things. The larger logs he will turn into bowls and ladles. This noise will go on all day.

I pour water from the jug and splash my face with the cool water. The cow will be bellowing if I do not soon relieve her of her swollen udders. Eli will be bellowing too when he sees there is no food upon the table. I have only one pair of hands, I shall tell him, and cannot do everything at once.

I go in search of him and find him in his private room where he counts his money. He is sat at his desk with his back to the window so I cannot make out his expression when I walk in. I apologise for rising late and say I will get his breakfast immediately before I go and milk the cow. He says nothing in answer to me but turns the pages of his ledger as if I have not spoken, as if I have become a ghost who he cannot see or hear.

"You need me!" I say to him, defiant. "Who else will you find to cook and clean for you now, eh?"

"You seem so sure Megan will not return that I begin to think you may have done away with her yourself," he says, looking up from his ledger and fixing me with the most hostile of glares.

"And when would I have done that? If she has been done away with as you say, then it was more likely you that did it."

I am frightened now at this idea. Is that what has happened to Megan, and him now looking to lay blame at my door? I've known men kill for less reason than Megan gave him.

"You can think again, if you think you can lay blame on me!" I go on with more courage in my voice than I am feeling inside. "If you do not treat me right then I shall pack my things and leave and then what will you do with no maid in house or dairy?"

I expect to see him back down at this, apologise, and declare he loves me still. But when he replies I know my days with him are over.

"I haven't told you the news, have I?" He says with a tight smile and slams the ledger shut. "Gwen is returning, now Megan is gone, and she will be bringing her cousin's niece with her to work in the dairy."

He pushes back his chair and gets to his feet. I watch as he takes up his jacket from the back of his chair and shrugs it on.

"And what am I to do?" I ask him, my voice wavering.

"You can pack your things as you have just now suggested."

I feel so small, suddenly, stood here in the middle of this cold room with its smell of mouldering books and damp mortar. And as I stand there wringing my hands and struggling to find the words to persuade him otherwise, I have a vision of myself lying in my grave and the smell of that grave is the very same as this room. It is a vision of my own impending death, I fear, when I am cast out from here.

"But you know I will find nothing but field work, if that. No one will be looking for a new dairy-maid at summer's end." I make a move towards him and see him stiffen. "Eli, please, you surely must love me a little, still. Have pity. The field work is so hard, and the cold is enough to kill."

"I no longer have a position for you, Branwen. Gwen and her niece are arriving tomorrow."

I detect a softening in his expression and voice, and this gives me hope and courage. I rush to him and grasp his hand in both of mine and smile up at him.

"Remember the times we had at your Uncle's farm! Such happy times they were! We can be happy again, Eli, you and me, like we used to be before you took up with Megan."

Just then there is a banging on the front door which makes me leap with fright. He pulls his hand away and tells me to be ready to leave next dawning. He will take me in the trap to Dinasffraint but I must make my own way from there. He goes to answer the door and comes back with the miller and Morgan Jones trailing behind him. They do no more than glance at me, as if I am of no consequence.

"I believe you have a cow waiting to be milked," Eli says, dismissing me as if I am and have never been anything but his dairy-maid.

I hesitate before turning on my heel and flouncing out with as much dignity as I can muster. Eli closes the door behind me and I linger in the hallway, waiting to hear if there is news of Megan. The miller tells Eli they have discovered that Megan has gone to stay with a friend in Dinasffraint but has left there and made her way alone, along the drover's road that heads over the Elenydd to the coast. They and a few others will be leaving soon to go in search of her but she started out some days ago and they fear she will have come to harm.

"I will go and get my horse," Eli says.

There is a loud scuffling and the sound of a chair being overturned. Morgan Jones speaks then and his voice is a snarl.

"You stay right where you are or it will not just be your nose I smash this time," he says. So that is how Eli got his injury!

The miller tells Morgan to let go of Eli.

"I will kill you with my bare hands if any harm has come to her, I promise you that," Morgan Jones says to Eli.

"Come, Morgan, let us make haste," I hear the miller say, and I make haste myself lest they find me listening outside the door.

I scurry up to the dairy to fetch the pail and milking stool and peek my head out of the dairy door. I watch the miller and Morgan Jones mount their horses and set off. Eli emerges a short time after, loosening his collar, his face drained of all colour. The men are still carving up the sycamore at the back of the barn and he goes over there. I go to milk the poor cow and tell her not to complain so at having been kept waiting. She will have an easier life than me because she has some value to the man who owns her. She is not the worthless wretch that I am.

Chapter Twenty-Two

And the scapegoat carried their sins into the wilderness.

It is at the sight of Myfanwy waving me farewell that I am made aware of my aloneness in a world that is suddenly grown too large and alien to me. On this journey I must make, there is not one I can turn to; no friend, no brother, no husband. There is only me and this poor dog that trots on ahead of me, looking back over his shoulder at intervals as if he knows the way he leads and is checking to make sure I follow.

The green road ascends through a grove of ancient hawthorns. Their berries are beginning to ripen; not yet the shade of bright, fresh blood but the dark colour of blood that has spilled and dried in the sun, as after the killing of the pig. The short turf of sheep-cropped grass is scattered with pale-blue harebells and clusters of creamy-white yarrow. They are the only witnesses to my passing.

It is a kind of dying, to be separated from all who have ever known me; to cease to exist in the lives of others; to no longer play a part in the ongoing saga of their lives. How strange it is to long to go home and have no home to go to. If I become lost in this wilderness which looms ahead of me, who would ever find me?

Such are my thoughts as the road rises steeper through the foothills of the great mountain which lies ahead. At times, I glimpse the valleys below, between gaps in jagged outcrops of rock. All the world seems then to stretch out behind me; the entire world to which I can no longer belong. Toward the distant horizon I see a range of hills and wonder if one of those is Carregwyn where resides the daughter I will never see again.

This thought brings a wave of grief, so strong it overwhelms me, and I begin to weep as though I shall never cease. I cannot see my way ahead for the torrent which blurs my vision. I lean against a rocky outcrop and close my eyes. My mind is filled with images of her; laughing, talking, holding my hand, skipping along ahead of me.... I hold each image in my mind so that the memories of her shall never fade and she will reside in my heart wherever I go, whether I live or die.

The dog waits patiently at my feet until I am ready to go on. He seems unperturbed by my outpouring of grief. When he sees me pick up the bundles I have dropped to the ground, he spins around in front of me, anxious to be moving on. It seems we have walked for hours already, judging by the height of the sun in the sky, and yet we are still climbing. With each hour that passes, though the sun is strong, the breeze grows cooler and stronger so that the sweat on my body chills and I must pause to pull yet another shawl from my bundle and wrap it around me.

By midday, the green road has all but disappeared and we are surrounded by a limitless expanse of pale grass stretching toward every horizon. There is nothing to be seen but this on every side. Yet, the clever little dog continues to steer a way ahead though I cannot tell north from south or east from west. He seems to be following his nose, tracing a scented path where others have trodden before us. I place all my trust in him to find our way across this mountain for there is no other to guide me.

Only when he stops abruptly and then veers off in another direction do I begin to doubt him. I call him back but he does not stop, only looks over his shoulder as if to urge me to follow. I have no choice but to follow but as time goes on I begin to fear we are now heading in the wrong direction entirely, and shall not cross this mountain before nightfall. Panic begins to rise within me for I am sure that when the sun goes down, all the clothes I carry in my bundles will not keep me from freezing to death up here.

Then I see a cairn up ahead on a ridge, and another further on. When we reach the highest part of the ridge, I see the most beautiful sight I have ever seen. Rolling hills stretch out before us and between two hills on the horizon I see a vast expanse of water which I know must be the sea, though I have never seen it before in my life. I gasp at the sight of it. Looking back the way we have come, I see why the dog had taken this route; he had avoided taking us through a vast expanse of peat bog where we would surely have been up to our necks in icy, peaty water.

"You clever, clever boy!" I tell him, ruffling his ears and head.

We sit together for a short time, gazing out at the landscape below as we eat bread and cheese to strengthen us for the rest of our journey. As we sit there, I silently thank God for the dog without which I know I would not have safely found my way. Like my brother before him, he had probably saved my life.

It is with great alarm that I see the sun is close to the horizon. I do not know how much further we must tramp before we begin to descend this mountain. I am so tired and weary, I can barely place one foot in front of the other, but the dog keeps going. I hear howling in the distance and the dog pauses, puts its nose to the air and begins a low growl. It is the howling of wolves, I think, that I've heard tell still roam upon these uplands. Am I to end my days like a small child in a fairy tale?

Chapter Twenty-Three

No chance to raise a hand and wave, no time to say farewell.

The oats are ripe and ready for the reaping. There is no time or men to spare for the search for Megan. Morgan and I set out alone, trusting in our neighbours to reap Morgan's harvest while he is gone. We throw blankets and packs of food over our ponies' backs, to sustain us on our journey. Mary is up in arms, scolding me for wasting my time chasing after a woman who so shamelessly abandoned her husband. I have not bid her farewell for I have run out of words to say to the wife I neither understand nor love.

On the eve of our departure, Mary announces her plan to send our oldest daughter to work as housekeeper to Eli.

"Mark my words," she said, "now Megan is out of the way, he is bound to fall for Eleri."

I tell her no daughter of mine would go and work for that scoundrel. Eli could rot for all I cared. And, I pointed out to her; Eli was not free to marry another if Megan was still alive.

"Scoundrel you call him? It is that wife of his that you should be blaming, taking off without a bye or leave and causing no end of scandal with her wild ways."

And why did she think Megan ran off? I ask her.

Mary stands with her hands on her hips inside the mill door, barring my exit. I've heard enough and am weary to my bones. I want no argument but Mary was in the mood for a fight from the moment I told her I was going with Morgan to search for Megan.

"You don't know what you're speaking of," I say to her, unable to help myself from speaking in defence of Megan, though I know too well that any good I said about Megan would only serve to rile Mary all the more. "If Eli had treated her right, she would not have had need to run away."

I go back to my task of shovelling flour into the sack at my feet. Mary snorts with contempt. "If he did not 'treat her right' as you say, then it will be for the reasons I've suspected all along. You think butter wouldn't melt in Megan's mouth but that child up at Carregwyn is her bastard, I'm sure of that! Poor Eli is all I can say."

She thrusts her chin towards me, her nose in the air as if she has smelt something rotten. I shovel more flour into the sack, unable to bring myself to look at her any longer, for the sight of her self-righteousness is more than I can bear. She appears to have cast from her mind the conversation we had a while ago. She takes my silence as a cue to carry on with her tirade.

"She is no better than she should be. She brought all her troubles on herself the day she begat that bastard living up there on the hill. And don't you tell me I am wrong about who the mother of that child is, it is as clear as day it is Megan's."

"And for one mistake she must be punished to end of her days," I say, throwing my shovel on the ground.

She opens her mouth to respond, then pauses, and I see the realisation flash across her eyes that she is again treading dangerous waters. I cannot resist temptation to press my meaning upon her.

"There is one rule for yourself but quite another for Megan, is that how you see it, Mary?"

Her face twitches with indignation but she is silenced now.

"You are too fond of punishing the rest of us for our sins while excusing yourself from all blame," I say, and push past her to get out into the fresh air, for the dust from the flour is stuck in my nose and throat so that I can barely breathe and my chest pains me.

I go to sit by the water-wheel, breathing deep of the clean, fresh air and listening to the rhythmical slap-slap as the wheel goes on turning. I watch Mary walk, stiff-backed, in the direction of the house. No doubt, I shall be punished with cold and stony silence for speaking the truth she would deny. I wish I had Megan's courage to walk and go on walking, as far as my legs can take me, but I fear I would not get far. I am too old now to escape the chains of marriage; this is how things will be for the rest of my days.

Morgan is silent and brooding after his altercation with Eli down at Wildwater. I tell him to put all thoughts of the scoundrel from his mind and think on the task ahead, but as so many things are, it is easier said than done. I leave him to his own thoughts; I have enough thoughts of my own to occupy me.

He does not speak until we are on the drover's road heading out of Dinasffraint. When I see the green road stretching up over the mountains before us, I wonder how poor Megan must have felt when faced with it alone.

"Reckon I'll be going home to an empty house," Morgan says to me, as we start the steady climb up the Elenydd.

"Why'd you reckon that?" I ask him with a quizzical look.

His pony stumbles on a stone and he is thrown forward in his saddle. When he is straight again in his seat, he heaves a heavy sigh.

"I asked Beulah, last night, if she would marry me," he says, a flush of colour rising in his cheeks.

"She turned you down?"

"She says now is not the right time to be asking."

"That doesn't sound like a no exactly."

"No, but it is the same thing she says every time I ask."

"Ah." I do not enquire further as to how many times he has asked her.

"Seems to me there never will be a right time. I suspect she is fobbing me off because she doesn't want to hurt my feelings by giving me an outright no."

"Well, that maybe so."

He shifts in his saddle and gazes up to the road ahead. "I never really thought about the work Megan did until she upped and married Eli. Beulah isn't cut out for it."

"And marrying you wouldn't make things easier, I suppose, for then she'd likely have a batch of young 'uns to look after, and all."

"It would make no difference if she loved me, though, would it? All I get is 'now is not the right time to ask because you're asking for the wrong reasons, Morgan'. I feel she is talking in riddles for I don't have a clue what she means."

No one knows better than me, the penalty that is paid for the rest of one's days if you go marrying the wrong person. Beulah is a wise woman, I think, to not rush into marriage with Morgan or any other. More toil is what it will bring her, for certain, if it does not kill her. How many woman have I seen die of the childbirth? Five or six in my lifetime, and that just in our parish. One of them died with her very first, the others were all on their eighth or ninth babe when the toll was too much on their worn out bodies. Aye, Beulah is wise not to rush, but what else will she do if not marry? Go back to the poverty of knitting stockings for no more than to keep bread on the table? And I wouldn't keep Morgan waiting too long for an answer for there are plenty who will be looking to him as a husband.

"I wouldn't be surprised if she is no longer there when I get back," Morgan goes on, "I reckon she will look upon my absence as a chance to leave without having to face me."

"You're talking daft, man. There is the little one; she wouldn't leave her there alone."

"I reckon she'll take the little one, and all, for she has grown very fond of her, and then I am done for."

Once a man gets a fear in his head, it is a hard thing to shift. There is not much I can say which will make him think differently.

"Let us hope you are wrong, Morgan. I fear you are letting your imagination run away with you."

We ride along in silence for a time. The path here is overhung on both sides with overgrown hazel trees, forming an arch over our heads. I turn in my saddle to look down on the valley we have left behind.

Dinasffraint nestles below the mountain, the church spire reaching above the scattered rows of houses. Beyond is a stretch of rolling hills leading to a distant mountain range, somewhere amidst of which is our little parish.

The path beneath us is pock-marked with the crescent shapes of the countless hooves of cattle that have trodden here for centuries. When a young man, I often thought I would like the life of a drover, but that was not to be for I was duty bound to take over the mill from my
father, as he was from his father before him. They say our lives are all mapped out for us before we arrive on this earth, that it is all part of God's great plan. I fear it is nought but hollow words. Not that I'm complaining. A miller's life is easier than the toil of working the land and the earnings are a great deal better.

"Megan told me you were not against Sian before she threw herself in the Wildwater," Morgan says, breaking into my thoughts.

I glance at him. "No, I was not. I had nothing but sympathy for her, and for Megan, too."

"Are you saying the Bible and our preacher are both wrong, then?"

I am not in the mood to discuss religion with him so hope he is not looking for a long debate. I tell him the preacher is a man like any other, and just as prone to be wrong.

"All I know, Morgan, is that our preacher may have succeeded in putting the fear of God into all, but I have yet to see fear bring out the good in anyone. I've seen the words of the Bible used to persecute and constrain the vulnerable by those who like nothing better to do so. I'm sorry, Morgan, but I cannot believe that is the will of God. That is the will of the worst side of human nature."

I see my words have shocked him, for I have contradicted all that his Mam beat into his head his whole life. Esther and Mary detested each other. I believe it was because they saw in each other what was most detestable in themselves; namely, their rank hypocrisy.

"Did Megan tell you what I told her about your Mam?" I ask him.

His expression is one of puzzlement. "No, what?"

I hesitate, unsure if I am being cruel to shatter all his illusions about his Mam. But, like Megan says, no good ever came of lies. It's time for a few home truths.

"Your Mam was in the family way when she married your father...."

He pulls up his pony and wheels round to face me. "You're lying," he says, but I can see by his face he knows I would never tell him a lie.

"...and so was Mary when she married me!" I say, carrying on without him. There, I have said it, and

286

did not know how heavy weighs unspoken truth until I spoke it.

We are close to the top of the mountain now, the trees and valleys left far behind. The top of this mountain is as flat as a table and soon there is nothing to see on all sides but a vast expanse of bleached and sparse grasses blown sideways by the wind, and nought but sky beyond. It is a good deal colder up here and the bleakness of the landscape is daunting. What must Megan have felt when faced with this wilderness before her, poor mite?

Morgan's pony catches up with mine. I tell him Beulah is right to be cautious, that the greatest unhappiness and loneliness of all lies in a loveless marriage. It is best to be sure before you take the leap.

"I married Mary because I'd got her in the family way, not because I loved her. She wanted me for the easier life she would have as a miller's wife, not because she loved me, I realised that, very soon after we were married. It is a miserable way to live one's life, Morgan. There are far worse things than staying unmarried."

He is silent and grave, no doubt mulling over what I have told him. I have been keeping my eyes peeled for a sign of Megan even though I know it unlikely we will see her here. If she survived this journey unscathed she will be on the other side by now and in the safety of some village or town there. I suggest to him that we set our ponies at a gallop so as to speed up our journey. We want to be lower down, on our descent, before night falls. I think how Megan would have been on foot, and wonder if she was stranded up here overnight. I pray she was not.

We gallop across the wilderness until I see a vast expanse of cotton grass up ahead, denoting boggy ground. We pull the ponies to a halt. There was no knowing how deep the bog was and nothing for it but to go across. The ponies flared their nostrils and twitched with fear as we pressed them forward. It took all my strength to keep my pony from turning and heading back the way we came.

The further in we got, the deeper we sank until we were in brown peaty water up to the pony's shoulders. I got scared then, I don't mind telling you, for I feared we would end up stuck in the middle of that icy bog. I shouted at my pony, flaying the reins and digging my heels into her sides, urging her to keep going, keep going. My heart was pounding and a shooting pain across my chest near took my breath away. Behind me, I could hear Morgan shouting at his pony, too.

Relief sweeps through me when the bog grows shallower and the pony speeds forward to carry me out.

"We must have strayed from the path at some point," Morgan says to me, "the drovers surely would never get their cattle to cross there."

I cannot think how or where we must have strayed but if we could lose the track then so could Megan.

"Damn this god-forsaken place! Which way are we meant to go now?" I say, looking as far as I could see and seeing nothing but more of the same. I no longer knew if we were even heading in the right direction.

"Look where the sun is in the sky. It will be setting over there," Morgan says, pointing. "The drover's road will pass east to west. So long as we keep heading west we should catch up with the road again," Morgan says, surprising me with his wisdom. Perhaps there was more to him than I'd thought; he'd kept his wits about him when I was close to losing mine.

We walk the ponies from there, for they are foamed up around the mouth and sweating from their distress. The wilderness seems endless and I cannot help but think that Megan would be frightened half to death if she had been lost up here. After a time, we come to a cairn on a ridge and catch up with the drover's road again. The road follows the ridge and soon we come to another cairn where the ridge rises sharply.

As we reach the top of this rise, a vista opens up before us like no other I have seen in my life. Hills rise and fall like islands in the mist-filled valleys, as far as the eye can see. And a long way off in the distance, between the hills, I see a vast expanse of water on the horizon.

"That's the sea way over there!" Morgan shouts, and my breath catches in my throat. It is something I never thought I would live to see for I have never been further than Dinasffraint my whole life long before.

"Well, I'll be damned," I say, taking my cap from my head to gaze in awe.

"The wool-picking girls have often told me of it, I never thought I would ever see it for myself," Morgan says.

The sun is getting low in the sky and we decide to make haste and begin our descent while there is still daylight.

"How far do you think Megan will have got on foot before nightfall?" Morgan asks me, voicing my own anxiety.

"With no pony, I cannot say for sure, but she would not have covered half the distance we have."

"She'll have spent the night on the top, then."

We look at each other, both thinking the same thing.

"I wouldn't want to have been caught up there after nightfall," I say.

Packs of wolves still roam these mountains, albeit in smaller numbers than in the past, killing and feeding off numbers of stray sheep. Though wolves are wary of people, there is no guarantee they will not attack a person walking alone, if driven by hunger or when they have young to feed. It is not only to ward off thieves that the drovers arm themselves before setting off over these mountains.

"The wool-pickers told me the most dangerous place is on this side of the mountain; thieves lie in wait for the drovers who are coming home with their purses full of money from having delivered the cattle down to England."

"Well, they'll find no money to steal from us," I tell him.

"No, but they would have found plenty on Megan," he says, and I shiver as though someone has walked over my grave.

The drover's road winds its way around great slabs of rock on this side of the mountain. I tell Morgan we will have to start looking for a sheltered place to rest for the night for I don't think we will get down before nightfall. He says we should press on as far as we can, hoping we will at least get down so far as to where there will be some woodland. It is then we spot the shepherd's hut, in a hollow between two outcrops of rock, some distance off.

It is almost dark when we reach it. We tether the ponies to graze and I climb the steps up to the door.

Chapter Twenty-Four

Tamed and tethered.

As I climb the steps of the shepherd's hut I hear the snarling and barking of a dog from the other side of the door. I feel my spirits sink for I am bone-weary and my head pains me. I long to lie me down to rest but another has taken shelter here before us. Morgan is stood at the bottom of the steps.

"Knock on the door and ask within if there is somewhere else near where we can take shelter for the night," he tells me.

My knocking brings no answer but more frantic barking from the dog. Thinking the dog has been left here alone, I push at the door, calling hello. The dog is stood just inside the door, barring my way, and snarls a warning at me to come no further. There, there, boy, we mean no harm, I tell him, and then I recognise him for Eli's dog, the one that went missing. And then I see her, huddled up in the corner of the cot which stands in the corner of the room. The room is unlit, save from the light from the little fire that is burning, but I see her eyes wide with fear, like a rabbit caught in a snare.

"It's me, Meg. It's Dafydd," I tell her.

She tells us to go, she does not want to be found. She says she will never go back.

"Don't talk daft, Megan," Morgan tells her, "you can't stay in this shack forever and where else will you go?"

She shrugs her shoulders and uses a stick to poke at the fire in the stove. "I've managed alright, so far," she says, casting a defiant glance at him.

"And what will you do when your food runs out? You'll have to leave, then. Besides, it is not safe for you here, you must know that. Imagine if we had been thieves who were looking for shelter this night. We would have robbed you, or worse, and left you for dead."

"The dog protects me."

Morgan laughs derisively. "That dog would be no match for a grown man determined to have what he wants."

I am sat on a makeshift stool by the fire, watching and listening. How many days has she been here? Three or four? She is as dirty and unkempt as an urchin. It breaks my heart to see our little Megan so reduced by circumstance.

"Morgan is right," I tell her. "You must come back with us, Meg. You cannot live like this."

Those eyes of hers flash at me with anger. "Cannot live like this? This is paradise compared to the alternative. Neither of you understand what you are asking me to return to."

She hugs herself with her arms, her shoulders hunched.

"Things will be different from now on, Megan, I promise you that," Morgan says.

"Promise me, do you? My husband can do what he likes with me. He is my keeper now, not you," she says.

Her tone is bitter, and her words hit their mark. Morgan's expression is one of chagrin which quickly alters to one of annoyance.

I hold my hand up to him, to stay him before he says some words of retaliation, as he is want to do when placed upon a hook and forced to examine his own conscience. They do not know it but they are alike in many ways, not least in their ability to blame themselves while broaching no blame from any other quarter. When one is apt to heap stones upon one's own head, one will quickly be buried if others do likewise.

"I am tired from our journey. Let us discuss this in the morning," I tell them, for I have the most terrible pain in my head and long for rest.

Megan tells me I do not look well and insists I have the bed, saying she will lie on the floor. I am ashamed to do so, but feel too ill to argue.

In the light of dawn, Megan is intractable. I send Morgan out to look for kindling and to attend to the needs of the ponies which are still tethered outside and in need of water. Megan tells him of a stream she has found a little way down the hill. My chances of persuading her will be greatly increased by his absence.

I watch her as she reaches up for the small bundle of food she has hung from a beam above our heads. When she sits down on the stool by the fire and places the bundle upon her lap, I see there is only a small portion of bread, a bite of cheese, and a piece of ham which she promptly gives to the dog. She sees I have noticed how little food she has left and quickly wraps up the bundle with the shame-faced look of a child who has been caught out.

"I am going to the coast and will find refuge with the wool-picking girls when I get there," she says with a recalcitrant shrug, in answer to my question as to where she is planning to go now her supply of food has run out.

"And you know where to find them and how to get there?"

This question is met with silence.

"Meg, you have reached the end of this particular road. You know it as well as I. You have to come home, like it or not."

Her eyes well with tears but she does not weep.

"I have money, I shall not want, wherever I go," she says, and then adds with a look of shame, "I stole from Eli, a great quantity of money."

"I know you did, cariad, and don't blame you one bit, but this world is not a safe place for a woman alone, whether she has money or no."

"I cannot go back to him, Dafydd. Every day he torments me, him and that dairy maid. They would have me put away for a lunatic but it is not I who is consumed by madness, it is he."

"Morgan and I will see to it that he is brought to his senses, Megan. He will mistreat you no longer."

"And can you protect me from the misery I feel at the absence of love I see every time I look in his eyes? I think not," she says.

"Do you imagine every couple to be living in the light of love, Megan? If you do, you are sorely misguided."

"Do not tell me that! Where is the purpose in any of it if there is not love?"

"I have asked myself the same question often, of late. But it is not for us to question life's purpose, Megan, for that question leads us down a dark and dismal path, as well you know."

"What would you have me do, then? You, who I thought understood me better than any? Would you have me go back to a man who loves me not, and live a lie pretending I am not the mother of that little girl upon the hill?"

Once upon a time, I would have said no, but now I see she has no choice, for the world is what it is and if I lived another fifty years it would not be long enough to change it. It grieves me to give up the fight for her but for her own sake, I must do it.

"Your situation could be far worse, Megan. At the least, Eli does not beat you with his fists as so many men do to their wives."

She looks at me askance, and I see she feels my words are a betrayal.

"There are many ways a man beats a woman, Dafydd, and not all require the crunch of fist or boot on tender bones and teeth."

Eli Jenkins does not deserve her and he will die by my own hand if he mistreats her again; he will know my wrath by the end of this day, and I shall ensure he fears it. I do not tell Megan this for my duty is to save her from herself, not him. It is time she ceased kicking against, or running from, a world which will only punish her all the more if she does. The time has come for Megan to accept her lot in this life, as we all must do. There is no changing or running from what has passed, the only thing to be done is to repair the broken pieces as best we can.

"You are Eli's wife, for better or for worse, and things could be a lot worse, Megan. You will not know a day's hunger as his wife. You will never live in a hovel with mud beneath your feet and a leaking thatch over your head, which is how your wool-picking friends will live. You will not be cast-out as the mother of your illegitimate daughter, because Morgan has stepped up to the task. You will not have to spend the rest of your days living off stolen money – and I'm sure you know, as well as I, no good will come from doing that. You will not know a day's true freedom if you choose that route. Be thankful for your blessings, Megan, for in my experience, those who are not thankful for what they have end up with a great deal less than they hanker for."

She sits on the stool, stroking the dog that sits by her side, his head resting on her knee, his eyes upon her face. Outside the hut, a bird is singing a merry song, the sound so at odds with the sombre atmosphere within. After a while, she straightens her shoulders, sighs heavily, and turns to me with a look of resignation and defeat. She says nothing but nods her head in assent and gets to her feet. It is with a heavy heart that I watch her gather her bundles together for I see that she does it with heaviness in her own.

Chapter Twenty-Five

A bird in a cage is worth two in the hand.

I'm only here for him. Known him since he were a boy, I have, and his parents, Eleanor and Rees, were good to me. *She* is my cross to bear, the debt I pay for a lifetime in their service. We all carry on as if nothing happened. It is best that way. No mention is made of the quarrel or her running off like she did and leaving him to fend for himself. He doesn't feel the same way about her, of course he doesn't, how could he? But he makes the best of a bad decision, there's not much else he can do.

She's carrying, I know that, I remember all the signs from when his mother was carrying him. I worked for them from the day they married, saw Eli come into this world. Eleanor and I had been friends from childhood. I thought the world of her and gave my whole life to her service. What need did I have for a husband and children of my own when I had everything I needed right here in this house? Fine, upstanding, chapel people they were. They'll be turning in their graves at the way things have turned out.

How this one was made, heaven only knows, for they no longer share the same bed. But then, his chamber is right next door to hers, so I dare say it wasn't far to wander along the landing in the dead of night. A man has his needs, after all, and it is his right to fulfil them.

She eats no more than a spoonful of breakfast before she leaps from the table and rushes outside to be sick. I don't know what is wrong with me, she says, but she must know, surely, for she is no innocent in such matters, after all. She has been like this for months now, yet Eli has not said a word to me so I do wonder if he knows. If it goes on much longer, I shall feel it my duty to tell him.

She never goes up there anymore, not since the day the miller and that brother of hers brought her back. At the time, I thought they should have left her to her fate, but now she is carrying, well, things are different now. If Eli should have a son to take over from him one day, then perhaps it was for the best they brought her back. People are stupid, mind. By and large, they seem to believe that bastard is her brother's progeny. I'd like to tell them the truth, and I would and all if it wasn't for Eli.

You should see them on a Sunday, at chapel. She stands next to Eli, looking for all the world like a good and proper farmer's wife. And she doesn't even glance in her brother's direction, where he is stood with her daughter and that housekeeper of his, Beulah her name is. I don't believe that one is any better than she should be either, living up there with a single man and her with no ring on her finger. Rumours abound about those two and I know the preacher has had words with Morgan about how it looks in the eyes of the parish, especially as he has already transgressed, or so everyone thinks.

Megan is a dull-witted thing. What Eli ever saw in her, I don't know. There is something about her that makes me want to take her by the shoulders and shake her. I know what it is that irks me so; I think, how dare she look unhappy when she has caught the best of all men? For I never see a smile on her face. She has no spirit, that is the trouble; no spring in her step, no brightness of eye, no enthusiasm for anything. She is a trial to look upon.

Oh, she smiles when spoken to, bestows a little smile when she greets me but there is nothing behind it, if you see what I mean. She is all pretence, that one. She should be happy, grateful for her lot, for most men would not have taken her back as Eli has done. Not after all she has done, the madam.

"Gwen," she says to me this morning, "Eli is going to a horse sale, today, and will need a parcel of bread and cheese to take along with him."

As if I need telling. It's just her way of reminding me who is mistress of the house, that's what it is. I ignored her request and turned my back, so as to let her know, in return, I don't need orders from her. I will do things in my own good time, not when she says so. Eli would have told me himself, soon enough, where he was going. There was no need for her interference. I hear her sigh in that way that she does, as if her patience is sorely tried.

I watch her from the corner of my eye as she drifts away into the parlour. She is like a ghost walking about the rooms, moving ornaments from their places and putting them somewhere else so that I must go after and put them back where they should rightfully be. She will throw on her cloak now and go wandering about the farm, watching the men at their work, getting in the way. Or she will go walking beside the Wildwater and come back with a basketful of golden crab-apples or some such, as she did the other day.

"And what are you proposing I do with those?" I ask her.

She tells me she is not proposing *I* do anything with them; she is going to prepare them herself and make a crab-apple jelly. They are still lying in the basket in the corner, turning brown. All I said was that I hoped she wouldn't be getting in my way because I have quite enough to think about without tripping over her clod-hopping feet every five minutes.

But she never goes *there*, oh no, not where she would have to face the evidence of her guilt. Not that Eli would permit it, anyway. I heard him, one night, when they were in the parlour and I stood listening this side of the door. It was the night after they brought her back – and you should have seen the state she was in, no better than a tramp, with her hair not brushed and her clothes all torn and filthy. I gave her such a look, I can tell you, a look that told her exactly what I thought of her.

She doesn't know the half that I know about what goes on in this house.

"Congratulations, Megan, you have succeeded in turning the miller against me with your tall tales of woe," he says to her.

He must have been standing near the door, by the painting of his mother and father, for I could hear him clear as day. She is farther away, so I have to lean in closer to the door to hear her reply.

"I spoke only the truth," she says, so quietly I barely hear it. The truth, indeed!

"It seems I am to take you back, no matter that you have disgraced me. So be it, but I warn you, Megan, I'll not be humiliated further. Your friend the miller and your brother can say what they like, but you are my wife, and therefore subject to my command.

She doesn't have anything to say to that!

"I want every farthing of the money you stole from me repaid, and you shall stay away from your bastard at Carregwyn."

She is quiet for so long, my feet begin to ache from the standing. When I am about to give up waiting, thinking there is no more to be heard, she speaks.

"I cannot repay all your money. I gave some of it away."

He asks her who she gave it to, and adds it had better not have been to that brother of hers.

"I gave it to a beggar who was in the marketplace at Dinasffraint," she says.

I hear the slap of his hand on her face and she yelps.

"I want your word that you will not visit Carregwyn again."

"For pity's sake, have mercy, Eli," she beseeches him.

When he does not answer, she issues a threat, telling him that Dafydd and Morgan will not allow him to treat her so cruelly.

"It is your choice, Megan. I cannot watch you every hour of the day. But no harm will come to your bastard if you give me your word."

I hear her gasp. Now he has her, I think with glee. She will not disobey him anymore.

I do not catch what she says next for she is sobbing as she speaks but I hear Eli's answer clear enough.

"I have nothing to be ashamed of. It is you that has brought shame on us all and now it is you that must pay a price. You are lucky not to find yourself behind bars, so please do not admonish me for cruelty when I have been far less harsh than I could have been."

It is all I can do not to push the door open and tell him how right he is, but I do not want either of them to know I am stood hear listening to all.

"But I am behind bars, as surely as if you had put me in the madhouse or the gaol," she says, and it was a silly thing to say, for here she is as free as a bird, wandering about the place like a lamb that has lost its mother, getting in everyone's way and casting a pall over all with her down-in-the-mouth demeanour. That mother of hers must have spoiled her is all I can say, for she appreciates not how fortunate she is to have married so well when she is, after all is said and done, nothing but a harlot and not good enough to lick his boots.

I hear the front door slam. So, she is off out again. I lean across the windowsill to see which way she goes. There she is, heading off down to the river, and it all swollen with the recent rain. That dog comes running out of the barn to greet her; follows her everywhere, it does. Eli has threatened to shoot the thing for she has spoiled it as a working dog. It will do nothing for Eli, now. Her cloak billows out behind her for the wind is high and roaring through the trees. I watch as she pauses and throws back her hood and turns her face up to the white clouds scudding across the sky.

There is something of the night creatures about that woman. Well, it isn't natural is it, to want to be out there in all weathers? She should be sat in the parlour, sewing and mending, as a good wife should. Or spinning at her wheel. Why does she never do that anymore, I wonder? Though, even that she used to do outdoors, every chance she got. She'd sit up there in the orchard for hours at a time. Strange, that's what she is. We can only hope the child takes after its father.

I noticed this morning, she's showing and all; round and plump her belly is, like a plum pudding. So she's further along than I thought. Has Eli not noticed? But then, he is a man and has had little to do with pregnant women before now, so perhaps he is blind to the signs. I must tell him as soon as I get a moment alone with him. He'll put a stop to her wanderings, then. There's no telling what harm she might be doing to that unborn child, running off all over the place like she is. It's time she quietened down, and thought of others instead of herself.

She's gone out of sight now, has followed the bend in the river, the dog trotting along beside her. She'll be gone for hours as she has gone that way. What does she do up there, I wonder? She's taken no food along with her, as I can see. Eli will be furious when he discovers she has not been looking after his unborn child. Taming, that's what that one needs.

Chapter Twenty-Six

Blow, wind, blow, and carry my words upon the
backs of careless clouds.

With winter comes the group of clog-makers to the
spinney below our gorge. Beulah says Fortune must have
some clogs, for yesterday she stubbed her toe on the
kitchen table. That is what comes from running bare-foot
through the house, Beulah told her. Fortune replied, as
quick as you like, she would not have been running bare-
foot if Beulah let her wear her boots.

"You would sleep in those boots if I let you!"
Beulah scolded her. "They are not for wearing night and
day else they will be worn out before you grow them
out."

So, hand-in-hand, we go down to the alder
spinney. The men have been there these past two days
and there are already two large stacks of short planks of
wood, all ready for the carving. Fortune sits on an
upturned log while a clog-maker fetches two pieces of
wood to mark out to the shape of her foot. Her toe is still
sore so she winces when he pulls of her boot and takes
her bare foot in his hand to place it on the wooden plank.
With a charcoal stump he draws a line around each foot.

"There you are, young lady," he says, "I will carve these out for you today. Dai over there will tack the leather on, and you shall have your clogs before the days end."

I have to nudge her to remind her to thank him for she is still not happy that she is not allowed to wear her boots at all times. If it were down to me alone, I would let her do whatever she liked, but Beulah says it isn't spoiling Fortune that will make things better. She doesn't tell me what will, though.

It is when we are on our way back to the house that I see Elgan riding up our track. He jumps from his pony and tethers it to the gate, striding over to where I am stood with Fortune. When I see his face, I tell Fortune to go on ahead to the house, for I can see he has come with bad news. I brace myself for whatever it is now but I am unprepared for it when it comes.

"It's Dafydd," he says, "he's collapsed this morning, they don't think he will last the day."

The shock of it strikes me with such a force that I am stunned as though from a blow to the head. My first reaction is one of disbelief.

"Don't talk daft, man, I saw him just yesterday!"

"I'm sorry, Morgan lad, I know you and he were close. I'd make haste if I were you, if you want to see him once more in this world. I'll wait if you like, while you fetch your pony."

"No, you go on ahead," I tell him, for I need time; to gather my wits and tell Beulah, and to get a grip on myself for I fear that I am breaking.

No. No. No. Not Dafydd! Not now! These are the words that repeat themselves over and over in my mind as I run to the stable and bridle the pony with trembling hands. He will be alright. Elgan does not know what he is saying. It would take more than whatever it is that has struck Dafydd down to kill him. Dafydd is a mighty oak. Dafydd will not be broken.

I walk over to the house with the pony. Beulah comes to the door and asks whatever is the matter.

"Something's happened to Dafydd," I tell her. "Elgan says he will not last the day but Elgan is talking daft."

"Oh, Morgan, I'm so sorry," she says, reaching out and placing her hand on my arm and I am overwhelmed by fear and grief then, for her sympathy makes the possibility of losing Dafydd the more real, and I do not want to accept it might be so. I mount my pony and take off at a pace for I am now in a panic that if he should die it will be before I get there.

His mouth is pulled down at one side and one hand lies limp on the counterpane. His eyes are closed when I enter the room and for a moment I fear I am too late, but as I step across the room, and the polished floorboard creaks beneath my weight, he opens his eyes and squints at me, and relief washes over me. Mary is sat in a chair by his bed, her face an unreadable mask.

The shutters are closed and the light from outside is divided into narrow slits casting stripes of light and shade upon the wall, and the room is thus dim though it is a bright sunny day outside. I yearn to throw open the shutters and cast the gloom from this room which seems prepared for death. A candle is lit and sits upon a small table by his bed. A corpse candle, I think, to light the path for the dying from this world into the next.

"Leave me and Morgan alone!" Dafydd says to Mary, with a dismissive wave of his good hand. His speech is slurred like one who has drunk too much mead. Mary gets up from the chair by his bed and casts a look of such hatred at me that I feel it like a knife in my heart. I take my place in the still-warm chair by Dafydd's bed and swallow hard on the lump that has risen in my throat. The poor old bugger has been cast one hell of a blow. I see now why Elgan said they don't think he will see the day out.

"What in hell happened to you, Daf? Did Mary strike you over the head with a pan?" I say, trying to make light but my voice breaks on a sob.

The one side of his mouth turns up in a smile and his eyes show their old twinkle.

"Aye, that must be it," he slurs.

Tears spring to my eyes. "Well, you'll have to recover for I can't manage without you."

"Don't take on, lad. We all have to go, sometime."

"Not you! You're not going anywhere! You'll be right as rain in a couple of days, just you wait and see."

"There, now, don't weep, Morgan. Promise me you will look out for little Meg, won't you, there's a good lad."

Every word he speaks requires such effort that he gasps for breath between each one.

"I promise, Daf, but you can't go. You're the nearest I have to a Da," I tell him.

"And you've been like a son to me."

He motions for me to come closer and I lean further across the bed, with my ear to his mouth.

"There's a surprise for you…"

It is the last thing he says before his last breath leaves him like a sigh. I feel a chasm open up inside me as I take his dead and wrinkled hand in mine. It is a gaping, overwhelming hollow and I don't know how it will ever be filled. Oh, Megan, Dafydd is gone, I think, and then I remember she is gone from me too, for she does not speak to me anymore, and it is more than I can bear. My tears fall like plump rain drops on the counterpane and my sobs all but rent my chest in two.

Mary comes in, takes one look at Dafydd and begins shouting at me, asking me am I happy now for it is all my doing. If I hadn't taken him off looking for my whore of a sister he would still be here, she says.

313

"He hasn't been right since the day he went off with you!" She shouts after me as I stumble out of the door.

I do not go home; I go to the top of our hill and howl like those wolves on the Elenydd. I howl out my grief and rage where the wind will carry my words upon the backs of careless clouds. I rail at the God who is so unjust that I want nothing more to do with him. In taking Dafydd he has taken the best and there is no longer rhyme or reason in this life.

Chapter Twenty-Seven

Tick-tock, tick-tock, a life measured by the
hands of the clock.

I pity the poor dog that spends all of its time tied up in
the barn. I tell him it is not forever, that this confinement
will soon be over, but he understands not, only wags his
tail and spins around, telling me he is eager to follow me
wherever I choose to wander. He does not know I have
no choices left to me. I dare not untie him and let him go
free, lest Eli should see and reach for his gun.

Gwen is standing in the doorway of the house
when I emerge from the barn and step out onto the snow
covered cobbles; eager for a chance to remind me I am
not allowed, should I choose to venture further. I am
hardly likely to need reminding when the threat of what
will happen, should I disobey, hangs over my head like
the sword of Damocles itself. She stands there with her
feet apart and her arms folded. Like great legs of ham
they are, her arms. She is like a ball and chain about my
ankle, placed there by my own husband. Oh, how she
enjoys seeing me cooped up like a hen in a cage.

"It's time you put a stop to her gallivanting," she said to Eli, "it is no way for an expectant mother to behave."

It was stupid of me to hope I could keep my condition hidden from him until the last. That interfering, bitter, old busybody was bound to notice. I shall never forget the look on his face as his mouth gaped open in surprise at her revelation. Though dismayed at her having told him, a peal of laughter escaped me at the comical look on his face as his eyes swivelled to my belly. I did not laugh for long. The smile was speedily swiped from my face when I saw enrapture in his own, which only served to repulse me, for I have not forgotten how that seed was planted in me, without so much as a please or thank you.

He has been almost solicitous towards me over the month since Gwen opened her trap and snared me like a rabbit. His attempts to ascertain that I am in good health serve only to sicken me, for I know it is not for my own sake that he enquires. It is the welfare of his child which concerns him, nothing else, and so he has me confined to the house, lest my 'gallivanting' causes some harm to his child. My value to him is like that of his herd of breeding cows down in the bottom pasture. They are put to the bull once a year to increase his herd, and should they fail to produce then 'pop' goes the gun he likes to so carelessly leave lying around the house.

Not once has he threatened to harm me, oh no, my husband is far too clever for that. From the night that Dafydd and Morgan brought me back here, he has let me know it is not I who will come to a sorry end at the end of a barrel, no not I. Should I transgress, it is my dear little Fortune and the poor dog who he will rid from his sight, once and for all.

I never know when or where I shall receive his reminder. And so it is always with a jolt that I encounter the gun, left for me to see in places it would never otherwise be. The first time I saw it, it was lying on the floor of the barn, its barrel pointing towards the dog where he lay tied up in the corner. That first time I saw it, I did not know it was left there as a message for me.

It is an incongruously beautiful thing, the gun, which belonged to his father before him. It has decorations of silver filigree all along its barrel. He has left it outside my bedchamber door so that it is the last thing I see before retiring at night. I have come upon it lying upon the seat beneath the apple tree in the orchard, a place where only I go and sit. In the drawer where I keep my needles and thread, he has placed little pouches of the deathly gun powder so that the smell of it assaults me when I go to take up my sewing.

I do not dare to so much as openly glance in Fortune's direction when they file into their pew in chapel of a Sunday. I wonder what they all must think of me, that I no longer so much as acknowledge their

317

presence. They will think me high and mighty, no doubt. I can all but hear Beulah saying 'who does she think she is?' When Eli kneels down and closes his eyes to pray; it is then I sneak a glance at her bonneted head, her chestnut curls cascading down her back, her fine-boned hands clasping the doll I made for her. This is how he keeps me imprisoned. The bars at my windows are wrought from fear and all routes of escape are blocked. He has bound me all the tighter for having tried to run from him.

It is as well that Dafydd does not know what he brought me back to. Dafydd advised what he truly believed was best for me. Dafydd is such a good man, and thinking Eli to be not a whole lot different to himself, he couldn't have known any better than I that Eli would go so far. Those times when I see Dafydd outside the chapel, he always raises an eyebrow in enquiry. I smile at him with a brief nod of my head, so that he will think all is well with me. The wink of his eye, in reply, always leaves me feeling I am drowning with not one straw to grasp to save me. I dare not tell Dafydd of the way things are for he will go straight to Eli with a few threats of his own, and then Eli will take his gun and carry out his threat. A man who is capable of making such a threat is capable of doing anything.

There are too many who so readily jump on the devil's horse-back. Branwen and Gwen have both been eager to help him do his dirty work against me.

Branwen, because she wanted him for herself; Gwen, because deep down she resents and envies me for having what she never had for herself – a husband and children, and she thinks her virginal self to have been far more deserving. Thus, I am the thorn in her side that digs deeper, every day, to remind her God never granted to her what he granted me. She has never said the words out loud to me, 'why you?' but I believe it is what she thinks every time she casts her hostile eyes upon me.

And Eli, who would have me believe it is I who have been the cause of his road to madness, yet, he would have done none of it if he had not sought to possess me, body and soul, and has sought to punish me for denying him what he believed was his right to do. In laying with another before him, he believes me to have given possession that was rightly his to another. It has never occurred to him that what I gave freely was mine to give, not his. In believing himself to own me, he entitles me with no more rights than his ponies, his cows, his dog, or his sheep, and thus renders me not equal to him as a human.

These are the thoughts which beset me, cooped up in this cage of fear and loathing where I have nothing to do but sew or knit the whole day long. The wheels of my mind do grind and turn like the great grinding stones in Dafydd's mill. The more I think, the further I travel down the tracks of Eli's misguided mind. With each stitch I knit or thread do sew, I draw my own conclusions. Thus, I think, while thinking me his possession, like his cow or his horse, he has no more need to ask my permission than he does theirs.

So, with the darkness of night obscuring his sight, he is able to enter my bedchamber and hoist my nightgown about my waist and thrust himself upon me until his lust is sated. He is as deaf to my protests as he is to the screeches of his pigs when he takes his knife to their sorry throats.

The more I sit here thinking, the deeper I must swallow my rage. It does not do to dwell on things we cannot change. And so, I speak to him when spoken to, as we sit by the fire of an evening with the light of the candles flickering in the draught that always blows from under the kitchen door. I answer with politeness when called upon to respond to some query he may have as to what I have done today.

I do not look at him when I speak for fear my eyes will betray the hatred that burns inside me. In the long silences between us, I listen to the clock ticking away the minutes and hours of my life. My hatred is not for what he has done to me but for the harm he would do she who is the most precious to me. From the moment he threatened Fortune's life, I have loathed him with an intensity which terrifies me, for the loathing is a thing of such power, I do not know for how much longer it will be mine to control.

Chapter Twenty-Eight

The miller's wheel keeps turning, even after
death.

"Don't you listen to that old bitch," Beulah says to me
when I finally go home and tell her it
is my fault that Dafydd is gone. "It was living with
Mary's venom all these years that killed him, more like.
I'll wager that poor man never knew a day's peace or
happiness with her."

I tell her what Dafydd told me when we were
crossing the Elenydd, but I make her swear first that she
will never repeat it. She curses me for making her swear
not to repeat a thing so heaven sent. If you want justice,
Morgan, she says to me, you will want to let the world
know what a hypocrite Mary is. I tell her that particular
justice is not ours to exact. It was Dafydd's, and he never
told a soul but me. It wasn't something he sought in this
life and so we have no right now to seek it after his
death. She picks up her apron that lies on the table and
throws it at me, while telling me that I test her to the
limits of her patience.

I tell Beulah how Dafydd made me promise to
look out for Megan. "I don't know how I am meant to do
that when she behaves as though none of us exist."

"It's just her way, Morgan, you know," she jerks her head towards the door, to where Fortune is playing outside. "It is easier for her to cut us off than have to come up here pretending she is someone she is not."

"Someone is going to have to tell her that Dafydd is gone."

Megan is pregnant, that's plain to see, and I think she will take the news very hard. Dafydd has been so good to her down the years.

"She will probably know already, news travels so fast in these parts. Someone will have told Eli by now and he will have passed it on."

It is at Dafydd's funeral that we next see Megan. She is stood between Eli and Gwen, her face the colour of the wet snow falling on the hood of her black cloak, her eyes red-rimmed from weeping. I hesitate in deciding whether I should approach her, and then the chance is gone for Eli steers her away by her elbow as soon as Dafydd is laid in the ground.

It is a few weeks later when I discover the surprise that Dafydd spoke of on his death bed. It seems Dafydd has exacted his own kind of justice, after all. In the absence of a son to take over the mill, he has left it to me, the nearest thing he ever had to a son, he wrote. Mary gets only the lump sum of his savings to live off for the rest of her days, his daughters will have to live off it too until they marry. No doubt, Mary will be looking to marry them off in haste, now.

Dafydd must have known his days were numbered for he left a letter for safe keeping with Twm, the Oaks, to be given to me in the event of his death. In it he says I am to forgive myself all past mistakes and begin my life anew, unfettered by the constraints of belief I have grown up with. I will have an easier life as a miller, he says, than I would ever have as a tenant farmer. Take all you have been taught thus far and throw it out of your mind, he says. Make up your own mind about things from now on, Morgan, and you will not go far wrong. You have a good and honest heart and I am proud to have known you. And if you don't take to the life of a miller, as I believe you will, I will not mind if you sell up and go back to your hill. From this day forth, you must do what is right for you, not what someone else tells you. And then he goes on to tell a secret he has kept for nigh on thirty years, and when I read of it, everything falls into place.

Following the reading of this letter I walk up to the topmost part of the hill. I sit myself down and think on what Dafydd has done. I have loved and worked every inch of this land as if it belonged to me. I have always said I will never give it up for anyone or anything. I was born here and have always thought to die here. Yet, it will never be mine. It belongs to the landlord who extracts his rent like teeth from me every

323

year. It has been nothing but struggle since I was a lad. I think on all this until it is properly sunk in and then I get to my feet and turn my head up to the sky. I shout 'thank you, Dafydd, from the bottom of my heart!' Though, I will wish for the rest of my days that my freedom this day had not depended upon his dying.

Beulah takes Fortune by the hands and takes her on a merry dance around the kitchen table.

"Morgan, the miller! Morgan, the miller! Oh, but it does sound grand, doesn't it?"

"It will take me a while to learn the ropes but old Twm used to help Dafydd in the mill, years ago, and he has promised he will show me all there is to learn."

"You are so bright, you will learn it in no time at all," she says, beaming at me with a pride I did not realise she felt for me.

"Mary is leaving with her girls to go and live with a cousin miles away."

"Pity help her poor cousin, then!"

"It's a big house, that miller's house. A miller would need a wife to look after a place like that."

"Would he, indeed?"

Beulah tells Fortune to go up to the dairy to fetch a jug of milk. Go slow with it mind, she tells her, I don't want to see a drop spilled. She goes to the fire and busies herself with stirring the pot of broth hanging over there, her face hidden from me.

"Aye, but his wife would not have to carry pails of water from the gorge, through mud or snow, for the water is right there beside the house."

"That is true," she says, and stirs the pot so furiously the liquid spills over the brim and falls hissing into the fire.

"And his wife would not have to make butter or cheese, nor milk the cow, for there is a maid to help with all that."

She has ceased stirring the pot but keeps her back to me, though I am willing her to turn and face me.

"Sounds like this miller's wife will have an easy life, to be certain."

"Aye, she would not have to toil too hard again, for the miller would tend to her every need and make sure she wants for nothing."

"And why would he do that?" She asks and turns at last to look at me. I see there are tears in her eyes.

"Because I love you, Beulah, and have from the first day you entered this house, like a gale blowing through, to blow away all the misery trapped between these walls."

A tears brims over and she swipes it away with an embarrassed laugh and sniffs.

"You daft bugger," she says in true Beulah fashion.

"Come here," I say, and reach out to her and pull her onto my knee. "Is that a yes, then?" I ask her.

"Aye, well, I suppose it is," she says, grinning through her tears.

"So you'll have me now I'm a wealthy miller, then?" I tease her.

"Aye, but not because you're wealthy but because you don't need me now. You could hire any woman you choose to keep house for you."

"That's true, I hadn't thought of that until you mentioned it."

She swipes me round the ear.

"You've kept me waiting for this yes for one hell of a long time."

"Aye, Morgan, because you never asked out of love before but out of need. I was waiting for you to ask me for the right reason."

I kiss her long and hard, like I've wanted to do for ever. I would take her upstairs right now but I want to make an honest woman of her first.

Chapter Twenty-Nine

What hope for one small voice against the chapel and the law?

My brother is the miller now, though Dafydd himself can never be replaced by any other. I cannot bear to think I will never see his kind face again, nor hear his voice speak words of wisdom and compassion. The loss of Dafydd is immense, for he was the best friend I ever had; not once did he judge me, or think ill of me; he simply loved and cared about me without condition. I was good enough for him, just the way I was. I never knew what a blessing that was until he was gone. His like I will never know again.

    Morgan has married Beulah at long last. I am told that Beulah looked beautiful, with her raven black hair strewn with a garland of snowdrops. It was one of the women of the village who told me, when she called here one day selling wooden spoons and pegs and such. She peered at me with a quizzical look, no doubt wondering why I did not attend my own brother's wedding. I blushed under her scrutiny as if the fault were truly mine, but it was Eli's decision that we would not go for he loathes Morgan with a passion, especially so since Morgan was left the mill.

It is with great relief that I watch Eli ride away with Gwen sat beside him on the trap. She has her winter cloak pulled up over the white of her hair, and a heavy woollen blanket over her knees. The wheels of the trap leave trails through the sparkling frost on the cobblestones, and their breaths form little clouds in the early morning air. I wave them off as a good wife would, while wishing neither of them would return. But she will return in just a few days, is only gone to attend a cousin's funeral. Eli is taking her to meet the stage-coach and then he too will return in a couple of hours.

The babe is not due for another month but my belly is huge and I am worn out with the carrying of it. I heard Gwen telling Eli that she does not mind one bit having the child to look after. My hands fly instinctively to protect my belly when I hear this. Surely, you have enough to do Gwen, he says. No indeed, I am quite able to tend to his needs while going about my chores, says she. After all, it is clear that Megan will not be up to the task. She will have to feed him, of course, for a short time, but I will tend to his every other need. We want him cared for properly, after all.

They presume it will be a boy so that I find myself hoping it will be a girl, just to see their disappointment. But then, I think, if it is a girl, he will subject me to all of this again, for it is a son he wants and nothing else will do. That is the way of men.

Gwen does not elaborate upon why she believes I am not capable of looking after my own child. Is it because I have been unwell? For if that is it, I am certain I shall be well again once the child is born, and this cough which drains my strength will surely leave me when spring arrives. She will have no excuse to take over when I am well. I am determined to be well, if only to thwart the ill-founded ambitions of the child-stealing thief that she is.

Yet, her words niggle and nibble away at me. What if? Is the question which plagues me. What if I do not get well? What then? I do not want this old woman tending my child. I do not want her clawed hands rocking the cradle, nor her great arms wrapped around. Yet how will I prevent her, if Eli should will it so? And will it he will, for his first and only concern will be for his precious son.

I looked after you when you were a babe, Gwen tells him, so I am perfectly versed in what is needed. She says this in a tone of voice that is meant to dispel any unspoken doubts he might have as to her ability. I grasp at the skirts of my dress lest my hands be tempted to grasp her throat instead. Does she not know that I can hear all from the parlour? She surely does, for I know that she likes nothing better than passing her time listening at the other side of the door when Eli and I are in there alone.

He is a mystery to me. When alone with me, he now behaves as if we are a proper husband and wife; as though he does not keep me bound to him by fear. I have seen bewilderment in his eyes when he attempts to converse with me in a normal fashion and I do not respond with anything but yay or nay. And I think; why does he feel bewilderment? It can only be that he thinks no wrong in taking the measures he has to ensure I obey him in all things. Moreover, it seems that he expects me to feel the same for him; the same as I did before he destroyed my love for him.

I cannot help but laugh at my own imaginings of how he would react if our situations were reversed. I do not laugh for long when I think upon the fact that he has the chapel and the law on his side. He has a right to do what he does, while I have no rights at all. Therein lies the brunt of it and he knows it only too well. The preacher, and therefore God, wills that I obey, and the law decrees Eli to have all necessary power to ensure I do so. While a man is confirmed of his cruel convictions from every corner, what hope for my small voice to be heard in objection?

The sound of wheels clattering over cobblestones tells me my jailer is returned. I go to the window and watch Eli leap down from the trap and land square upon his two feet with a theatrical flourish. An air of confidence has grown about him since dear Dafydd departed this world. It is as if he thinks God himself is on his side and did the miller in for having stood against him. Strutting about like a self-satisfied, barn-yard rooster, Eli was, when he heard of Dafydd's demise, while I felt a chasm had opened before me into which I would surely fall.

Even Morgan's close proximity, down at the mill, only served to dent Eli's confidence for a short while.

"If ever there was proof of the miller's stupidity, it is in his decision to will that brother of yours as successor," he dared to scoff to me when I was in the throes of grief over the loss of Dafydd.

"Your brother will be bankrupt within the year, mark my words."

Always, my husband is on the lookout for justification and validation of his beliefs, and where there is none he will conjure it by creating future scenarios which fit with his view of the world.

I see him stride from the trap, across to the house, and I quickly go to the sink so that he may think me industriously occupied when he enters. He goes to the pantry and cuts himself a hunk of bacon from the leg hanging there. He grabs some bread. Only then does he see I am standing there.

"I have just passed the cowherd; there is a cow taken sick in the bottom meadow. It will take all of us to lift her. I shall go to see to it, straightaway," he says, as if I may be interested to know.

I watch him go towards the door.

"I'll put the pony and trap away on my return but it would be a help if you were to give the pony some water for I may be gone for some time," he says without turning to me, as he is going out of the door.

I reach for the pail and go out to the well and attach the pail to the hook on the rope. There is a whirring inside my head as I turn the handle to lower the pail into the deep, dark hole below. As I hear the soft splash of the pail hitting the water, the thoughts in my head become like ravens, flapping their wings and cawing, demanding my attention. Slowly, I rewind the rope and lift the pail from the hook. The pony all but knocks it from my hand in her hurry to get to the water.

I race to the house as fast as my belly will allow. I pull my cloak from the hook behind the door and throw it around me. I am so panicked as I rush over to the barn that my breathing is ragged and my heart beats at a furious rate. I unleash the dog and urge him to come quick. Then we are up on the trap and I am urging the pony to make haste.

I do not think about where I am going, my only thought is that this is my one chance, perhaps the only chance I shall ever get, to free myself from this tyranny. I will not have another child stolen from me to feed the hunger for acrimony of a bitter, old woman. I know, in this moment, I would rather die than bring another child into this world for someone else to take.

As I round the bend and the mill comes into view in the distance, I pull the pony to a halt, for the sight of the mill brings me back to my senses. Seeing the mill is akin to running headlong into the bars of my prison and I am as surely winded by the sight. The minute he finds me gone, he will come here with his gun and carry out his threat. He will do it without fear of the consequences because he knows it is the one thing which will destroy me.

I see her then, in the meadow beyond the mill, chattering to the dairy maid who is returning with a pail of milk. I urge the pony along the lane and pull up where there is a hazel grove to obscure me from the view of anyone coming and going from the mill. Then I call her name, softly at first, then louder until she hears me and turns from the dairy maid to come skipping towards me.

"I have come to take you for a ride on the trap!" I tell her, patting the seat beside me, in a gap between me and the dog.

Her eyes widen with excitement. "I'll go and tell Mam and Da!"

"No need! I have told them already. Quickly, for I do not have much time."

She looks back over her shoulder at the mill, undecided. "Shall I just go and say goodbye, then?"

"There is no need, we won't be gone for as long as all that!"

"Alright, then!" she says, and grasps the rails to pull herself up.

I wait until she is sat firmly on the seat with her doll sat beside her, and then urge the pony forward.

"Where are we going?"

"We could go to market, if you like."

"I loves the market, I does! I got these boots in the market with the moneys the fairies did give me. They left me this dolly, too. I loves the fairies, I does."

She swings her feet out in front of her, turning them from side to side so I might see her boots from every angle.

"I's not supposed to wear them all the times for they will wear out in no time ifs I does, Mam says. I is supposed to wear my clogs for about the place but these boots is beginning to pinch my toes a bit, truly they are, and it would be a shame if I did grows out of 'em before hardly wearing 'em at all."

Her chattering makes my heart swell fit to burst and I cannot speak a word in return for the swelling in my throat. I swallow hard and fight back the tears that are blinding my eyes. What have I done? What have I done? It was done before I'd thought of the consequences. There is no turning back now.

Fortune sits quietly for a time, looking at the road ahead, admiring the clumps of snowdrops growing along the way.

"This is much better than Da's rickety ol' cart. Da's going to get a trap too, as does befits a miller!" She says, turning every which way in her seat and admiring the trap. "That Eli Jenkins won't be able to look down his nose at us then!"

I hear Morgan's voice in the words she speaks and smile.

"Why doesn't you come to visit us? Is it because you is a wealfy farmer's wife?"

I clear my throat and take a deep breath. "In a way, yes, but it is not that I don't want to, it is that my husband will not allow it."

"I is never going to allow my husband to tells me what I can or cannot do!" she says, pulling herself up straight in her seat and clasping her hands in her lap.

"I am glad to hear it. I very much hope you will have a husband who will not want to order you about but will want you to be free as those birds up there."

She follows my gaze to where a flock of starlings are making patterns in the sky, like a swarm of great bees.

"Oh, I will have such a husband, I has already decided."

Oh, if only the world was as straightforward as it is in the mind of a child; a world in which we get what we choose rather than one in which we only get what others decide we deserve. Children it is who have the wisdom, unfettered by tradition and indoctrination. Eli's contemptuous words ring in my ears. "You are an idealist, Megan, and therefore as naïve and simple as a child. It is as well that women are not the decision makers in this world!" I think if ever a man does scoff at Fortune so, I will want to take him by the neck and throttle him, like a rooster destined for the pot.

Chapter Thirty

On a wing and a prayer, the raven flies in search
of absolution.

Who would have thought it; me, the barren dairy-maid,
ending up with a house full of little children? They're
not mine, of course, but I love them all just as much as if
they were. The mistress knows all about the one I lost.
We had a real heart-to-heart, we did, when I first came
here. She's a more understanding soul than most.
There's plenty would have closed the door in my face
after all the things I've done. I never set out to be a
wrong 'un. I'm trying to make up for my past mistakes, I
am.

I didn't have much choice but to return to this
town of my birth after Eli Jenkins left me standing with
my bag on the side of the highway leading out of
Dinasffraint. He placed a sovereign in my hand to help
me on my way, and planted a kiss on top of my head.
That was all he could offer now he had no more use for
me. Where am I supposed to go now? I asked him. Go
home, Branwen, said he, and so I did.

Seeing as he'd given me money, I took the
stagecoach for the first time in my life. I felt like a real
lady, I did, handing the driver my bag and stepping up

into the coach. I'd never had two pennies to rub together before, and had to rely on my own two feet or a ride on some old farmer's cart to get where I wanted to be. I took a seat in the corner of the coach, smoothed back my hair, sat up straight, and adjusted my bodice to set off my milky-white throat to its best advantage. I was as good as any of them, I told myself, for I had money in my pocket the same as they.

My thrill at such extravagance was to be short-lived. As the coach rocked and stumbled over every bump and hole in the road, I was jiggled about and thrown from side to side, and jostled against my fellow passengers. Beside me sat a man with fleshy lips and a paunch that protruded from his waistcoat. As I was thrown against him, he took the liberty of thrusting his hand up my skirts and grasping me between my legs. I wrenched the vile creature's hand away and slapped him hard against his head, not wanting any of our fellow passengers to think I was such easy pickings as all that. My slap did nothing to dampen his ardour but made him laugh most heartily.

I felt as low as that time when my Da threw me out, though the reason was no fault of mine that time. I had no such excuse this time around. I had brought it all on myself, chasing after a man who belonged to another; a man without an ounce of compassion in his selfish heart. Humiliation made me angry and bitter towards Eli, but beneath all of that, I knew I was not without blame in it all.

As I stepped from the coach onto the cobbled square, I found that Cardigan town had flourished during the fifteen years since my departure, sprouting grand looking houses in the latest fashion. Da was long gone, I was soon to discover; died no more than two year after I left. It was an apoplexy, so my brother says, brought on by the worry I'd caused. It wasn't me that caused it, I spat back at him, it was our very own Uncle that sowed that seed in my belly. That shut him up. I left him gawping like those floundering fish in the nets down in the harbour. I had to laugh. I've not been back to see him since, though he is living only a few streets away.

It was on account of him living not far away that I told my mistress of my past. I thought she'd find out for herself soon enough, through gossip and tittle-tattle. So I got my ten-pence worth in, before someone else told her half the story. I wanted her to know; I wasn't that sort of girl back then, I was young and taken advantage of by my wicked uncle. I told her I was sorry for the wrongs I had done but didn't think I was wholly to blame for the way I've turned out.

I feared she would look to make trouble for me; blacken my name about the place so that I would not be able to get work. After all, I have behaved badly and am not worthy of pity or forgiveness. There is enough misery in this world without my adding to it, she said.

She took me in and placed me in charge of the children she has given refuge here, so their mothers are free to earn their living. They are women she has picked up off the streets, women who would have ended up in the workhouse, or the sea, if she had not come upon them, pregnant and destitute. She has opened her doors to those who found every other door locked against them.

"What greater gift can I give to one who cannot have children of her own but a houseful of children to nurture?" She said to me.

Meurwen is my mistress's name. She is the most beautiful creature I ever set my eyes upon. Her skin is as fine as a porcelain cup and she is fine-boned as a kitten. And then she has these pale-grey eyes framed by the longest, thickest lashes I have ever seen. I no longer look in mirrors for now I've seen true beauty, I know myself to be ugly by comparison.

She says she never met her father but her mother was a maid at one of those big mansions the landowners live in. Her mother told her that her father was a wealthy French man, a friend of the Lord somebody or other who employed her. This French man stayed often and helped himself to the maids in the same way he helped himself to the roasted pheasants on the dining table.

The master, Llewelyn, is due home any hour, so there is great excitement amongst them. He has been gone three weeks, droving cattle over the border. I have not said so much as a bye or leave to him since I've been here. I make myself scarce when he is around. I've learned my lesson and my place, I have, and want no truck with any man again, let alone with another's husband. Not that this one would look twice at me. He has eyes only for his wife.

I peek into the front hallway when I hear him arrive. He tears off his great, oilskin coat, throws his hat on the ground, and wraps his arms around her, nuzzling his face in the curve of her neck, murmuring how much he has missed her. It always brings tears to my eyes, seeing the two of them together, for I know I shall never know such love for myself. She gently pushes him away and holds him at arm's length, her hands resting on his shoulders, gazing up at him, drinking in the sight of him. I watch as she takes a lock of his hair and pushes it back behind his ear. I turn away and go about my business when he leans in to kiss her.

It's best if I don't say too much about how the women in this house make their living, nor how they came to make their children. Meurwen won't hear of them having their lives put at risk through trying to get rid of their unborn babes with poisons, or worse, and so the numbers of children have grown, year on year. Meurwen can't have any children of her own for she once went to an abortionist who near tore her to pieces.

Llewelyn knows all about Meurwen's past; how she once made her living by hoisting her skirts down the narrow, cobbled alleyways near the harbour, for that is how he met her. He loves her none the less for it and does not seek to punish her for the error of her ways. She agreed to marry him on condition that she could use this big house of his to give refuge to other women of the streets who were less fortunate than her. He was so besotted with her, he could refuse her nothing.

How I wish I had met Meurwen when I was destitute. Perhaps my child would have lived. I don't think it is such a bad way to make a living; I would only have been getting paid for something I've given away my whole life for free. The women do catch diseases, from time to time, of which some have died over the years, Meurwen has told me. It's the sailors, she says, travelling all over the world and spreading disease from port to port.

I'm sure I am dying, anyway, so it would make no odds to me. It is God's punishment that no sooner have I landed upon my feet than I am struck down again. I am wasting away; my clothes hang from my shoulders and hips as though they were draped from pegs, and I have a constant pain in my stomach as if there are rats trapped in my belly and they are trying to chew and tear their way out.

Meurwen doesn't say in so many words that she knows I'm done for; instead, she tells me I must make my peace with those I feel I have wronged. You will feel better in yourself when you have apologised to Megan, she tells me.

So it is that I am back on the stagecoach with money in my purse which Meurwen has given me for my journey. My companions this time are a young man, sat opposite me, who has the smell of a sailor about him, and is probably visiting relatives while on leave; and a middle-aged woman with a young boy who has to stick his head out of the window every half hour or so to be sick. I huddle into the corner of my seat and gaze out of the window, or sit with my eyes closed when the boy is sick lest the sight of him should make me do the same.

Each time I open my eyes, I catch sight of the sailor looking at me. He blushes and quickly looks away when I catch his eye. I feel my old wickedness rise up in me and adjust my bodice so there is more of me on display. I shift forward in my seat and part my knees a little. My knees brush against his and the groin of his trousers swells appreciably. I look from his groin to his face and see it is satisfyingly swollen with lust. It has been such a long time, if it were not for our companions, I would lay me down and spread my legs right there on the floor of the carriage.

I turn to the woman and ask if she is travelling all the way to Dinasffraint. Her eyes travel from my face to my bodice and she purses her mouth. We are not, she answers, with a haughty glare and turns away to look out of the grimy window. I run my tongue around my lips and give the sailor a look, which I am certain conveys my meaning because he begins to grin like a village dolt.

343

He shall be mine, if not on this journey, then when we get to Dinasffraint. My knees have turned to water at the thought.

It is an hour or more of waiting before the woman and boy alight with their bags at a coaching inn in a small town on the way. To my dismay, an elderly gentleman takes their place. He is soon followed by a blue-eyed, young maid with golden locks who looks no better than she should be. She lifts her skirts high above her ankles as she climbs the steps onto the coach. I look sharply at the sailor and see he has noticed her. He does not look at me again for the rest of the journey. Such is the fickleness of men, or perhaps I am getting too long in the tooth. I almost weep with disappointment for I would have liked to know one more night of rapture before I have to leave this world.

There is a weakness in me which has been there since my Uncle planted his seed in me. It is a wanting for men to want me; a longing for a man's love which can only be gained through their lust. Or so I once thought. Surely, I have long since learned the one and the other are not the same; not one man I have lain with has ever loved me like Llewelyn loves Meurwen. Yet, I cannot seem to help myself from throwing myself at any man who looks at me twice. I am a woe-begotten, hopeless creature. I shall never be loved.

There are a few hours of daylight left when the stage-coach halts outside the coaching inn at

Dinasffraint. I see the main street is filled with cattle so I know there has been a sale here this day. I wonder if Eli is here, and hope I do not run into him. I thread my way through the market. As always on a market day, it is filled to bursting with farmers and their labourers, and my bag is an encumbrance, knocking into people's knees, as I try to weave my way through the throng.

I catch sight of that friend of Megan's, standing knitting stockings on the other side of the square. But she has seen me first and I see her face darken. I think I shall turn and run, and then decide to stand my ground as I see her jostling her way towards me through the crowd. This is not the time for running from the past, this is the time to meet it head on.

"I don't know what you're up to, coming back to these parts," she says to me, "but you can hurry right back the way you came, else you shall have my boot up your backside to help you along."

Then she looks me up and down, frowning, taking in the sorry sight of me, shadow of my former self that I am.

"I've come to tell Megan I'm sorry," I say, and I can tell by her face that she knows the reason why.

"Sorry won't alter anything. She's back with her husband now, so her friend Beulah tells me, so you'd do best to leave well alone."

"I haven't come to make trouble."

"That's as well, you've made more than enough of that, already."

How wicked I was, I think now, remembering all the times when Eli took me off to market, leaving Megan at home, alone. So pleased with myself, I was, that it was me he wanted alongside of him, not her. Cruel it was what we did. It was worse than cruel what we planned together; to deny her sanity and liberty so that we could lust after each other with impunity; out of sight and out of mind was where we wanted her. I sold my soul for a man who loved me not and now it is only Megan's forgiveness that will save my soul from eternal torment.

I turn from Myfanwy with a heavy heart. I need to make haste if I am to reach Wildwater before dark. I head for the road out, the road I used to hurtle along beside Eli in the trap, where I had no right to sit for it was Megan's place, not mine. The surface of the road beneath my feet is hard and uneven. Stones jut up to trip me up and I fear I shall twist my ankles in its potholes. Though the day is chill, my hair beneath the hood of my cloak is soon wet with sweat, and I am weary from tripping my way along, with my bag becoming entangled in my skirts or bruising my shins.

The sound of cart wheels trundling up behind me gives me a start, for I have been lost in memories. It is the blacksmith, returning from the market, and I beg him to let me ride along. He knows me straight off, asking if I was not the dairy maid who used to work at Wildwater.

But he seems to know nothing of my affair with Eli, for he is friendly enough and polite.

"Back for a visit, are ye? I hear Megan is in the family way. Did you know her brother is the miller now? He married that housekeeper of his. What is her name? Beulah, that'll be it."

So, things have come right between Megan and Eli, I think. He has forgiven her, at last, and now she is to have his child. I begin to doubt my wisdom in returning, for I will be a reminder of bad times they will not wish to remember. But if I do not receive Megan's forgiveness, then I am doomed. I have no right to ask for it but ask for it I must.

The blacksmith turns off the lane and down a farm track, where I must wait while he shoes two carthorses at a farm along the way. I sit on the cart and take a shawl from my bag to drape over my knees. I begin to feel anxious, afraid to turn up at their door without warning, especially after dark, which it will surely be by the time the blacksmith is finished here. He is but half way done, the farmer leading the second horse towards him to be shod. They then stand and talk for a time, so that I wonder if the blacksmith has forgotten altogether that I am sitting here waiting.

While I wait, I watch the sun drop lower in the sky, tinging the billowing grey clouds with a rose coloured hue. Pigs are rooting in the earth beneath the oak tree in the field below the farmhouse, but the rooster is gathering his hens about him and leading them into the barn for the night. My agitation grows so that I can no longer sit still. I am beginning to wonder if it might not be quicker to walk the rest of the way, when I see with relief that the horse is shod and the blacksmith is returning to the cart.

He drops me at the turn for the village and it is only a short walk from there to the mill, and Wildwater beyond. As I come closer to the mill so that I can hear the paddles of the wheel turning through the water, I hear voices calling, over and over, and they are calling Fortune's name. As I round the turn in the track, I see Beulah is coming down the track towards me and the dairy maid is coming up from the meadow from the evening's milking of the cow. Beulah's anxious expression turns to one of astonishment when she lays eyes on me. She opens her mouth to speak but then sees the dairy maid approach and asks her if she has seen Fortune anywhere for she has been missing for hours and they cannot find her.

"Isn't she back yet?" the dairy maid asks.

"Back from where?" Beulah asks her.

"She went off with Megan in the trap. I thought you knew," the dairy maid says, "I heard Megan telling Fortune she had asked you if it was alright for her to go."

"Did she now! Oh, God help us. What has she taken into her head to do now?"

Beulah turns back to the mill, calling for Morgan to come quick. I follow on behind her, not knowing what else to do.

"Megan has taken Fortune!" Beulah shouts at Morgan when he comes running up from the orchard, and tells him what the dairy maid has told her.

"Perhaps she's taken her to Wildwater," Morgan says but the dairy maid contradicts him, saying Megan was headed the other way and seemed in a hurry for the pony was going at full trot.

It is only then that he sees me standing behind Beulah and his face turns dark.

"You! What trouble have you been causing now, eh?"

"I've only just now arrived!" I tell him.

"What in hell's name is she doing back here?" He asks Beulah.

Beulah takes one look at me and declares that I look terrible and must come into the house at once.

"She's not coming in any house of mine!" Morgan splutters.

Beulah ushers me inside, and tells Morgan to cease complaining and to set his mind to thinking what they were going to do about Megan and Fortune.

"Why and where on earth would Megan have taken her without telling us? And not bring her back before nightfall?"

Beulah ladles broth into a bowl, from the pan hanging over the fire, while she speaks. She tells me to sit at the table and places the bowl in front of me. She cuts me large chunks of bread and cheese, all the while talking to Morgan as if I am not there.

"You'd better go to Wildwater, see if Eli can shed some light on where she has gone. I wouldn't mind if she'd told us she was taking her, or if she'd brought her home before dark. But really, she must know we'd be worried sick by now."

The pain in my stomach is terrible bad, but I concentrate on getting some food inside me, for I am feeling as weak as a new-born kitten. Lord only knows, Morgan may take it into his head to throw me out of the door, any minute, and I want some food inside me before that happens. I'll not be able to go to Wildwater if Megan is not there for I don't want a moment alone with Eli if I can help it.

As speaking of the devil will so often conjure him up, there is a loud banging on the mill door and Eli's voice demanding Morgan open up. Morgan goes to the door and I am thankful I cannot be seen from the doorway.

"Where is she, Jones?" I hear Eli ask Morgan.

"I was about to ask you the same thing," Morgan answers.

Beulah goes to stand beside Morgan and tells Eli that Megan was seen leaving in his trap.

"I know that already. I came home from the fields to find both my wife and the trap were gone," he says to her. Then he addresses Morgan. "If you have put her up to this, so help me, I'll see you swing."

"Put her up to what? She's gone for a ride in the trap, man! It's nothing to get yourself upset about, surely!" Morgan scoffs at him.

To my surprise, Eli falls silent, for I thought he would surely take offence at Morgan's sneering tone. I don't twitch one muscle where I'm sat. I fear that any minute Eli will put his head round the door and see me sat at Morgan's table. Then Beulah tells Eli not to worry as she is certain Megan will be home soon as she will not want to keep Fortune out for long after dark.

"She has just misjudged how long it would take them to get back, that is all," she tells him.

Just as I'm thinking Eli will go now when he realises he has made a fool of himself, there is an almighty bang which makes me leap from my seat and run for the corner, for I think it is a gun going off. I raise my head and see Beulah is lying on the floor and the door near kicked off its hinges, while Morgan, who was holding the door in one hand, is now clutching his arm and groaning as if it is broken.

"You're a madman!" Morgan shouts at Eli, then goes to help Beulah to her feet.

"Where has she gone? I'll not leave until you tell me."

Eli can barely speak for he is panting with rage.

The dairy maid pokes her head around the scullery door with a vexed look on her face, and says she thought she heard Megan tell Fortune they were going to the market.

"There you are, man! What in hell's name is wrong with you? Can't my sister go to the market without you losing your head? There's something wrong with you!" Morgan is jeering now, rubbing salt into Eli's humiliation.

Eli steps forward into the room, and raises his fist.

"Aye! Come on, then, hit me! As I recall, you came off the worst last time, and all!"

Beulah steps between them, shouting there will be no fighting in her house. Eli glowers at the both of them and then turns around to leave. It is then that he sees me, cowering in the corner. He gawps at me as though I am an apparition.

"You! I should have known. What have you been saying to Megan, eh? What trouble have you come here to stir up now?"

I cannot speak, cannot even swallow, for my mouth is as dry as a slice of stale bread. It is Beulah that answers him.

"She arrived here only minutes before you, Eli, so don't look to lay blame at her door. For pity's sake, man, can't you see she is ill?"

352

Do I look as bad as all that, I think, when he takes another look at me for I see he is shocked by the sight of me. He turns on his heel and makes one last aside to Morgan before going out the door.

"We shall see who laughs last if my wife is not returned this evening, for it is the law who shall be after you if she is not."

"After me? What in hell would they be after me for?" Morgan shouts after Eli as he leaves.

Beulah comes over to me and helps me to my feet.

"Come," she says, "don't be afraid. Come and sit here by the fire for you are shivering."

She tells Morgan to close the broken door as best he can for there is a freezing draught blowing in from outside. Though it is not the draught that has made me shiver but the dangerous rage I saw in Eli's eyes for it is out of control and I fear he will do some terrible harm to someone if Megan does not soon return. Does he guard her so jealously then, that he should so react to her having gone off without him? I only know I have spoken this thought aloud when Beulah replies.

"I think you have hit on the source of what we've seen here tonight, Branwen," she says.

"Did you ever see the like?" she asks Morgan, who is still nursing his arm. "Let me take a look at that!" she says, pulling off his jacket and rolling up his sleeve.

A large bruise is already forming on his forearm. "I don't think it is broken. I will make a poultice," she says.

"Are you alright? That madmen knocked you clean off your feet when he kicked the door," Morgan says to her, his eyes filled with such tender concern that I have to look away.

"I'm alright! Plenty of padding I've got since coming here! It'll take more than a fall on my backside to hurt me!"

He smiles on her with a fondness I never knew he was capable of. I feel I ought to get up and leave but I have no strength left in me. Then a cloud of worry passes over his face and he frowns.

"You don't think Megan has run off again, do you? Surely she wouldn't take the little one with her if she was going to do that, would she?"

Beulah turns to the table and busies herself with clearing away my plate and bowl, hiding from him the anxiety I can see in her face. I can see she is struggling to decide whether she should speak her mind or not. She picks up the plates, then places them firmly back down on the table, and turns back to speak to him.

"I don't know, Morgan, but what I shall ask you is this; why didn't Megan tell us she was taking Fortune with her?"

Morgan shrugs his shoulders and hazards a guess. "Fortune is hers; perhaps she didn't think she needed to ask?"

Beulah stares at him with a look that tells him not to be stupid.

"She doesn't acknowledge our existence, or Fortune's, for months, then at the drop of a hat she decides to take Fortune for a ride with her to market. Don't you think that strange?"

Beulah goes in search of the dairy maid to ask her again what she heard. She tells them she distinctly heard Fortune say she would go and tell her Mam and Da she was going and that Megan had replied there was no need for she had already told them.

"I know what I heard! I could hear as clear as day. Mrs Jenkins was in the trap, just behind the hazel grove, and I on my way back from the meadow."

"She's run off again!" Beulah says with a certainty that jolts me from my torpor. I had been listening to all but not really taking it all in for I had grown sleepy sitting so close to the fire.

"But why would she do that now?" I blurt out, and Morgan Jones looks at me with disdain.

"Now that you're not there causing trouble, you mean?" he says.

Chapter Thirty-One

The road to redemption; through a night of lengthening shadows.

"I saw her this very day! That woman has one foot so firmly in the grave she looks like a ghost already!"

Myfanwy is the perfect picture of indignation. She knits furiously as she talks, her knitting needles flying like shuttles in a loom.

"Oh, the poor thing," I say.

"Poor thing indeed! After all that she did! I told her to go back the way she'd come or I would help her on her way with my boot. I'm going to say sorry to Megan, she says, before it is too late. Sorry won't make a difference, I told her, what is done is done."

I gaze into the smouldering remains of Myfanwy's fire and choose my words carefully, not wanting to further incense my friend on whom I so depend.

"I beg to disagree. I think sorry makes all the difference in the world, for sorry lays the path to forgiveness, and I sorely want to forgive her."

She ceases knitting to gawp at me, her knitting falling to her lap as if it too has given up in despair of me.

"Don't be so soft in the brain, Megan. She turned your husband's head. How can you forgive her that?"

"She is not to blame for the choices Eli makes. Why is it that women must always be blamed for the sins of men? I know what she did, I know she encouraged him, but Eli is a man with a will of iron, that I know, and no one can lead that man where he does not choose to go."

"Oh! Well…" Myfanwy says, and falls silent, her expression crestfallen.

She fidgets with her knitting and turns her woeful expression towards the bed in the corner. Fortune is sleeping there, where I slept the last time I was here. She is worn out by the day's excitement and only laid down to rest. In the blink of an eye she was asleep and it is a blessing for I will not have to explain to her that I am leaving her here.

"Does he know *she* is with you?" she asks, for I have not yet told her my reason for coming here with Fortune.

I know I am testing her friendship to its limits by bringing trouble, once again, to her door.

"No, he does not, and I didn't tell him I was leaving, either," I say, watching closely for her reaction.

"I guessed as much," she says with a sharp nod of her head.

The clacking noise of the weaver's loom drifts through the walls. It is the only sound, bar the hissing of the fire and the wheezing of my own breathing.

Her gaze wanders to my belly. "You don't look well. How long before this one is due?"

"A month, perhaps a little more, I think."

"What did he do this time?"

I take a deep breath and then I tell it all.

"You do understand, don't you? I will not let another babe be stole from me. When I saw the pony and trap, it seemed like a gift from God and I grasped it and took it, and then I was driving past the mill and I saw her and I knew that if I was to leave, I would have to take her too, or he would do her in as he had threatened he would."

"Your brother and his wife will be wondering what's happened to her. They will be worried sick."

"I know, I know. I was in such a state of agitation, I did not think beyond the moment. I must go back and let them know she is safe."

"That husband of yours will be looking for you. What if he comes here?"

"That is why I must hurry, to tell Beulah not to divulge your whereabouts to him."

"I don't know, Megan, love. Perhaps you should both go back. Apologise to him, isn't it, for not telling him where you were going."

She is wringing her hands, her eyes darting from one corner of the room to another, as if she sees danger lurking all around us.

I think long and hard on what she says. I imagine myself going back and grovelling for his forgiveness and promising to obey him in all things in future. I see Gwen taking over the care of the babe who will soon come into this world, and I standing by and being able to do nothing, for as long as I lived I would never be sure he would not carry out his threat to harm Fortune.

I feel a rage that wants to scream its name build inside my aching chest. Is it any wonder that I can hardly breathe, and cough and wheeze through night and day, for am I not suffocating under his callous rule so that my whole body does protest against it? I do not know what I shall do or where it is I will find peace and refuge. I only know that the life he would have me live is not worth the living.

I look up to see Myfanwy has been closely watching me and in my face she has seen my despair for next she asks, "what will I tell the little one when she wakes?"

"Tell her I shall return soon."

"Be careful, Megan. There is no telling what that man will do when he has found you gone."

"He cannot harm her if he cannot find her."

She gives me a queer look and opens her mouth as if to speak but says nothing. I light a taper from her fire and take it outside to light the lamps on the trap for it is now dark. Myfanwy follows me out into the cobblestoned street and squeezes my hands in hers, her face filled with anxiety which does nothing to alleviate my own. I call to the dog and pull myself up onto the trap and flick the reins.

The moon is full and scuds in and out of racing clouds. It gives more light than the spluttering lamps on the trap and I am grateful for it. So many times, I have made this journey in daylight, and yet it all looks so different at night that I barely recognise the road I am on. The stone walls appear to be luminous and looming in the moonlight. The limbs of trees are black silhouettes against the ink blue of the horizon. A frost covers all, glinting and sparkling by the light of the moon. Shadows along the way are as black as the night itself, as if evil lurks within each one. Of course, the pony knows the way and would get me there whether I can see or no, but I am glad I am not being hurtled along in darkness for I am frightened enough without that.

I half expect and fear to see Eli leap from each shadow as I come round every bend in the road, afraid that he has already set out in pursuit of me. But beneath my fear there is something else, a gnawing thing as when something has been forgotten or unattended. It is lurking there at the back of my mind but I do not know what it is. It reminds me of the day leading up to our Da's accident and death. All day, I had the feeling that something was amiss; the feeling grew stronger as the day went on until I was filled with foreboding, though for what I did not know.

Mam said it was no more than coincidence; that it was not a premonition, but I have often wondered if God was trying to warn me of impending disaster.

"We can all be wise after the event, can't we, Morgan?" Mam said to my brother, claiming I was making it up to gain attention.

She did not say the like to a neighbour who said he had seen a corpse candle on our very track, earlier on the night when Da died. To him she said that God reveals his plans in mysterious ways. So, I kept to myself the same feeling I'd had since waking, on the day when a neighbour was struck down by lightening when ploughing his field.

I have often wondered why I should be given some forewarning of danger when there was not a thing I could do to prevent it. Perhaps Mam was right, and it was no more than coincidence which was only made to seem significant by the events which followed. This is what I tell myself as we hurtle along the lanes by guttering lamplight and moonshine. Yet, the nearer I get to my destination, the stronger the feeling grows, so that I find myself praying for God to protect me in this night of lengthening shadows.

At first, I think it must be later than I imagined, or I had lost track of time, for it seems the dawn is breaking with the red glow that warns all shepherds of bad weather coming. It is only when I see sparks flying up to mingle with the stars do I know there is a fire. It is a strange time of year for a rick to alight, I think. The moonlight is now obscured by thickening cloud, giving no more than a faint glow of light to the landscape.

The mill comes into view ahead as we turn the bend in the lane, and it is then I see the fire is further along the road which means it can only be at Wildwater. I see a large group of the parish men are gathered outside Morgan's door. Lamp light spills out of the door and illuminates their faces. I see Morgan follow them out, pulling on his coat, and hurrying with the other men in the direction of Wildwater. They are all carrying two pails apiece, to bear water from the river. They are all gone out of sight by the time I arrive at the mill's door. I gaze at the glowing sky in wonder that a burning hayrick can so light up the night sky.

Chapter Thirty-Two

Hark, the call of the raven, harbinger of doom.

I dream there is someone banging on our door. I open it and there is a raven standing there. The raven opens its mouth and words spill out of its withered beak onto the flagstones beneath my feet. I cannot read the words for Morgan has not taught me to read, as he promised he would. I call to him to come and read the words the raven has spoken. He gets down upon his hands and knees, running his fingers along the lines of letters, just as he does when he reads the bible. Then he scoops up the words in his hands and tries to push them back inside the raven's mouth, telling it to take them back for he does not want to know. What is it you do not want to know, Morgan, I ask him. I do not want to hear of death, he says, I have heard enough of death. I turn back to the raven but the bird is no longer there. In its place stands Branwen, spitting words from her withered lips. Morgan takes her by the shoulders and pushes her out of the door.

The banging at the door begins again and is accompanied by shouts that pull me from my slumbers. It is no dream. I shake Morgan awake and tell him there is someone at the door, perhaps it is Megan come back with Fortune. Befuddled, he fumbles to light the candle in the dark, and stumbles down the stairs. We have lain awake for hours, waiting for Megan to return with Fortune, and finally succumbed to restless sleep. I go to pull back the shutters, thinking it must be near dawn. At first, I think I am looking at a blazing sunset, though I know the sun cannot be setting in the middle of the night.

Alarmed, I grab my shawl and pull it about my nightgown, and rush down the stairs. Twm, the Oaks, is in the porch and a large number of men are standing behind him; every man of the parish it looks like. Morgan tells them to go on ahead and races upstairs to clothe himself. Twm tells me Wildwater is burning and they are going there to try to put out the fire.

Morgan has pulled on his coat and boots and gone out of the door before I have a chance to say goodbye, or to remind him to be careful.

Branwen calls down to me from the top of the stairs, asking to know what has happened.

"There is a fire at Wildwater. The sky is lit up!" I tell her, going back up the stairs to get dressed for there will be no sleeping done again in this house tonight.

No sooner am I at my chamber door than there is knocking on the door again. Branwen offers to go answer it while I throw on some clothes. It is Megan's voice I hear, this time, as I am coming back out onto the landing. Thank God, I think, they have returned! My thanks are short-lived when I see she is standing at the bottom of the stairs alone.

"Where is Fortune?" I ask her.

"She is safe. I will explain all later. Right now, I must go to Wildwater."

She turns to go back out of the door. "You can't go tramping up there in the dark when you are so heavy with child," I tell her.

"I have the trap. I will be there in minutes."

She must see the doubt and concern in my face for she steps forward to kiss my cheek, before turning to lift the latch on the door.

"Don't worry, I shall be alright!" is the last thing she says.

Too late, I gather my wits. I run out into the night, to ask her to tell Morgan to be careful, but she is gone and I am left listening to the wheels of the trap clattering over the stones of the road. A shiver runs down my spine as I look to the glowing sky above Wildwater. I pull my shawl tighter around me and hurry back to the house.

Chapter Thirty-Three

The wheel of destiny will turn, whatever we may do.

Sparks, caught on the breeze, spin and twirl across the sky. As I get closer to Wildwater, I can hear the shouts of the men carrying up from the river. They have formed a line from the river to the house. Pails of water are being passed rapidly up the line while a young lad is running back and forth, returning each empty bucket from the end of the line to the man at the water's edge. I have seen them quench the fire in a hayrick this way, many times. But a house was a far greater challenge than they'd ever faced.

I jump down from the trap, the dog at my heels. I scan the line of men, looking for Morgan. Where is Morgan? I ask the men. If they hear me they do not answer, too immersed in the task at hand to notice my presence. I walk quickly, unable to run with this belly of mine, up the line of men, looking for Morgan's face among them. They spill hardly a drop of the precious water as they pass the pails along the line. I reach the end of the line where twenty or more buckets of water are lined up on the ground.

Then I see him. He is one of the men who are up close to the house, hurling the water from the pails into the flames which are leaping out from the kitchen window. I am a good distance from him and yet I feel the heat from the fire. I want to run to him and tell him to come home. Let the place burn! I want to shout at them all. Why risk life for stones and mortar?

I see other wives are coming now, tramping along the track. They come and stand with me and I am relieved and grateful for this show of solidarity. We are all a-feared of what this night may bring a-knocking on our doors. Just don't do anything foolhardy, is what we all are thinking. And so we keep vigil, watching our men as they try to beat back the hell-fire flames, ready to leap forward in an instant, if necessary, with a staying hand.

I look around the sea of faces but see no sign of Eli. Where is Eli, I hear someone ask, and then another, further away, asks the same question. Is Eli inside, a voice shouts out and I see Morgan pause in his task and look from the voice to the house. I am trying to push my way through the crowd, not taking my eyes from Morgan as he slowly places the pail of water on the ground. Get out of my way, I shout, trying to push people out of the way as Morgan looks up again at the house. Get out of my way, I scream, my arms flailing at someone's unmoving back.

And then I am through and stumbling towards Morgan as he walks towards the flames. Don't you dare,

Morgan Jones, don't you dare risk your life for that scoundrel, don't you dare! I yell his name and a strong arm grabs me from behind. I turn, only for a second, to wrench myself free, and when I look back, Morgan is gone.

Chapter Thirty-Four

Beulah fears the worst.

Branwen sits hugging herself by the fire while I am too agitated to sit down for a moment. I have brought in water and placed the kettle over the fire, for Morgan, when he returns. I have brought in enough peat to keep the fire going all day. I have laid the table ready for when Morgan comes back, for he will be hungry. Morgan. I should have gone with him when he left. I should have gone with him for he is no good at looking after himself. He is a man that acts first and thinks later.

I cannot bear the waiting any longer. I grab my cloak from the peg and throw it about me.

"I have to go and see that he is alright," I tell Branwen, "else I shall go mad with the waiting.

"I'll go if you want. It's the least I can do."

"He won't heed you, Branwen."

The heavens have opened and a heavy rain is falling. The hem of my cloak trails behind me, dragging through the dirt churned up by the rain. I am not half way there when I see a small huddle of women coming towards me through the rain. Between them, bent over and barely able to walk, her hair soaked through with the rain, Megan is being held on either side.

I rush towards them, alarmed at the sight of Megan and enquiring what has happened.

"The child is coming," one of the women informs me; an old crone with her mouth set in a rigid line of disapproval.

Megan moans and grasps her belly. "Let's get you indoors," they say to her, "the midwife is on her way."

We help Megan back to the mill and lay her down on my bed. Her skin is pale as snow and she grasps my hand. "The baby is coming too soon," she says.

"Don't worry, Meg, I'll stay with you, and the midwife has arrived."

Old Angharad begins issuing orders as soon as she is inside my door, asking for boiled water and all the clean sheets I can spare. God help me, I've never attended a birth before and have not a clue what I should do.

"Oh, Beulah, Morgan and Eli are missing!" Megan tells me, and I feel my heart clench like a fist.

Branwen offers to go to Wildwater for news and there is nothing I can do but sit by Megan's side and wait. All the while, in the back of my mind, I hear the words of a saying of old; as one soul leaves this world, another arrives to take its place. As I listen to Megan's screams of pain, I pray God will bring Morgan home safe to me.

Chapter Thirty-Five

Branwen scorched by cruel words.

When I come upon Wildwater, the sight before me
makes me gasp. Charred, black, gaping holes are all that
remain of the kitchen window and the one above. Curls
of smoke furl up from a yawning chasm in the roof. The
air is rank with a smell like that of an old charcoal pit,
stumbled upon in the woods. On the slick cobblestones
outside the house, men are sat or lying about, without a
care that they are being soaked through by the rain. They
look for all the world as if they have just fought in a
fierce battle, as well they might. They talk among
themselves, speaking of the rain as a gift from God for
they would never have managed to put out the fire
without his help.

I pull my cloak closer around me, hoisting it off
the wet ground, and make my way around them, looking
for a glimpse of Morgan's face. I see a group of women
are huddled inside the shelter of the barn and go to them,
asking if anyone has seen Morgan. The faces which look
back at me are openly hostile, their eyes looking me up
and down with contempt.

"I am a friend of Megan's" I say, to explain my
presence, "she has sent me to look for Morgan."

"Friend she calls herself!" one among them shouts with a harsh laugh of derision, and laughter breaks out among them. "We know who you are and what you are. You're not wanted around these parts."

Other voices join the affray, mumbling the words 'harlot' and 'Eli's whore'. I feel a flush of humiliation and shame heat my cheeks. I would deny their accusations but that I know them to be true. That is all I ever was and ever shall be. From the day my Uncle said 'lay down', my sorry fate was sealed. Yet, looking from one face to another, all condemning and judging me, I am at a loss to understand why God chooses to go on punishing me for a sin that was committed by another. I turn my back on them with a flounce of as much dignity as I can muster, hot tears welling up in my eyes. Megan, who I so wronged, is the only woman to have befriended me in this life. I shall find her brother and take him home, if it is the last thing I shall do.

I skirt my way around the lolling, exhausted men, ignoring a shout of warning not to go in as I push my way through the front door. Inside, the walls of the hallway are blackened with soot. I push open the door to the parlour. It too is blackened with smoke, a coating of soot on every surface. The portrait of Eli's sombre parents still hangs upon the wall, but the glass is cracked through, a jagged break between husband and wife. The kitchen door is smouldering still and I kick it back. With a creak it comes loose from its hinges and falls to the floor with a crash.

The kitchen floor is covered with a thick layer of ash and soot. Only one smouldering leg of the table remains. The ceiling is burned through and I look up into the room above, my old bed chamber, and out through the hole in the roof to the flinty sky beyond. Rain beats down into what is left of the kitchen where I took meals with Eli so many times. There is a loud groan and a creaking noise from above and I see the beam of the bedroom ceiling is burned through, and one end drops down a little and hangs precariously.

I call their names. Eli! Morgan! I listen, head cocked, for an answer. The only sound is the soft pitter-patter of the rain falling, and the ticking of the clock, which by some miracle is unscathed and goes on ticking. Life goes on, whatever may befall us.

I go to the bottom of the small stairway that leads up to the bedroom above. Its surface is blistered in places but not burnt through, and I think it will take my weight. I take off my cloak, lest I trip over it, and climb the stairs, testing each step to see if it is strong. Up here, in this little room, is where Eli and I went at it like a bull and cow. When I see the smouldering remains of the bed, I think God himself has struck this place like a bolt of lightning. If I had slept here last night and not at the mill, I would have been burned like a witch at the stake for my sins. Edging my way closer to what remains of the bed, around the cavernous hole in the floorboards, I see it is not God but human hand that set the bed alight, for the tell-tale remains of a lamp lie there in the smouldering heap.

The beam above my head creaks and shifts again and I turn to hurry back down the stairs. It is then I see him, lying in the corner of the room, and the sight so horrifies me that I scream. I stand, transfixed, shaking like an aspen leaf, my knees turned soft as dough. I hear shouts downstairs and boots on the staircase. I wish I had stayed in Cardigan, wish I had never come back to this God-fearing place. Whatever am I to tell Beulah?

Chapter Thirty-Six

Down in the woods, the beautiful woods, beside
the babbling brook,
the slumbering madman dreams he hears the
calling of a raven.

She never knows, will never feel quite safe. We walk alongside the Wildwater, beneath the blossoming hawthorns where they arch above the path. Megan's babe is slung in a shawl, its downy head resting on her breast. Clusters of the frothy blossoms get caught on a gust of breeze and swirl about our heads, making Fortune exclaim that it is snowing. Fortune skips from mill to Wildwater and back again, at will, now the repairs are done. Sometimes, Fortune will make her bed at Wildwater with the woman she now calls Mam, sometimes not. She goes wherever the wind blows, as free as the birds in the sky.

Megan bolts the doors when we are indoors, and checks every window is fastened tight at fall of night. Eli's gun she has concealed beneath her mattress but says that is no comfort, given what Eli did to Morgan with his bare hands. Even out here, on such a beautiful day, I see her glance over her shoulder often; always she is on her guard. I tell her no harm will come to her as long as I am in this world, for I would lay down my life in defence of she who has been my whole salvation. But she never feels safe, for they still haven't found him.

An eye for an eye, Eli told her brother on the night of the fire. He gouged out Morgan's eye with his fingers and left him there for dead. I tell Megan that Eli will never dare to return, for he will be made to pay for what he has done. I can see by the shakiness of her smile that she does not believe me. Every day, we live in hope of his body being found so that she will at last be truly free.

As for his housekeeper, Gwen, she got her orders to leave and never return, the moment she arrived back from her cousin's funeral to find the house still smouldering from the fire and blaming Megan for it all.

"At least I have nothing left to hide," Megan says. "Even though I may never live free from fear, I am free to be myself and that is a precious freedom."

For as long as I live, I shall never forget the pride I felt when she called for a meeting at the chapel. Courageous, she stood in front of them all and told them more than they ever bargained to hear. I stood watching, my face awash with tears and my heart soaring at the words she spoke in defence of all we sorry women.

Morgan it was who stood first, and told them all that his sister had some things she wanted to tell them.

"And if when she is finished you shun her, then you shun me, too, for she is my flesh and blood and I am proud to call myself her brother."

His voice cracked, then, and he had to fumble in his waistcoat pocket for a handkerchief to dab at his remaining eye. There wasn't a whisper nor a cough among the people gathered there. They sat, transfixed by the sight of their one-eyed miller breaking down in front of them all. He returned to his place beside us, and Beulah took his hand in hers and squeezed it tight.

They can do what they want now, he'd said the night before, for I no longer depend on them as I did. Where will they go for their oats to be ground if they shun me? he asked. Still, he knew he was taking a risk, knew he might lose their custom to another parish's mill, however inconvenient that would be for them. He is kinder to me now. He says if it were not for me he would be dead, for no one else had thought to look inside the house for him.

Megan walks slowly to the front of the chapel and I can feel everyone is holding their breath, just as I am. Feet shuffle as people turn in their seats to watch her rise from her seat and walk to the front. She does not hang her head in shame but stands straight and dignified, and boldly looks upon each face, greeting them each by name. Then she begins to speak;

I once knew a young girl with spun gold hair who lived on a hill beyond Carregwyn. That house where she lived is empty now. The garden gate lies a-rotting on the ground. The stone-wall boundaries have crumbled and are overgrown with bracken. Moss grows on the rotting window frames and saplings have taken root in the gutters. Dust has settled on the un-swept floors where children's feet once scampered. An eerie silence hangs about that place which once rang out with the joyful squeals of children. If you stand outside the door, as I did yesterday, you will feel the sense of someone watching and waiting. That someone, I believe, is Sian Williams, and she is waiting for absolution.

There is some embarrassed shuffling in the pews, but their faces remain turned up towards Megan, and no one interrupts.

I once walked through that garden gate and leapt the brook with Sian, though I was not supposed to go there, was forbidden from speaking to her, for the whole parish had shunned her for being with child out of wedlock. The preacher was baying to have her thrown out and made an example of. I am the weed he must cast out from his Eden, Sian told me.

I've often had cause to think of Sian over the seven years in between, and when I do, it is with a heavy heart, for I think if I'd had courage I may have prevented her sorry death. For she threw herself in the Wildwater because she believed herself to be all alone and unloved in the only world she had ever known. But she was not alone in her predicament. If only she had known, if only

I had told her, I was with child too, and the father of mine was the same man who seduced our little Sian. That child is now seven years old and Morgan, God bless him, has claimed her as his own to save me from being shunned as Sian was.

You should have seen their faces, then! I would have been trembling in my boots if I had been Megan but she carries on, her voice rising to be heard over the kerfuffle her words have caused.

What kind of world is this we have created here; a world that drives daughters to suicide, and forces the likes of me and my brother to live a fearful life of deception and pretence? It is a world of rules laid down by men for the benefit of their own kind, no matter that so many abuse those very rules to subjugate us women. We work alongside you in your fields. We bake your bread. We bear your children. We are your equal in all things an, yet; you afford us no more rights to err than the horses in your stables.

Voices rise up then, men denying what she says is true, and a few brave women who have the courage to agree with Megan.

"I think it was terrible what happened to Sian," Blodwen rises up to say, "it still haunts me to this day."

"I, too," Bess shouts from the back, "there is not enough compassion, if you ask me!"

Elgan's wife stands up, red in the face. "Men have it all ways. They can do what they like but we women can do no wrong. We are rejected if we don't give them what they want and punished if we do."

Elgan tells her to shut up and sit down or he will take her home. He grabs her arm but she pulls away.

"We have three daughters at home! How would you like it if it was one of them that ended up like poor Sian?" she asks him.

"If you raise them right, they don't go astray!" he tells her, puffing out his chest, and looking about him for agreement. She swipes his shoulder and tells him not to talk such tosh.

Old Twm, the Oaks, gets to his feet, blushing and turning his hat between his hands. He looks at the floor when he speaks, his voice trembling.

"My sister hanged herself from a beam in our barn. She were but fourteen year old, and I was ten. It was me that found her. She hadn't dared tell us, we had no idea. She'd been in service less than a year. We believed it was her employer that done it but we never knew for certain."

Twm sits back down in his seat, wiping the tears from his wrinkled face with the back of his hand.

It is Geraint who gets to his feet next, turning this way and that, addressing everyone, his eyes twinkling with mischief. "I don't know why it is us men who are being blamed for it all! You women are far worse, if you ask me! You lot are the first to leap onto the wagon and condemn, if there is some poor woman gone astray."

Cerudwen gets to her feet, her hands fisted on her hips. "Aye, Geraint, it's true enough, what you say. But why do you think that is, eh? The preacher is right! Pull out the weed before it contaminates the rest, for if you do not then what you get is one like that one amongst you!"

It is a moment before I realise she is pointing her finger at me. When I see it is me she is referring to, I blush to the roots of my hair.

"Please do not speak of Branwen in that way," Megan tells her, "for she is as much a victim as any of us."

Megan knows all about what happened to me at the hands of my Uncle, for I told her all when I asked for her forgiveness.

Cerudwen splutters and turns her mocking face to the crowd, searching for allies I am certain she will find, her voice rising to fever pitch.

"Megan dares to come here and preach to us when she keeps a harlot in her house, a harlot that led her husband astray, by all accounts!"

"No man was led astray that did not choose to be," Megan says to her, "and Eli used Branwen to punish me, as surely as he used a stick to punish his dog."

Megan's words take the wind from Cerudwen and she knows not what to say. It is now her turn to back down and she returns to her seat.

"Geraint speaks the truth. We women are often our worst enemies. Instead of pulling together, or helping each other, we are the first to turn our backs, or turn the screw, and all that we do we do out of fear."

"What is she talking about, now?" I hear Cerudwen mutter, loudly enough for all to hear.

Megan looks at her and says, "It is for you to say what your fear is, Cerudwen, but if I should have to presume, I would say fear of abandonment was your greatest fear. And who can blame you for that? Not I. We are all dependant on our men from the moment we marry and have children. For what would happen to us and our children if our men ceased to work and provide? We would end up in some workhouse, or begging along the roads, watching our children die of starvation or disease. By the very virtue of us being women, we are rendered dependant on our men. Is it not imperative, then, that those men on whose goodwill and responsibility we depend upon should treat us with sympathy, compassion and as equals?"

To my astonishment, Cerudwen's face crumples and she begins to weep. "It's all so wrong," she sobs "it is all so unjust. I'm worn out with it all. Babies, year in and year out. And all so that he gets what he needs and doesn't go somewhere else."

"Where else did you think I would go?" Geraint asks her. "Come here, you daft woman," he says, and wraps his arms around her, his eyes swimming with tears.

It is then that I first think that I would lay down my life for Megan, for through her honesty she is bringing people together as I've never seen in my life. She is working a miracle amongst these god-fearing people. Yet, she wholly believes in God, she told me so herself. It is not God that is the problem, Branwen, she says, it is the things which people choose to do in his name.

Megan begins to speak again, and there is not one in that chapel who is not listening now.

"The greatest and truest friend I had in this world cannot speak for himself this day, for he is no longer with us. So, I shall leave you with the words which Dafydd Williams once spoke to me. 'The preacher is but a man, and can be as wrong as any other. It is compassion this world needs more of, not cruelty'.

Megan's voice wavers when she speaks Dafydd's name. Her brother has shown her the letter the miller wrote, to be read after he died. She will never get over it, she says, she thinks of the miller every day. He walks beside me in spirit, she says, the father I never knew I had until he was gone.

"I feel he his right here," she says, patting her shoulder, "looking out for me, still."

Megan's Mam, Esther, had been a wild one in her youth, apparently, and lay with the miller whilst betrothed to the man who Megan had grown up believing was her Da. Dafydd had wanted to marry

Esther, but Esther swore him to secrecy and went and married the other. She had plenty of reason to regret her decision, so they say. Megan says she always felt that Dafydd was like a Da to her but she never suspected the truth.

"I always believed Mam despised me because I reminded her of the man I thought was my Da," she told me. "But now, I think it was because I was a daily reminder to her of her sins. When she looked upon me, she saw her own shame."

Megan longs to return to Carregwyn but fears we would be in more danger there for there are no near neighbours. Fortune has her own pony now and would be able to come and go from Carregwyn as she pleased. Morgan is to be a father. He and Beulah are like a pair of young lovers since his accident. I have never seen a man and woman better matched.

Megan travels every week to a new parish and repeats what she said that day in the chapel. I travel along with the babe in my lap and Fortune travels wherever we go. Megan gathers large crowds; people come from all over to hear what she has to say. Whether on village square or on some open slope of hill, there she stands before them with the dog sat at her side.

They call it a revival but instead of instilling fear of hell and damnation in the people, Megan is ridding these parishes of the fear that has bound them for too long. When they see this woman, so slight of frame, having the courage to speak against the tyranny of preachers and men, they take courage themselves to stand up against the injustices perpetrated against their own. She is changing the lives of womankind for the better, in one small part of this world.

If Eli is still alive, I know where he will have gone into hiding. There is an old quarry on his Uncle's farm, the stones from which went to build his Uncle's house, he said. A strange place it is, down in the woods; great boulders of stone strewn over the ground from which ferns and such grow from the crevices in the rock. So quiet it is, peaceful, with nought but a babbling brook to trickle the silence. He used to go there when he was in one of his brooding moods and wanting to be alone. Only once did he show it to me for it was a private place for him. There was a small cave behind one of the boulders of rock where he had made a bed of bracken. Sometimes, he would stay the whole night there, and one time he had me for company.

I would be dead now if not for Megan, for I have flourished under her wing when all believed I was dying. I know now, it was my own guilt eating away at me that made me ill, and it is her forgiveness which has healed me. In return, I shall gift her freedom to live again without fear. It is my calling in this life.

The Cambrian Times.

On the day of our Lord, thirteenth of June, 1832, the remains of Mr Eli Jenkins were found in a quarry on the farm of his late Uncle. Mr Jenkins, who went missing some months ago following a fire at his farm, Wildwater, was said to have been wanted in connection with a brutal assault on his brother-in-law, Morgan Jones, who lost the sight of one eye as a result of the attack. Reputed to have been of unsound mind, it is believed that Mr Jenkins died of wounds to the head from his own gun which was found beside him in a small cave inside the quarry.

Printed in Great Britain
by Amazon.co.uk, Ltd.,
Marston Gate.